HZ 20/10

Please return/renew this item by the last date shown
on this label, or on your self-service receipt.

To renew this item, visit **www.librarieswest.org.uk**
or contact your library

Your borrower number and PIN are required.

LibrariesWest

QUIET
ACTS OF
VIOLENCE

CATH STAINCLIFFE

QUIET ACTS OF VIOLENCE

CONSTABLE

CONSTABLE

First published in Great Britain in 2020 by Constable

A CIP catalogue record for this book is available from the British Library.

ISBN: 978-1-47213-211-6

Typeset in Times New Roman by Initial Typesetting Services, Edinburgh
Printed and bound in Great Britain by Clays Ltd, Elcograf S.p.A.

Papers used by Constable are from well-managed forests and
other responsible sources.

Constable
An imprint of
Little, Brown Book Group
Carmelite House
50 Victoria Embankment
London EC4Y 0DZ

An Hachette UK Company
www.hachette.co.uk

www.littlebrown.co.uk

To Sara – agent extraordinaire

Chapter 1

Jade was buzzing, little shocks and fizzes of adrenalin sparking through her blood. Always the way when they were called to a death. The end of everything for somebody. The start of something for Jade.

She joined the boss, DI Donna Bell, in the line of figures ranged along the cordon. All attention was focused on an industrial-sized bin sited at the near end of the alley, which ran between the backs of two rows of terraced houses to the railway line across the bottom.

The terraces had small backyards and the alley served as access for people to get bikes and bins up and down. Handy for drug-dealing, and burglaries too, out of sight. In some areas of the city the alleys were gated now, while other residents agitated for barriers to be installed.

In the dark, hastily erected floodlights illuminated the container and the area around. The white radiance was punctuated by flashes of red and blue light from the stationary patrol cars. The bin was about five feet by four. The sort of thing that looked like a big chest on wheels with a roll-over top. Painted offal red, the name of the firm on the side. CleanSolve. Beneath that, General Waste. A mobile-phone number.

A gust of wind, warm for October, sent scraps of litter around the bin scattering in a spiral. Plastic coffee lids, cigarette packets, polystyrene food trays.

Jade zipped up her leather jacket: she could do without it flapping about.

The boss held her hand over her hair, which was flying in her eyes. Jade kept hers short, these days – saved so much bother.

She could smell onions, spices and fat lingering from the takeaways dotted along the road. Woodsmoke too: a bonfire, maybe, or someone with a log-burning stove.

Passing traffic on the main road slowed to gawp at the clutch of police vehicles and the forensics team, in their protective overalls, photographing the scene.

A freight train clackety-clacked over the tracks at the end of the street, about level with the upstairs storeys of the houses.

'It was found in the bin?' Jade asked the boss.

'Yes. A baby girl.' The boss gave a little shake of her head. 'In a bin bag,' she added.

'The mother?' With an infant, the mother was always top of the list for those-most-likely-to.

'No sign.'

Jade stepped back to take in the area. To the left of the scene were a fried chicken shop, a nail bar and two curry houses (one of which used to do a decent tikka masala). To the right a Super Saver, a lettings agency and a minimarket.

On the opposite side of the road more of the same, shuffled into a different order: takeaways, nail bar, betting shop, barber, shisha lounge.

Two cars drove past, heading north towards the city at excessive speed, exhausts roaring, not deterred by the police presence.

One of the children's homes Jade had lived in was along there, further towards Stockport. One of the first places. Just a fistful of images in her head: a Barbie duvet cover (Barbie FFS); a swing hung from a tree in the garden, an orange plastic disc with a rope going through the middle; Jade hurling the swing at the girl who whispered, 'Paki,' each time she passed Jade, and feeling a burst of triumph when the girl's nose dripped blood; a day trip to some forest where the mist hung between tall, spindly trees with black trunks and spiky needles, like some horror-movie set.

She shook away the thoughts. 'Whose bin?'

'Shared by the Chuckie Chicken and the Super Saver.' The boss gestured to the two businesses immediately to the left and right of the alley, one on the corner with Rosa Street, the other on Grace Street. Both premises had at one time been family homes. 'Mr Siddique runs the Chuckie Chicken. He says there's always people dumping their stuff in the bin.'

Jade looked up to the corners of the roofs, the chicken joint, the Super Saver. No CCTV cameras pointed in this direction.

There were fewer gawkers than usual. Perhaps because it was close to midnight, people tucked up in bed. And none of the residents down these two side streets would be able to see the activity at the end of their road without coming out of their houses. She surveyed the onlookers. Mixed bunch, young and old, white and Asian; one looked mixed race, like she was. Eyes wide, like this was the best thing she'd seen all year.

'Any witnesses here?' Jade asked the boss.

'No one so far. We'll be knocking on doors tomorrow but none of this lot claims to have seen anything. We've taken names and addresses anyhow.' Hoovering up information, because who knew what might be useful in days to come?

'Could be someone passing?' Jade said. 'Opportunistic. They saw the bin.'

'They already had the child in the bin bag?' the boss said.

'No filming!' one of the uniformed officers shouted, sounding cranky, as if she'd already had to repeat it a few times. Citizen journalists were a mixed blessing. Mobile-phone footage was often crucial in documenting crimes and identifying perpetrators. But filming during an investigation could cause problems down the line when the case came to court. Material detrimental to a fair trial.

'Anthea?' The boss called over the crime-scene manager. When she drew close the boss said, 'Can we do a complete lift and load?' nodding to the bin.

'Yes, of course. And, Donna, I asked someone to recover the child, the bag and contents from the station and transfer them to the mortuary,' Anthea said quietly.

3

'We're off to the station now.' The boss glanced at Jade. 'Interview the witness.'

It was a woman who had found the newborn baby's body in the bin and taken it to the police station.

Jade wondered why she'd done that instead of calling them out. Didn't she know that she'd have messed up all sorts of evidence by moving stuff? Maybe it was her kid. And she'd hurt it, or it had been stillborn, and she was making up stories.

Time to find out.

Chapter 2

Donna had brought a flask of coffee with her, not prepared to settle for the foul concoction in plastic cups dispensed by the machine. She drank some in her office while she logged on to the system and opened a file on the new case.

The station had become increasingly corporate over her years at work. Canteen and staff lounges had closed and the place had been kitted out like some low-budget conference centre with every carpet tile, stacking chair and window blind sourced at the lowest possible price with no regard for style or comfort.

When Jade arrived Donna waved her through. 'Coffee?'

'Sorted.' Jade held up a can of some energy drink. The sort of thing that Donna's twin sons threw money away on, claiming it helped their sporting performances.

'The witness?' Jade said, bright-eyed. She looked like she'd just had a good night's sleep and a nourishing breakfast, not been dragged out at the fag-end of the evening to face an all-nighter. Maybe it was a jolt from the energy drink or, more likely, given what Donna knew of Jade, impatience glittering in her gaze. Always champing at the bit to get stuck in, passionate for the job, no matter what it threw at them.

'She's ready to give us a statement. Been fed and watered. Not that she could eat.' Donna finished entering the initial details into the pro-forma on her screen.

'How come?'

'Seriously, Jade? She just found a dead baby in a bin. Not exactly going to buck up your appetite, is it?'

Jade wasn't wired like most people, the empathy gene missing or disabled. But she needed to grasp that part of being a good detective was being able to put yourself in someone else's shoes. It required the ability to hold someone's hand and walk them over the stepping stones of truth, steadily and with care, because no matter what horrors they had witnessed or perpetrated they were human. Like you. Could Jade learn any of that? Was the capacity in there, hidden beneath the surface?

Jade drained her drink, crushed the can. 'Shall we go, then?'

'Yes. I'll just let Jim know,' Donna said. 'See you down there.'

She could phone: he'd still be up. He didn't turn in till one or two in the morning, these days. Not back at work yet after a heart attack in the car had incapacitated him, leading to a collision and the death of a pedestrian. A horrible accident. And the inquest still to come.

While Jim's broken leg healed, and he waited for further tests on his heart, he was still getting up early enough to help the younger kids get ready for school and to referee squabbles about time in the bathroom for the older three.

We really need another bathroom, she thought. Five kids. We should have sorted it years ago. But now? By the time they got round to it the kids would probably all have left home.

She slid her phone-screen to unlock it. A text would be so much easier. No chance to resume the argument they'd been in the middle of when she'd been called to work, no nagging or point scoring on either side.

How had it come to this? How come they were now on different sides? What had happened to unity, to being in it together? To love and to cherish, for better or worse? What had changed? Was it her? Him? OK, after twenty-four years of marriage you couldn't expect the intensity of love and passion of the early years, but surely it wasn't right that now when she thought of Jim, her first uncensored feelings were of irritation and disappointment rather than any deeper love or even sympathy.

Going to be all night, she typed. *See you sometime tomorrow. D x*

***

6

Colette Pritchard was a wreck. She'd been given a change of clothes so the forensics lab could examine what she'd been wearing, if required. But her appearance, matted brown hair, chapped lips and mottled skin, decaying teeth and an ugly cut on her jawline, all bore witness to the deprivations of life sleeping rough.

That, along with the sickly sour smell that humans exude when they go for a long time with no access to regular washing facilities.

Donna felt a pinch of guilt at her earlier thoughts about the lack of bathrooms at home.

Colette sat on the edge of a small sofa, huddled forward as if she couldn't get warm. Stiff hanks of light brown hair shielded her eyes. Hiding? Or just wishing herself out of sight? Away from this, from here, from what she had found.

Donna checked her details, her date of birth made her thirty-seven years old. Address NFA. No fixed abode. 'No fucking address,' more than one homeless person had said to Donna in the past, with a grim flash of humour.

'I need to let you know we're video recording this interview,' Donna said. 'It will also be used as a basis for your witness statement. OK?'

The camera was set up on a shelf in the corner, pointing down at Colette but far enough away to capture footage of Donna seated in a chair to one side of her and a bit of Jade on the other taking handwritten notes. A coffee-table in the middle.

'I know you've had a terrible shock,' Donna said. 'Do you feel well enough to talk to me about it?'

'I think so,' Colette said. Her voice was husky, raw. A smoker's voice? Or a bad throat?

Donna led her gently, building a general picture of her circumstances.

'How long have you been homeless, Colette?'

'Three years.'

'And before that, did you live in Manchester?'

'Northenden.' A southern suburb, close to the airport.

'You were working?' Donna said.

'Yes. Wages department for Lunds. In Wythenshawe. They went bust. I had to sign on.' She stopped, swallowed, reached for the cup of water on the table. Donna noticed the dirt around her fingernails, the rough, reddened skin across her knuckles.

'I borrowed on the credit card to cover my bills. I thought it would all come right once I found a new job, but there was nothing out there. I got very down. Anxious, you know, stressed. I'd maxed out my cards. I did what I could, applied for every job going. They put me on universal credit. The landlord – that was no good for him. He evicted me.'

'That was three years ago?' Donna said.

'Nearly, yeah.' There was flat defeat in her voice. She blinked, and rubbed at her forehead. 'I've had some time in hostels and I was in a B-and-B for a bit, emergency housing. That was awful. These last nine, ten months . . . Since just after Christmas I've been on the streets.'

'In Levenshulme?'

'Here and there. Over Fallowfield way in the summer. That wasn't bad. The heatwave, you know.' She gave a tremulous grin.

Donna returned a smile. 'That was something, that was,' she said. Weeks of sunshine in a city known for its incessant rain. A hosepipe ban, even. Her kids getting tans ahead of their family holiday to Spain. Meals in the garden. Staying outside till dusk fell, savouring the scents of cypress and jasmine. The flick and twist of a bat passing overhead.

'So, how long in Levenshulme?'

'Last few weeks. I was in Withington in September but—' A spasm twisted her face and her body jerked as though she'd had an electric shock. Donna almost jumped, caught unawares.

Colette pressed her fists to her mouth, eyes shut.

'Take your time,' Donna said.

Jade looked at Donna, querying, eager. Donna gave her a stare: *Wait.*

Colette's breathing was ragged. 'They beat me up. They . . . they assaulted me, you know. Sexually. Rape.'

8

Oh, God. 'I'm so sorry that happened to you, Colette. That's awful.'

The woman's face worked. She blinked rapidly.

'Did you report it?' Donna asked.

Colette blew out a long sigh. 'I thought about it. Even set off for the police station one time.' She shook her head.

'It's not too late,' Donna said. 'If you want to make a report, we can refer you. We have a specialist team. They're very good.'

'I don't know,' Colette said.

'The offer's there. No pressure. And you don't have to decide now.' Donna's heart went out to her. She understood how the prospect of reporting the crime would feel like another trial, another burden, freighted with the anxiety of reliving the trauma, revisiting the violence that had come from nowhere and against which she had had no defence, no protection. And on top of all that, the rates for successful prosecution and conviction were pitifully low.

'That's why I started sleeping in the bin,' Colette said. 'It's not safe on the street. You're out there, on a bit of cardboard in a sleeping bag, and you're a target. People – they're like animals.' She stared at Donna, the first time she'd made full eye contact. 'They chuck their takeaways at you, piss on you, throw matches.' She raised her face to the ceiling. Grime ringed the creases in her neck.

Donna's attention was on Colette but she could feel the tension rising off Jade beside her. Was there something in Colette's story that resonated with her?

Colette looked straight at Donna again. 'I had a home. I paid taxes. I had a direct debit to Marie Curie and another to the Dogs Trust. Holidays abroad.' Her voice grew louder. 'A fucking cherry tree in the garden. And now that's all gone. So what? I'm not human any more?' She broke off abruptly, her angry plea echoing in the small room. 'Sorry,' she added.

Oh, love. 'You've been sleeping in the same bin over these weeks?' Donna said, after a moment.

'Yes. Some nights if I'm on edge, know I won't sleep and it's dry,

9

I'll just walk. Keep moving. But most nights, yes. It stinks, it's horrible. And it's hard to sleep sometimes with the noise.'

'Go on,' Donna said.

'There's a street-sweeper truck comes in the night. There's a dog, a yappy one across the road, barks its head off. And others on the industrial estate. Always lots of coming and going there.'

'In the night?'

'Yes. I think some of those units run shifts. Then there's pubs chucking out. The trains. Don't mind them so much. And you never know if someone's going to throw something in the bin. But at least I'm out of sight. And I know when it gets emptied. I remember reading about that man, the one who was crushed? We talked about it at work. I never thought . . .' She studied the backs of her hands, one finger tracing the raised veins.

'When is it emptied?' Donna said.

'Tuesday, the wagon comes.'

Tomorrow morning.

'So tonight. What time did you get there?' Donna said.

'Just after eleven. I waited until the takeaway had closed.' Colette shifted on her seat, rubbed at her forehead again. 'I can't . . . I just . . . Can I use the loo?' Blinking and twitching. Nervous as the questions drew closer to her finding the baby.

'Of course.' If this was a suspect, Donna might ask them to complete their account, not allowing time for them to regroup or to think up a cover story. But this was a witness. A good citizen who'd come in to report a death. A suspicious death – that's all they had so far. Not murder, or manslaughter, or infanticide. Not yet. Only if the forensics led them that way.

Donna paused the video and went herself to escort Colette to the visitors' toilets, waiting in the corridor outside to walk her back.

In the interview lounge, Colette sat on the sofa and took another drink of water.

Donna resumed, 'So you climbed into the bin just after eleven p.m. What happened next?'

'I . . . I was moving the bags, seeing what was there – you've got

10

to be careful with broken glass and stuff like that. Cans. People put dog mess in sometimes an—' Tears filled her eyes and again she pressed her fist to her nose and mouth, shaking her head slowly. 'I'm sorry.' She blurted a muffled sob.

Out of the corner of her eye Donna could see Jade scribbling on the edge of her notebook, jagged little black lines, like a drawing of dense spiky grass. Doodling. Was she even aware she was doing it?

Donna reached forward and took some tissues from the box, which was regularly restocked for this room. 'Here.' She leaned over to hand them to Colette. The smell radiating from her was so strong that Donna moved swiftly back in her seat. She cupped her hand to her chin, as if she was deliberating over what to ask next, but giving herself the chance to inhale the trace of perfume rising from the cuff of her shirt.

Colette wiped her eyes, blew her nose noisily. She lowered her head, staring down at the carpet, the tissues balled tightly in her fingers.

'Sometimes there's leftovers, stuff that can't be reheated. Oh, God . . .' She shuddered. 'That bag . . . I was hungry and . . . I thought—' She wept again, a desolate sound. Mopped at her eyes with the sodden tissues.

Donna swallowed and waited.

'You can't see anything in there,' Colette whispered. 'I thought maybe it— I thought— Oh, God . . . I thought it was a chicken.' She dropped the wad of tissues on the table, held her hands out, a foot apart, shaking. Fingers gently curled, indicating size.

'You didn't know what it was,' Donna said. A statement and an absolution.

'No. I rolled back the lid to get a bit of light, so I could see to open the bag.' She met Donna's eyes, her own harrowed, shimmering with tears. Her nose red and puffy. 'It was a baby, a little baby. And it was . . . it wasn't right.'

Donna wondered what they'd face when they visited the mortuary. Some physical disfigurement? The skull unformed or features missing? A reason for the mother to abandon it? She remembered the hope she had clung to throughout each of her pregnancies, during each labour – just let it be healthy.

'It wasn't right?' she echoed Colette.

'It wasn't moving. It was . . . so still.' Crying blurred her words. 'So still. And cold.'

'Can you tell me where you touched the baby?' Donna said.

'On its . . . Here.' She pressed her palm to her chest. 'For the heartbeat.' Tears streamed down her cheeks.

Once Colette had wiped her face with fresh tissues, Donna said, 'Tell me what you did next.'

'I brought it out. The baby and the bag.'

'The baby was dressed?'

'In a jumpsuit. A white Babygro,' Colette said.

'Can you describe the bag?'

'A bin liner, those heavy-duty ones.'

'Was there anything else in the bag?' Donna said.

'Some papers. Newspapers and card and that.'

'OK. And then?'

'I brought it here,' Colette said.

'You walked?'

'Yes.'

'Thank you. I'd like to ask you some more questions if you feel OK to keep going,' Donna said.

'Yes.' She was less agitated now she'd recounted the worst of it.

'Do you want another drink or anything to eat?' Donna said.

'Coffee would be good, thanks.'

'Milk, sugar?' Donna asked.

'Yes, three, please,' Colette said.

'OK. DC Bradshaw will get that,' sending Jade to fetch the order. 'And then we'll carry on.'

Chapter 3

'Colette, just to be clear, have you any idea who the baby is?' Donna said, once Jade was back.

'No.' Colette frowned.

'Or who its mother might be?'

'No.'

'You've been sleeping in the area for several weeks, do you recognise any of the people thereabouts?'

'Yes, a few. But I take myself off first thing and only come back when it's dark.'

'Where do you go?' Donna said.

'The libraries, they're good – they let you use the computers for claims and that. You can read the papers or a book. There's the Whitworth too, the gallery. And the parks when it's fine. I know a couple of churches that do hot meals.'

'Thinking about Levenshulme, do you remember seeing any pregnant women around where you were sleeping?' Donna said.

'No, I don't think so,' Colette said.

'When you came to the area tonight, did you see anyone? Think for a minute. People on foot, walking to the bus, getting off the bus, anyone in the alley, anyone stopping a car? Coming into or out of the takeaways?'

'There was a bike delivery.' She nodded slowly. 'You know the ones with the big square bags on the back? They went down Rosa Street. And before that I saw Odelia, this woman I know. She was down the road. She has these two little pugs. Walks them every night. They have those Day-glo collars for the dark. She goes as far as the park, round the block and back. She stops when she sees me, has a word. She's kind like that.'

'Do you know where Odelia lives?' Donna said.

'Rosa Street but I don't know which number,' Colette said.

'Can you describe her, please?'

'A black woman, in her sixties maybe. She's got grey hair.'

'Tall? Short?' Donna said.

'Short, a bit overweight,' Colette said.

'Did you talk?' Donna said.

'Not tonight, just waved. She was on the other side, and I was walking down from Longsight,' Colette said.

'Did you see anyone else tonight?'

'Not that I remember.'

'Notice any cars or vans stopping?' Donna said.

'No.'

'Anything unusual, anything odd, anything at all catch your attention?'

'Nothing,' Colette said. 'I'm sorry.'

'No. This is really helpful,' Donna said. 'Thank you.' She paused a moment to give Colette a chance to catch her breath before turning to fresh questions. 'What about last night? What do you remember from then?'

'I saw Odelia. We had a quick chat. And there were some kids hanging round the alley. So I walked past and came back later when they were gone.'

'What were they doing?' Donna said.

'Smoking, drinking maybe.' Colette shrugged. 'I could smell skunk.'

'Did you recognise any of them?'

'I only glanced. There's quite often kids there. I keep a low profile.'

'Is there anything else you can think of that might help us?' Donna said.

'No.'

'OK. If you do remember anything after today, please get in touch. For now, we'll have this typed up for you to check and sign. Thank you for your help, for coming in. For bringing the baby.'

Donna stopped the recording.

'Why would someone do that?' Colette's voice rose. 'Why wouldn't they want a proper funeral if they lost the baby? To just throw it in a bin bag?'

'That's what we aim to find out,' Donna said. Foul play might be one explanation. A secret pregnancy another. Or a tragedy: the baby dying and the mother panicking.

'While we write your statement up maybe you'd like a hot shower.'

'That'd be great. Thank you,' Colette said.

Donna felt Jade's eyes on her: showers at the station were strictly for staff. 'And we'll see if we can fix you up with some emergency accommodation. Would you be willing to do that?'

'Yes. Not Withington, though.' Sudden tears sprang in her eyes.

'Of course. And if you do ever want to report that, Colette – next month, next year, whenever – we can do that. I can put you in touch with the specialist unit. They really are very good. And they do understand.'

Colette's lips tightened, eyes swimming. She nodded. Then she said quickly, her face colouring, 'My stuff. I don't like to ask but my blanket and that, I'm sorry – it's in the bin.' Her embarrassment burned through the air.

'We'll sort out replacements,' Donna said. 'Don't worry about that. It's the least we can do.'

Chapter 4

Jade had typed up the witness statement for Colette and given it to
the boss.

Next she checked that there were no reports from any of the hospitals of a baby abduction, or of a new mother going walkabout when
she shouldn't.

Then she made calls to the emergency shelters, looking for somewhere that would take Colette. Even though half the night was over.

The answers were the same. Night-duty staff answered with
whispery tones or yawned down the line. *All full, no beds, waiting
lists, refer you to the new scheme tomorrow, we lost half our spaces,
full tonight, try tomorrow, sorry, sorry.* No room at the inn.

Jade sought out the boss and found her in the corridor coming out
from getting Colette's statement signed. Jade passed on the news.
'We could give her a cell for the night?' she suggested.

The boss rolled her eyes. 'Would you sleep in one of our cells?'

Jade shrugged. 'Depends how tired I was. Better than a bin.'

The boss raised an eyebrow. She got out her phone, tapped at it,
found a number and dialled. 'I'd like to book a room for tonight. One
adult. Colette Pritchard. I'm paying for the room. My name is Donna
Bell. I'll give you my card number.'

'You're putting her up? With your own cash?' Jade said, when the
boss had finished.

'Call it my good deed for the day.'

'At a hotel?' *Talk about a soft touch.*

'Jade, it's a pile of a place that hasn't seen a paintbrush since

16

nineteen eighty-five. The rooms are full of construction workers from the airport expansion, sex workers, stag parties waiting for their flights, frazzled wedding hosts who had to settle for cheap and cheerful because of the truckloads of relatives coming from Ireland or wherever. It's hardly the Hilton.'

'Isn't it against the rules?' Jade said.

The boss gave one of her stares, her eyes going round and hard like marbles, head tilted forward and down a bit, as if she was about to give Jade a head butt. 'Are you talking to me about rules?'

Jade said nothing.

The boss made a sound in her throat, straightened her neck. 'You can give her a lift down there.'

Jade wanted to protest. She was a detective, not a cabbie. But she just grunted. At least it would give her a chance to grab some scran on the way back. 'You want any takeout?' she asked the boss.

'Sausage bap,' the boss said.

It was Jade's turn to raise her eyebrows. The boss was always banging on about healthy eating.

'Well, you're hardly going to find anywhere serving lentil soup at this hour, are you?' She got her purse out, gave Jade two fivers. 'Give one to Colette. The other's for the food.'

Jade drove through the dark, enjoying the novelty of not being stuck in traffic. Manchester by day was insane, permanent gridlock. And with a train service that had been plagued by delays, cancellations and strikes for months on end it sometimes seemed as if the whole city was going to grind to a halt and stop functioning altogether.

But now the roads were almost empty.

Colette didn't chat, which suited Jade just fine. But she said thank you loads of times when Jade dropped her off. Jade waited until she saw them buzz Colette in through the plate-glass doors. The foyer beyond was already fancied up with Christmas decorations. Or maybe no one had been arsed to take them down after last year. She bumped the car back through the car park, which was pitted with holes, still filled with water though it hadn't rained for a few days.

Driving to the all-night café on Bolton Street, Jade thought there was something brilliant about being up and out when the rest of the world was sleeping. A wild edge to it. Probably from the nights she had spent out of bounds, out of hours and often out of her head. Jade and her mate DD. Riders on the storm. A girl and a boy who'd found each other in the ruins of their childhoods. Taken on the world. Kids whose only sense of direction was towards kicks, sensation, danger.

She shook her head. Ten years on and they were divided by the paths they had taken. Jade on the straight and narrow, the sunny side of the street, proper job, catching killers, DD still wheeling, dealing, stealing in the shadows.

The boss's line, 'Are you talking to me about rules?' Was it a threat? The boss knew Jade had lied on her medical, that she was taking anti-psychotics, because a member of their team had squealed to her, diverting attention from his own wrongdoing. He'd been neck deep in a cover-up, protecting his son from a murder charge, destroying evidence. Now *that* was rule-breaking.

They'd brought the bastard down, her and the boss. But the boss was aware of Jade's secret. Not an ideal situation but then again the fact that the boss had kept shtum and hadn't gone blabbing to HR meant she was party to it now. Collusion. She couldn't expose Jade without dobbing herself in too.

The all-night café was busy. It always was. A feeding station for night workers, mainly cleaners and door staff, drivers and security guards.

Jade's mouth watered as soon as she stepped through the door. She ordered a chicken burger and chips for herself and the boss's butty. Listened to the babble of conversations, little explosions of laughter. Polish she thought she recognised, and something that might have been Arabic, and English in heavy African accents.

Several of the customers wore the same fleece tops, *U dream We clean* emblazoned on the back.

Jade headed off, leaving the steamy fug of the café. Outside the wind still blew, fresher now. A handful of gritty stars was visible overhead. The scream of a siren faint in the distance.

18

Her thoughts were on the case. Who was the baby? Where was the mother tonight? Long gone, putting as much distance as she could between herself and the child? Or somewhere in the city, sleeping, hoping not to be found?

Or dead, like her daughter?

Chapter 5

So small, thought Donna, when she saw the baby through the mortuary window from the anteroom. A scrap of a thing curled on the table. Naked. Vulnerable.

She and Jade were donning protective suits, masks and overshoes when the pathologist opened the door, pulling his mask down to greet them with a smile. Django was relatively new, a German Turk whose Scottish wife was also a pathologist working in Manchester. He had a lively enthusiasm for his work, which might have seemed out of place in such surroundings but which Donna found refreshing.

'The external examination is completed,' he said, leading them through.

The infant had pale, wrinkled skin, a cap of very fine straight brown hair. Her knees were bent and fists closed in a foetal position. At first glance you might think she was sleeping, until you noticed how very still she was.

'She is small in size and weight, two point four kilos,' Django said. He translated it into pounds when Donna frowned. 'Five pounds five ounces.'

'Premature?' Donna asked.

'No, full term, I think. Just on the smaller side. The age between two and four days old I estimate, and I'm basing that partly on the appearance of the umbilical stump here. It has begun to dry out and darken but only a little. It takes about a week to shrivel and drop off. The other factor that supports this age is meconium found in the nappy.' Django gestured to the counter along the side of the wall where the nappy and the sleepsuit were placed.

'Meconium?' Jade asked.

'This is first faecal waste. It is passed for the days after birth before feeding is properly established. Then the stools change,' Django said.

Donna nodded. 'It's very sticky, almost black.'

Django touched the baby's head. 'Also, please see how the skull is still elongated from the birth. But no traces of vernix so I think the baby has been washed.'

For a moment Donna had a rush of sense memory. Those leaky, achy, amazing, overwhelming days after birth. The visceral connection, as if she and the baby were still part of the same entity, still sharing blood and oxygen. Exhaustion and pain and elation. The hot, dense weight of a newborn. The pull that tugged at Donna's womb as the baby fed, the smell of her scalp.

'Now the umbilical cord has been tied off with a piece of household string. In hospital or at a home birth, midwives would use a plastic peg.'

'An unreported birth, then,' Donna said. 'Estimated time of death?'

'Hard to tell,' he said. 'The rigor has passed. This is not always detectable in an infant. With a small body mass the process is quicker. It is early onset and quick to dissipate. There is no sign of putrefaction so I am estimating sometime in the twenty-four hours before she was found. Internal examination might support that window. Cause of death can be particularly difficult to determine in infants. Initially I am seeing no obvious signs of trauma, no abrasions or puncture wounds. But here . . .' Django slid a hand under the baby's head, tilting it to raise the chin, then pointing, '. . . bruising around the mouth and inflammation of the nostrils.' He spoke excitedly, eyes bright.

Faint discoloration, a dusky bluish tinge spotted the skin in four places: three daubs to the right side of the nose and mouth and one to the left of the nose. Nothing obvious or dramatic. A layperson might very well have overlooked it.

'And here . . .' He released the head and used his little finger to draw back the lower lip. 'Petechial bleeds.'

Donna recognised the little pinprick marks, brought to the surface by pressure breaking the blood vessels. She was used to seeing similar marks in the eyes, in cases of strangulation.

'She was smothered,' Jade said.

'That would explain these injuries,' he said.

'Could they have been made by someone sitting or falling on her, crushing her?' Jade said.

'Then we would see a wider area of damage,' Django said.

'Any prints?' Donna said.

'Yes. We have two partials.' He pointed to the edge of the baby's jaw below the left ear. 'And one on the temple, here. And we swabbed everything for DNA and trace evidence. We may recover more fingerprints from the clothing and nappy.'

'We should check them against Colette,' Jade said.

'Colette?' Django asked.

'The woman who found her,' Donna said. 'She only touched her briefly but we need to see if there is a match.'

'I am performing the internal exam now,' Django said. 'Do you wish to stay?'

'No, we're briefing in an hour,' Donna said. 'But please let me know if you find anything else of particular significance.'

'I will do. We will be able to tell if she has been fed or not.'

The prospect of a child starving felt as awful to Donna as that of her being smothered.

'So it's murder,' Jade said.

'Or infanticide,' Donna reminded her. 'If it was the mother.' The law stretched to encompass some understanding for those women driven senseless in the aftermath of childbirth. The ones who were tormented by psychosis and acute depression. Those no longer of sound mind. 'Either way it's not a natural death. Someone's responsible for it,' Donna said.

And with that certainty came the knowledge that the hunt for the culprit would consume her energy, her efforts and those of her team over the days and weeks to come.

'Call her Baby Rosa,' Donna said to Django. 'I've cleared that with the press office. They're just waiting for my go-ahead to issue an appeal for information.' She hoped naming the child now would help fix the case in the public's mind and mitigate against any baby-in-the-bin style headlines once further details about the location of the discovery of Rosa's body were released.

'My daughter is Rosa,' Django said softly.

'We can change it?' Donna said quickly, looking at him.

'It is OK,' he said.

For a few moments no one spoke. Donna reached out a hand to cup the child's head before taking her leave.

Chapter 6

Once introductions had been made, Donna talked the team through
the known facts, referring to the map and images on the wall.

'Is the witness a person of interest?' asked Calvin. Donna had
worked with him twice before and at first had thought him a bit too
laid-back, dreamy, dozy almost, until she realised that he often took
his time thinking things through before he spoke. The opposite of
Jade. When he did contribute it was invariably valuable, identifying
a connection or anomaly in the evidence that others had missed.

'Not at present,' Donna said.

Calvin had done something different with his hair: the short Afro
he used to sport was replaced with a boxy cut, shaved at the sides. A
flat top? A fade? Her kids would know. It made him look fuller in the
face, even sturdier than he was.

'No inconsistencies in her statement, fully cooperative,' Donna
continued. 'We've taken DNA swabs and fingerprints. We've asked
her to keep us informed of her whereabouts so if anything does arise
we can talk to her again.'

Calvin gave a nod, wrote something in his notebook.

'Any evidence of abuse or trauma?' Isla looked up from her tablet.
Apple-cheeked with a mane of blonde hair, she was the very picture
of the healthy outdoors type. She was also tech savvy and one of the
best detectives at using a computer for forensic investigation. She
talked the same language as the digital forensics unit.

'No signs,' Donna said. 'The pathology report tells us that Rosa
was fed, there was partially digested formula in the stomach. She

24

was washed and clothed. Her umbilical cord was tied. She was cared for in those hours before her death.' Donna paused for a moment, letting that sink in. 'So what changed? You all appreciate that identifying the victim is our first priority. It can sometimes be a difficult challenge. Even more so when we're talking about an infant.'

'No dental records,' Jade said.

'Exactly. Little history on the body. No scars or medical implants. No chance of a criminal record. No mobile phone, house keys, bank cards and the like. So we start with what we do have. Where was the sleepsuit made and sold? And the brand of nappies?'

'What about the rubbish, the wastepaper in the bag?' Calvin said.

'That too,' Donna said. 'It's with the lab. We don't know yet what it consists of but we hope it will help us direct enquiries.'

'There might not be a connection,' Isla said. 'Whoever disposed of the baby might have found the bag of rubbish there in the bin already.'

Jade was nodding. She had said something similar to Donna earlier.

'It's possible,' Donna said. 'Everything is wide open at the moment so for now we focus on the following tasks. First we want to find Rosa's mother. At this stage we don't know if she's culpable or not but she's certainly a vulnerable person. So, when talking to people keep that in mind. Do they have customers, neighbours, clients who were expecting? If forensics link any of the evidence recovered to that area then we may look at liaising with local maternity services – find out if any expectant mothers have suddenly fallen off the grid.

'Second, I want to build up a timeline of who was coming and going near the scene yesterday. There are cameras on some nearby businesses and we talk to the owners, collect the footage for analysis. We do house calls in Rosa Street and Grace Street as well as the closest properties on Stockport Road. Have they heard a baby crying? Seen anyone loitering near the bin? We need to establish a pattern of activity around the site between eleven p.m. on Sunday and last night when Colette Pritchard arrived. Third, we—'

25

Donna's message alert sounded and she held up her hand to pause the meeting while she checked her phone. An email from the lab. 'No match on the fingerprints to anyone on the database,' she relayed.

A second email arrived. 'Positive match between Colette Pritchard's fingerprints and those recovered from the chest of the sleepsuit.'

'Like she said.' Jade leaned forward in her chair.

'Yes,' Donna said. Donna took comfort from that. She'd believed Colette, and if the science had contradicted her story, Donna would have been dismayed.

'The DNA profile of Colette is still running but shouldn't be much longer.' She glanced at her notes. 'Third line of enquiry is the clothing and the nappy. Now, an appeal for information is going out at ten.' Donna saw it was ten minutes to ten. 'So those of you on the phones get ready. We're including a request for people who were in the area during the relevant period to come forward. Anyone passing through and using dashcams will be asked to submit them for viewing as well. We aren't releasing the fact that Rosa was in the bin yet, although it's inevitable that word will spread, given the locals who were present at the scene last night. It's a baby. There'll be a lot of concern, a lot of interest. We want information not speculation. I don't want to panic the mother. We need to give her every chance to come forward. So for now, outside this room, we refer to this as an unexplained death. Is that clear?'

People nodded, understanding the need for discretion.

'Jade, we'll speak to the owners of the nearest properties, Mr Siddique at the Chuckie Chicken, and whoever we can find at Super Saver, then move on to Rosa Street. Isla, retrieve footage from the traffic cameras along that section of Stockport Road and get us as much as you can on the immediate area, who owns what, activity, criminal or otherwise, residents and businesses, and let's flesh out this map – everywhere from the church at that end to the mosque at the other. Calvin, please follow up on the sleepsuit and the nappies. The rest of you are on house calls on Grace Street and Stockport Road. Note all responses on the system. Let's meet again at six unless you hear otherwise, and in the meantime, if anything of interest comes up, feed it through to me, soon as.'

There was a racket as people pushed back their chairs and gathered up their files and notes.

'What happened to you?' Donna spotted the cast on Isla's leg. Jim's was off now. He'd worn it for ten weeks.

'Broken ankle,' Isla said.

'Snowboarding?' Isla and her girlfriend were adrenalin junkies, fixated on anything fast or potentially perilous or both.

'Hang-gliding. We fancied something new,' Isla said.

'Good job I'm not sending you out on house-to-house, then,' Donna said.

Isla grinned. 'I'm gutted.'

Jade was waiting by the door. Donna could see from her stance that she was impatient to get going. Her attitude reminded Donna of her eldest, Bryony, seventeen and forever infuriated by Donna. Though in Bryony's case, when she wasn't wound up by Donna 'taking like ages', she was a teenage sloth, who had to be prised from her bed with shouts of 'I told you when we were leaving', 'We'll be late' and 'We're going NOW!'

Donna nodded across to Jade, *I'm coming – keep your hair on*, and said goodbye to Isla.

Chapter 7

Mr Siddique seemed shaken by it all. In between their questions he would swing his head and stroke his beard and say, 'A terrible thing. This is a terrible thing.' At first Jade wondered if he was just bothered about the effect on his business, like he didn't want to be associated with a scandal, but then he was saying, 'To do this to your own flesh and blood.'

'We don't know who did what,' Jade said.

'But the mother must—' he began.

The boss interrupted him, 'We don't have all the facts so we concentrate on what we do know.'

He gave a shrug, like he didn't agree but he wasn't going to say so out loud.

'What time did you close?' the boss said.

'Eleven o'clock.'

'And how many of you were working last night?'

'Just two. My brother Waheed does the cooking and I'm on the counter.'

'What about deliveries?' Jade said.

'My nephew lives just over the road. We call him when he's needed but Mondays are our quietest night,' Mr Siddique said. With his long, narrow face, crinkly forehead and pointy beard he put Jade in mind of a goat.

She shifted in her seat. They were crammed into a small room at the back, next to the kitchen. Three of them around a rickety table, a row of coat hooks on one wall, the rest lined with tins of corn oil, five-litre containers of multi-surface cleaner, and boxes of polysty-rene takeaway trays. More boxes on the top shelf were wrapped in bin liners.

There was no window, just a fluorescent strip that sizzled and gave off a pitiless glare, making them all look sickly. At least, the boss and Mr Siddique did, so Jade expected she must too.

'And did you use the bin at all?' the boss said.

'Yes. At the end of the night all the rubbish is cleared away.'

'What time is that?'

'Ten forty-five, ten fifty,' Mr Siddique said.

'And who did that job last night?'

'I did,' he said.

'Did you see anyone?' the boss said.

'No,' he said quickly, with barely time to register the question.

'You sound very certain.'

'I have been thinking about this all night.' He sounded chippy. And then, 'A terrible thing.'

'How many bags did you put out?' the boss asked.

'Just the one. We clear up every night. It's important for food hygiene.'

'And what type of bags do you use?'

'Grey ones, heavy duty,' Mr Siddique said.

'Like those?' Jade pointed up to the ones covering the boxes.

'Yes.' He coughed and cleared his throat.

'What did the bag contain?' the boss said.

'Food scraps, disposable trays and cutlery, packaging, cans, bottles.'

'You don't recycle?' the boss said.

'CleanSolve take everything. I don't know if they sort it,' he said.

The strip light buzzed louder, sounding like a mini chainsaw. Jade wondered if it would blow.

'We'd like to take fingerprints from you, and your brother, for purpose of elimination,' the boss said.

'Really? Well – I suppose so.'

'Someone will be round later to do that. When are you expecting your brother?' the boss said.

'Soon. He's at the cash-and-carry.'

'OK. What time did you open yesterday?'

'Midday. As usual,' he said.

'And do you recall anything odd in the course of the day, anyone acting suspiciously, any cars pulling up but no one coming in? Anything out of the ordinary?'

'Not a thing.'

'Do you live in the area?' the boss said.

'No. Over in Reddish,' he said.

How long have you run the business here?'

'Fifteen years.'

'So you have regular customers?' the boss said.

'Yes, some.'

'Anyone recently who was heavily pregnant?'

'No, I don't think so,' Mr Siddique said.

'We'd like to take a look at the CCTV,' the boss said.

'Why?' He gripped his beard.

'Until we know the identity of the baby, we're having to focus on who was around. Try to find a connection, trace the mother.'

'Like I said, no one pregnant came in. Anyway, it's not working. I keep meaning to get it fixed but it's not like we carry much cash.' He was smiling then, showing all his teeth, bright and white apart from one at the front, which was cracked and stained with tobacco or coffee or something.

'We'll check it anyway,' the boss said, getting to her feet, one hand on the table, which rocked, making the dirty cups there rattle.

'If you want to waste your time,' Mr Siddique said, all huffy.

'Time is not an issue,' the boss said. 'We're talking about a child, an unexplained death. It takes as long as it takes.' Words sharp as knives.

He scratched at his beard, gave a breathy laugh. 'For sure, yes. A terrible thing. All I'm saying is if there's nothing on there, there's not much point . . . It's not . . .' He dribbled to a halt.

'We'll take the CCTV now.' The boss edged her chair out of the way and moved to the door, forcing him to do the same.

'He's hiding something,' Jade said, as they walked away from the shop.

'I'm with you there,' the boss said.

Jade looked back to see Mr Siddique still at the shop doorway. The scowl on his face changing to his fake smile as he saw her watching. He raised a hand and waved.

'Crap actor, too,' Jade said.

Chapter 8

They passed the area where the bin had been, still cordoned off with tape, to reach Super Saver, the business on the next corner, at the junction of Stockport Road and Grace Street.

The woman behind the counter was scrawny, the skin on her neck all wrinkly, everything mottled, freckled, like she'd spent too much time in the sun. She had pink and blue streaks in her grey hair, a big silver-coloured man's watch on her wrist. Jade recognised her from the onlookers last night.

'Mandy Myers.' She gave her name. 'I didn't know if I should have opened, what with everything . . . Is it all right? Only no one said anything and . . . I think it just . . .' She blinked fast. She had navy eyelashes. 'Sorry, sorry.'

'There's no problem opening up,' the boss said. 'But we'd like to talk to you and it'd be best if we weren't interrupted.'

The boss looked to the door just as a man came in. 'Mandy,' he said.

'George. I've got to close up for a bit.'

'I'll take my paper,' he said, 'and a Lucky Dip.'

Mandy looked worried, but the boss gave a nod and Mandy served him.

Super Saver sold a bit of everything. Groceries, cleaning products, hardware, pet food, booze, medicines, cigs. There was even some fancy coffee machine. And a selection of sweets, old-fashioned ones like humbugs and sherbet fountains alongside the Haribo and Chupa Chups lollies.

A tray of Remembrance poppies by the till. The lampposts on the main roads had been decorated with large plastic versions to mark a hundred years since the end of the First World War.

One display was given over to Halloween goodies: fake fangs, dressing-up gear, decorations. Signs on the windows showed the shop was a collection point for parcels and an outlet for Western Union money transfers. A big fluorescent one behind the counter read, *You want it? We get it!*

'Are you here about the baby?' George said to them.

'That's right,' the boss said.

'They do that a lot in Asia, China and that. They want boys so if it's a girl they leave them to die. It was on the telly.'

No one spoke for a moment. Jade saw Mandy give a quick eye-roll as George counted out his money.

'You live locally?' the boss said.

'Number nine Rosa Street. George Peel. We're practically neighbours, aren't we?' he said to Mandy.

She grunted.

'We'll call round after this,' the boss said.

'House-to-house, is it?' George said, on his way out.

Everyone an expert.

Mandy turned the notice on the door to 'Closed' and put the latch on. Then she led them through to an office space at the back, furnished with a two-seater sofa, a desk and a chair. She perched on the chair and pulled an e-cigarette from her pocket. 'It's all right, if I . . .?'

'Sure,' the boss said.

'I probably smoke twice as much as I used to do, with these things.' Mandy waved the stick. 'But they say it's tons safer, so . . . Is it true someone was sleeping in the bin?'

'We can't divulge any information,' the boss said.

A smell, like raspberry jam, sweet and sickly, filled the space.

'Poor little thing. And the mother, do you think she's ill?' Mandy prattled on. 'She must be, to do that. It's sad, isn't it?'

'We don't know what happened yet,' the boss said. 'When did you last use the bin?'

'Yesterday. They empty them on a Tuesday so I put stuff in when I close up. About eight o'clock.'

'Can you describe what you had? How many bags? What they contained?' the boss said.

Jade made notes as Mandy talked. Two bags, black ones, tie-handled, yellow ties. Plastic packaging, cardboard and paper, waste coffee pods. Some broken cups. 'Dropped the box like an idiot,' Mandy said. 'Set of four shattered.' Other odds and sods.

'And did you see anyone around when you took it out?' the boss said.

'No, nothing. No one.'

'And when you put the bags in the bin did you notice anything different inside? Any unusual bags?'

'No, but I barely looked. Just slung them in.' She reddened. 'I'm sorry, that sounds awful, but I never thought . . . I never knew . . . If I'd thought for one moment—'

'Of course,' the boss said. 'What about earlier yesterday? Anything strike you as odd, different from usual? Anyone acting strangely?'

Mandy pulled a face. 'No. Not that I can remember.'

'We'd like to arrange to take your fingerprints. It will help us eliminate people who used the bin from our enquiries. And the prints would be kept on file only for the duration of the investigation. Is that OK?'

'Of course. No problem.'

'We'll send someone round to take those. You'll be here all day?' the boss said.

Mandy nodded.

'Have you got any CCTV?' Jade asked.

'Yes, I can give you that. I'll get it now.' She set down the e-cigarette and bent under the table, emerging a second later with a disc. 'That's got yesterday and today on.'

'Are you open every day?'

'I close Sundays and Wednesday afternoons – a lot of us still keep to the half-day closing. Open eight till eight the rest of the time.'

'Long days,' the boss said.

'It's the only way to survive now. At least I've not got to travel far. Only up the stairs.' She raised her eyes to the ceiling.

'What about your own rubbish? Does that go in the same bin?' Jade said.

'No. I've council ones in the backyard, for the recycling.' Mandy took a suck on her e-cig, let out a cloud of vapour.

'How long have you had the shop?' the boss said.

'Twenty-six years.' She laughed. 'It was my father's before that, sweets and tobacco, papers. But when Ken and I took over we expanded.' She fingered the watch on her wrist. Ken's, Jade guessed.

'I can't compete with the supermarkets. People tend to pop in if they run out of stuff. Then there's the regulars, like George, who come in every day for papers or cigs. And the kids who call for sweets after school. Some people just use it for parcels, internet shopping. Doing the coffee helps. Seems like we're all mad for coffee, these days. People walking round with a big beaker glued to their hands. I can't drink the stuff. It gets me hyper. I'd rather stay calm.' If this was calm, Jade would have hated to see the woman wired up.

'Are you here on your own?' the boss asked.

'Yes. Ken died. Eleven years ago now.'

'I'm sorry,' the boss said.

'Long time.' She took another suck.

'Mandy, do you know of anyone locally who was due to have a baby about now?'

'There was Carla. She's down near the end of Grace Street but she's had hers, twin boys, I heard. I can't think of anyone else that far along. You think it was someone round here?'

'We don't know yet.'

There was knocking from the front of the shop.

'I'll send them away.'

'It's all right. We've got what we need for now,' the boss said.

There were three kids at the door, a lad of ten or so and two little boys.

'All right, William? I can set my watch by you. You let these ladies out first,' Mandy said to the oldest lad. But the smallest kid had already shoved into Jade's knees and wriggled past. He made a beeline for the sweet counter.

'Mum not here?' Mandy said.

William shook his head.

'OK. Tell her it's a rollover. She never misses. Could be her lucky break.'

Outside, schoolchildren were drifting along the pavements in groups of two and three. Those with parents or carers moved more quickly. Jade saw how people switched pace when they passed the police tape, some slowing down, others speeding up. She watched an older woman, with a bunch of children, cross herself then kiss her thumb, as if she'd ward off evil. The gesture echoed in Jade's head. Someone she knew well used to do that. Who had it been? Back when she was small? Her mother? Another relative? It wasn't at school, she was sure of that. Ah, who cared? It didn't matter. The past, and everyone in it, was dead and gone. Or good as.

Chapter 9

George's house was only a minute's walk, halfway down Rosa Street, and while they waited for him to answer the door, Donna noticed a woman coming along the pavement opposite, with two black pugs on leads.

'Odelia,' Donna said to Jade, watching as Odelia went into the house to the right of the flats. A three-storey block with a level roof, they interrupted the terraced row. Donna judged that they occupied the space once filled by three houses.

'We could have a word with her after,' she said. Odelia's house looked spick and span, with a shiny blue door and white venetian blinds, in contrast to George's, whose old wooden window frames were crumbling, while grass and a lanky sycamore sapling adorned the roof guttering.

George took them into his front room where he settled himself in a chair facing the window and the TV in the corner. The sofa was strewn with papers, a carton of light-bulbs and a Tupperware box full of medicines. He didn't offer them a seat so they both remained standing.

'If I was you,' he said, 'I'd be talking to that lot in the flats.'

'Why's that, then?' Donna said.

'Coming and going all hours. Parking on the pavements. They shouldn't have built those flats there, not without proper parking. But money talks, I suppose.'

'Have you any reason to think someone living there might be able to help us with the inquiry?' Donna said.

'You know what they say, no smoke—'

Donna interrupted, 'We've a lot of people to talk to, Mr Peel, so we'd appreciate it if there's anything specific you can tell us.'

'Last night,' he said. 'Doors slamming and screaming, then someone goes roaring off in a car.' He gave a smirk, bowed his head at her, pleased with himself.

'What sort of car?' Donna said, eager to get as many details as she could.

'I don't know. By the time I looked out to see what all the commotion was, it was gone.'

'The screaming. Who was screaming?' Donna said.

'It sounded like a fight, a man and a woman. Shouts,' he said.

'Anything you could make out? Any words or phrases? Names?'

'No.'

'Were they speaking English?'

'Probably not.' Which was no sort of answer at all.

'What about the slamming? The doors. What sort of doors?' Donna said.

'Oh, I don't know.' He twitched his shoulders, as though irritated now by his own account.

'Car doors or a house door?' Jade said.

'Car door,' he said, off-hand. Donna's faith in his recollection grew shakier. She saw, out of the corner of her eye, Jade flex her fingers, like she was trying not to butt in, or to thump him.

'And when you did look out of the window, was it this window?' Donna said.

'Yes.'

'Did you see anything at all?' Donna said.

'I did!' Triumphant, as if he'd scored a point, he jabbed a finger in her direction. 'I saw lights going on in a flat at the top. The left-hand side. That's what I mean. You need to talk to them over there. I reckon whoever had been screaming, one of them drives off, the other goes in, slams the door and puts the light on.'

'I thought you said it was a car door?' Donna asked.

'Probably both. If you think about it.' He glared at her.

38

Donna softened her tone deliberately, not wanting to give him the satisfaction of appearing frustrated. 'Mr Peel, we can only deal with precise information. If you're not sure which type of door you heard, that's fine, but it would be helpful if you could be clear.'

'Both,' he said this time.

'What time was this?' Donna said.

'Seven. *The One Show* had just started.'

'And you heard it above the noise of the TV?'

He sighed. 'I heard something.' He spoke slowly, emphasising every word as if she was dense, patronising her. 'So I turned the TV down to make sure.'

'I see. Can you remember anything else?'

'No.'

'If you do, please get in touch,' Donna said. 'Do you know any of the residents in the flats?'

'No. They don't mix. They're always moving on. Students and what-have-you.'

'It's student accommodation?'

'It's an eyesore, that's what it is. They let the rubbish pile up, leaving it out. Then it gets knocked over. We have rats and foxes. Dirty beggars.' Donna wasn't sure whether he was talking about the vermin or the neighbours. There was nothing particularly untoward, from what Donna could see of the property across the road. George's house was probably shabbier than the flats.

She asked him to write down his movements for the twenty-four-hour period they were concentrating on, and include in his notes anyone he'd seen or spoken to.

'What for?' he said.

'We need to try to identify who was in the area and when,' Donna explained. 'Someone will call round in the next day or so for that.'

He sighed theatrically and shook his head slowly.

Outside, Jade said, 'If he's right and it was the people opposite, they'd have to have run up two flights of stairs like gold medallists to turn the lights on that quickly.'

'It could just be a coincidence,' Donna said.

'Or . . .' Jade said, her eyes gleaming.

'Go on.'

'Whoever was over there had turned the lights *off* to have a sneaky peek when *they* heard screaming. If it was screaming. And then they put them back on again when the car's gone and there's nothing more to see. If there was a car.'

Donna looked round, plenty of lampposts. 'But why turn their lights off? They'd be able to see well enough with the streetlights.'

'Because *they* don't want to be seen having a nosy. I always turn mine off before I look out if I think something's kicking off. No one outside can see you, that way. It's safer.'

Donna wasn't sure what to say to that, imagining Jade in the dark, tense and alert to danger. Jade had been attacked in her own home not long ago, which would make anyone cautious and careful. But then again, Donna suspected Jade had been in other dangerous situations long before that. She'd had a tough start in life and it had shaped her, made her streetwise, and distrustful. She never talked about it but Donna had pieced it together from little clues here and there.

'Good point,' Donna said.

'There could be a connection, couldn't there, between the fight, or row or whatever, and the death?' Jade said.

'There could be but that's a big leap at the moment. Let's not get ahead of ourselves, eh? There could be a dozen other explanations.'

'Yeah, I guess,' Jade said, the excitement fading from her voice.

'Let's see if there's anyone at the flats,' Donna said. 'Then we'll talk to Odelia.' She yawned. Seventeen hours straight since she'd been called to Rosa Street. She could feel the fatigue stiffening her neck and her shoulders. A mild ache behind her eyes, and a sour taste in her mouth.

At the entrance to the block of flats, Jade stabbed each buzzer in turn but no one answered the intercom.

'Odelia's, then,' Donna said.

When Jade pressed the bell at number six, a chorus of barking,

40

fast and high-pitched, came from inside, followed by a shout: 'Shut up! Eric! Ernie, shut up! Now!'

Odelia opened the door and Donna made the introductions. Odelia ushered them in, brow creased. 'I've put the dogs in the kitchen,' she said. 'Daft as a brush, the both of them.' She spoke with the Mancunian accent, a lilt of the Caribbean mixed in.

Drawings of the pugs dominated the living-room walls. 'My daughter does them. She's an artist.'

'She's good,' Donna said.

'So how can I help?' Odelia said.

'You know Colette Pritchard?' Donna said.

'Colette?' Odelia seemed surprised. 'Yes. Well, I didn't know her surname. But yes, why?'

'When did you last see her?' Donna said.

'Last night, late on, close to eleven.'

'Where?'

'On the road, the main road. I was bringing the dogs home,' Odelia said.

'Did you talk to her?' Donna said.

'No, we just waved. Is she all right? Has something happened to her?'

'She found the baby,' Donna said.

'No.' Odelia pressed a hand to her chest. 'Oh, Lord. That poor woman. She has no home, she has no . . . She has nowhere. Nothing.'

'Do you know where she was sleeping?' Donna said.

'Wherever she could find a dry place, I think. Doorways and that sort of thing. The railway arches,' Odelia said.

Donna could imagine Colette wouldn't have wanted anyone to know the real truth about where she was spending her nights, shame making her hide the worst of it.

'We're asking people if they know of anyone in the area who was expecting a baby,' Donna said.

'I don't. I mean there must be some,' she added. 'I'd probably have been able to tell you when I was still working. I taught at Oaks Primary so we knew all the families. There is Carla. She lives on

Grace Street – she's had twins, so she might know others. Do they still have the baby clinic in the prefab past the church? I lose track since I retired. But you could ask there.'

'We'll find out. Thank you. Did you see or hear anything unusual last night?' Donna said.

Whining came from the kitchen, growing in volume.

Odelia shook her head at the distraction. She smoothed her grey hair with one hand, pursing her lips. 'I don't think so. I was out, round at my daughter's, until about half past eight. There was nothing strange after that, I don't think.'

'Any noise and disturbance?' Donna said.

'No. But my hearing is not as good as it used to be. The dogs would usually bark if there was a lot of noise. They would let me know. And they didn't.'

'What about earlier in the day? Were you here?'

'Yes, most of the time. I took the dogs out after breakfast. And in the afternoon I went to the health centre – blood-pressure check.'

Donna asked her to note down who she'd seen and when for the investigation. 'We're asking everyone to do the same.'

'Fine. They're away next door, number four, Mr and Mrs Singleton,' Odelia said.

'Since when?' Jade said.

'Since Wednesday, holidays.'

'Thank you,' Donna said. 'Do you have any bother from the flats next door?'

'You've been talking to George?' she said. She raised an eyebrow.

Donna tried not to smile.

'That man has a whole hive of bees in his bonnet.' Odelia tutted. 'Now and then there's a party and they'll go on half the night, true enough, but it's not all the time. People have to live side by side. I've known worse.'

A savage snarling rang through the house. Deafening.

'Oh, Lord, excuse me.' Odelia moved to the hall and they heard her shouting to quieten the dogs. She came back in, saying, 'It's not like this house is the quietest in the street, either.'

'Does anyone else live here?' Donna said.

'My son Oscar. But he's away now. He works in catering on the cruise ships.'

Donna saw him in the clutch of family photos on top of the bookshelves. Odelia and her husband, presumably, two children. Images of the daughter's graduation, a Disney trip, a wildflower meadow with the two children performing handstands, a posed Christmas picture, the family all in seasonal sweaters.

'Just Oscar?' Donna ventured.

'That's right. My husband isn't around any more.' Her tone grew clipped and Donna chose not to ask her to elaborate. If he wasn't in the house it wasn't relevant. Did she keep the photos up for the children? Donna had a moment's disorientation, imagining her home, her family without Jim. Another heart attack ripping him from their lives. She quashed the thought.

On the way out, Donna noticed a stack of Labour Party pamphlets on the hall table. The headline, *MP CALLS FOR ACTION OVER POLICE CUTS. BRING BACK OUR BOBBIES.* If only, Donna thought. The violent crime rate was climbing, the drugs syndicates growing ever more bold, and young people were disproportionately the victims but, with the country still plagued by austerity and mired in the mess of Brexit, there was no chance of a significant increase in funding. Besides, working at the sharp end, Donna knew that violent crime was directly linked to poverty, poor education and domestic violence. Policing alone could only deal with the symptoms, not the causes.

Back at the flats, there was still no response. Then Donna's phone vibrated.

'Anthea?' she answered.

'The initial audit of the rubbish bag is through,' Anthea said.
Great!

'We're on our way,' Donna said. She turned to Jade. 'Call everyone back in.' And her blood began to move faster at the prospect of fresh evidence to add to the nuggets they'd recovered so far.

Chapter 10

Donna started the meeting even though Calvin hadn't arrived and neither had two of the house-to-house team.

'Lab report.' She held up the printout. 'They'll be carrying out further tests looking for trace evidence that could tell us who handled the papers, and the rubbish bag itself, but for now we have a list of the contents. Any thoughts as we go, please jump in.'

Donna began the list. 'Copies of the *Daily Mirror* for Wednesday, Thursday, Friday, Saturday, and the *Sunday Mirror*.'

'Only part of the week,' Isla said.

'The bins, the residential ones round there, they get emptied on a Wednesday morning,' Jade said. 'If the blue bins were done last week this could be all they had left.'

'Good point, but also true for anyone on the same rota elsewhere in the city,' Donna cautioned.

Jade shrugged. Donna couldn't tell whether she was accepting the idea, or dismissing it.

'We also have food packaging,' Donna said. 'Teabag and egg boxes, pizza box, fish-fingers packet, cartons of individual juice drinks.'

'Someone with kids?' Jade said.

'Though some adults like those,' Donna said.

'Calvin for one,' Isla said. 'He has those little drinks.'

'And Marks & Spencer's do fish-finger sandwiches. Retro, isn't it?' Tessa, one of the DCs, said.

Calvin walked in, mini Vimto in hand, and a gale of laughter rang round the room.

'What?' he said, unbuttoning his jacket. 'Did I miss something funny?'

'We'll catch you up later.' Donna smiled. 'So, possibly a household with kids – but don't get blinkered.' She scanned the list. 'Card inserts, the sort of thing found in clothing from online shopping, and shredded corrugated-cardboard packaging material. Toilet-roll centres. Used kitchen roll. Junk mail: flyers for carpet cleaning, one for windows replacement, and another for a free month's gym membership, three leaflets for takeaways, and a paving and patio firm.'

'If we contact these companies we can find out who was doing the distribution and where they've been active in the last few days,' Isla said.

'Calvin, you take that?' Donna said.

'Will do, boss.'

'Next, a Labour Party pamphlet,' Donna said.

'Odelia Johnson had a pile of those,' Jade said.

'She did,' Donna said. 'Obviously the latest bulletin for the ward. So, Isla, can we find out from the constituency office when and where they were delivered. Cross-referencing that with the other items should narrow down the geographical area. Nice job on the map, by the way.' Names and pertinent information had been added to properties in the immediate vicinity.

'We also have a calling card, someone touting for business as a dog-walker, sort of thing you can print off at home. Again, let's ask Lady and the Tramp—' A groan greeted the name of the business.

'Better than Paws for Walk,' someone shouted.

'Or Pound the Hound,' Isla said.

'Enough,' Donna said. 'Ask the dog-walker which addresses they've covered since Tuesday last. Finally a lottery ticket. Lotto.' Donna thought of Mandy's shop. The regulars buying their tickets like clockwork. 'Anyone here play the lottery?' she said.

A sprinkling of hands.

'Keep your hand up if you always buy tickets for the same game.'

A couple of hands went down.

'And relax. So most of us are creatures of habit. Remember that. Could this ticket point to someone?'

'Are there no receipts? Personal correspondence? Nothing addressed?' Calvin said.

'Nothing,' Donna said. 'And I'd imagine there would be some personal mail over that period.'

'Not necessarily,' Isla said. 'Lots of people go paperless, do everything electronically, on their phone.'

'Could be that. Or they made sure there was nothing left in there to identify them,' Donna said. 'That's it on the rubbish. Now, on house-to-house we've had no reports of a pregnant woman who could be Rosa's mother. Anyone else hear anything?'

General shaking of heads from the house-to-house teams.

'Anything over the phones?' She looked to Bob, who was coordinating the public response to the appeal.

'We've a few names to follow up,' he said. 'Nothing's come of any of them so far.'

'She's disappeared,' Donna said. 'Has she left the area? Or was she just passing through? Is someone sheltering her? Staying with house-to-house, what else did we learn. Jade?'

'Report of an argument at seven p.m. yesterday. A man and a woman, shouting and screaming, doors slamming, vehicle leaving at speed. But no visuals. The witness claims that lights going on in the flats over the road means they were involved, but that's from a curtain-twitcher with a chip on each shoulder.'

'Yes, Mr Peel is a bit of a Victor Meldrew, for those who remember the character,' Donna said, catching a combination of smiles and puzzled frowns. She gestured to Jade to continue.

'We're waiting to speak to the occupants there. Also, the owner of the Chuckie Chicken, Mr Siddique, got arsey when we removed his CCTV. Even though he said it was broken.'

'I want to know why,' Donna said. 'Tessa, will you take a look at it, please?'

'The sighting of Colette Pritchard just before eleven p.m. by

46

Odelia Johnson from six Rosa Street fits the account we had from Colette,' Jade said.

'And Colette's DNA profile is through now,' Donna said. 'So Forensics can use that when they're analysing evidence on the bin and paper waste. Please make sure you all feed in any timeline information so Isla can work her magic on that.'

'Boss,' Bob said, 'we had an alert through from neighbourhood police. Police Community Support Officer Evans attended an attempted break-in at thirteen Grace Street yesterday at eighteen forty-five.'

'Isla?' Donna said. Isla highlighted the property on the interactive map. It was the last house on Grace Street, next to the railway line.

'Suspect hadn't gained entry but substantial damage was done to the door and window there,' Bob said. 'The occupant got home from work at eighteen hundred hours and called it in.'

All eyes were on Bob. Donna imagined that, like her, they were trying to work out if this crime had any connection to their own investigation.

'PCSO Evans then went round to Rosa Street to ask if anyone in the houses at the bottom end had heard a disturbance or seen anything, given they share the back alley. No one had,' Bob said.

'Was the property alarmed?' Donna asked.

'No. But they'd have made a lot of noise, apparently. It looked like they'd been using a jemmy.'

'Maybe the doors banging that Mr Peel reported was actually the burglar,' Isla said.

'But the timing doesn't fit,' Jade said. 'Too soon.'

'Off by more than an hour,' Donna said. 'Can we ask Officer Evans to send us a full account, including who they talked to and when, and feed all that into our timetable?'

'Will do,' Bob said.

'Calvin, what have you got?' Donna said.

'Apart from a Vimto?' Jade slipped in.

'Both the nappy and the sleepsuit are own-brand Asda. There's a store in Levenshulme, half a mile from the scene. I asked them to do a search for sales of those items in the last month. There's also a branch in Longsight so I've done the same there.'

'Good. Anything else, anyone?' Donna said.

'The mother lives nearby,' Jade said. 'And it's someone with kids already.'

'Possibly,' Donna said.

'This stuff, it all fits. The clothes are in the Asda down the road, the paper waste is what anyone in those streets would have. I've just checked the council website and last week *was* blue bins.'

'As it would be further afield,' Donna said. 'Suppose you're right? Say it is someone local, why leave the baby so close? There's more risk of being traced.'

'It's the nearest place she thinks of. See, we know the baby was looked after before it was smothered. So something happens, she loses it, goes off on one, smothers the baby, then panics. She has to get rid, so she puts it in the rubbish bag and dumps it in the bin by the takeaway.' Jade was animated, intense, her face sharper with urgency. 'She knows the commercial bins get emptied this morning. And no one would expect people to start poking around in them.'

'Jade, I hope you're right. It would make it much easier for us if it was local, but until we've checked and cross-referenced everything we can't definitively say where that rubbish came from, or that baby. Or – that the mother is responsible.'

'It's obvious—'

'Jade,' Donna hardened her voice, 'I'm not saying you're wrong but I am saying we don't know yet. We let the evidence lead us. And as senior investigating officer I decide when we close off any lines of enquiry. Clear?'

Jade's face was wiped of any expression. Blank. The animation gone. Donna was aware of pulling rank but that was no bad thing. There were some in the room who would be biding their time before deciding if Donna was up to scratch. Everyone knew she'd been fooled by a bent colleague who had almost destroyed a previous investigation. Some might even know it was Jade Bradshaw who'd exposed the corruption and could mistake Donna's hard line with Jade as bitterness between them. So be it.

Donna looked round the room. 'Anything else?'

No one spoke.

'Then let's call it a day.' *A long one.* 'Except for those of you heading out for further house-to-house. It's a good start, people. Thank you. We'll pick up tomorrow, eight o'clock start, tasks as discussed.'

The meeting broke up. Donna watched Calvin hold up his drink, head angled in question, and Isla leaned over to explain.

Donna took a final look at the boards. The green crosses on the map that showed properties already interviewed. Question marks where officers judged enquiries still needed to be made. Photos of the bin in situ. And the picture of Rosa, pale, curled up, her true identity still a mystery to them all.

Chapter 11

Jade's lights were on as she parked outside her block. She always left them on. She wondered again about the lights coming on in the flat on Rosa Street. Would whoever lived there have seen anything significant? Was there a connection between the screaming George Peel claimed to have heard and the baby's death? And what about the attempted break-in on Grace Street?

Whatever – she was sure it was down to someone local. The boss had jumped down her throat for that. Jade knew they had to do it by the book, not allow hunches or bias to prejudice their enquiries, but at times like this she wished they could just get the fuck on with it and ramp up the action. 'Methodical': that was often the word the boss chucked at Jade when Jade was impatient because she knew, she just knew, what they should be digging into.

Jade climbed the concrete steps to her landing at the top, the third floor. She slowed her pace at her neighbour Mina's door and knocked four times. A signal that Jade was home, so if the old woman heard noises from Jade's flat she wouldn't need to come nosing around to make sure Jade wasn't being robbed. Or beaten up.

'It's not going to happen again,' Jade had told Mina. 'The guy is a shitbag . . .'

Mina had pursed her lips at 'shit'.

'He knew I was on to him, he knew where I lived, he lost the plot. And I brought him down.' OK, maybe she hadn't done it single-handed. She'd had a little help from her old mate, DD. But all the same. 'You don't need to check up on me every five minutes.'

'What if another come? You are chasing all bad people. Murderers.' Mina was Polish and her English got worse when she was agitated.

'And shitbags.' Jade couldn't resist.

Mina punched her arm. 'How do I know this is not a killer in there?'

So Jade had come up with the knock system.

'What if I don't hear you knock? If the television is loud?'

'Then ring me, or text me,' Jade said.

'No text.' Mina scowled. 'Too fiddly. Faffing. We would all be dead before.'

'So call. And not for a chat,' Jade warned. 'Just to check I'm home.'

'Mrs I'm-So-Busy,' Mina huffed.

Jade had just stared at Mina until she dropped her gaze and gave a shrug.

After a few false starts, when Mina had answered the door, calling hysterically, 'Yes? Hello? Who's there? Who is it?' as Jade reached her own flat, the arrangement seemed to be working.

Bert, her ancient neighbour opposite, was less fussy but probably more trouble. Pitching over and having to be hauled upright on a regular basis, he insisted to all and sundry that Jade was his unofficial carer, did all sorts, couldn't manage without her.

He was frailer every week. Had the shakes now, too.

'Look at that.' He'd shown her a crossword, the squiggles lurching all over the grid, like someone had knocked into a Scrabble board. 'Can't write, bloody useless.'

The GP had talked him into using a company who delivered ready meals so all he had to do was heat them in the microwave. He'd given Jade a couple to try – they weren't bad. But he was still shrinking. Jade wondered how skinny a person could get before their legs just snapped.

Inside, Jade locked and bolted her door, put down her bag and took off her jacket. One advantage of the attack, and the trashing of her flat in the fight with her assailant, was that she'd been forced to get some new stuff. Just the basics but a step up from what she'd had before. Table and matching chairs, sofa and flat-screen TV, bed, bedside table, chest of drawers, clothes rail.

'You need pictures and cushions, make it homey,' Mina had said, when she blagged her way in with a form for a blue badge that she wanted Jade's help with.

'You haven't got a car,' Jade said.

'*You* have a car. I can put the number down. Then if we go somewhere you can park with the badge. Even double yellow.'

'Where would we go?' Jade said, regretting the question the second she'd opened her stupid mouth.

'The seaside. The Trafford Centre.'

Kill me now.

'Mina, I don't have time. Don't start thinking I can take you here, there and everywhere. I'm fine doing your shopping but that's all.'

'Just do the form,' Mina had shouted.

'Fine. Jesus,' Jade had shouted back, snatching the paper.

A few weeks after, Mina had presented Jade with a crocheted blanket, woollen squares in primary colours. 'For your couch,' she said.

'You keep it,' Jade said.

'I have one,' Mina said. 'This is for you.'

'Right,' Jade said. 'Ta.'

She had stuffed it under her bed. Then one night she'd got cold watching telly and, rather than use her coat, she'd wrapped the blanket around her. So now it lived on the sofa. A blare of colour in the neutral greys and beiges of the rest of the place.

Jade heated some spag bol in the microwave, opened a can of Red Bull and washed down her tablets.

She watched the news while she ate, their case headlining the regional segment. Footage of the cordon at Rosa Street, a repeat of the appeal for information.

She pulled the blanket up and closed her eyes, images from work flickering in and out of view.

She woke stumbling from a dream where Bert was in the wheelie bin and Jade couldn't pull him out. The bin was on the edge of a mountain cliff with a sheer drop below.

It was three in the morning. Some quiz-show bollocks on the TV. Jade switched it off. She should go to bed. Get undressed. Lie down. *In a minute.*

She closed her eyes again.

Chapter 12

Donna lay awake. She was exhausted, bone tired, and her eyes were dry and gritty. She had tried to relax her muscles, to focus on her breathing, but her mind chattered on and her body danced to its tune.

Beside her Jim slumbered, apparently untroubled. She always envied his ability to sleep in a crisis. To get his eight hours in the midst of grief or stress or ructions with the kids.

Arriving home from work she'd seen the notice straight away: he'd left it on the kitchen table. To remind her? The inquest was going ahead. He was summoned to appear at ten a.m. on Thursday to give evidence as the driver of the car that had killed pedestrian Aaron Drummond.

They'd known this was coming but Donna still felt a surge of anxiety about it, and a backwash of pity and sorrow for the poor man who had died in the accident, for his wife and his two children. For Jim, too, because he would have to live through it all again. Cope with the guilt. If he'd only taken her advice and seen the GP about the chest pains he'd been suffering with, perhaps he wouldn't have had a heart attack and lost control of the car when he did. She remembered how he'd woken in the night, mumbling, 'Pain.' How clammy he'd been when she'd touched his forehead. And she felt angry afresh at how he'd batted away her concern, her suggestions. 'Indigestion,' he'd said.

This evening she had picked up the summons and found Jim in the armchair in front of the telly. Nine-year-old Matt was asleep on the sofa, his cheeks cherry red, sweat darkening his hairline.

'Nightmare?' she asked Jim, tilting her head towards Matt.

'Zombie cats,' Jim said.

'Two for one,' Donna said. Matt had a long list of things that scared him, and plagued his dreams.

'I'll take him up when I've had something to eat. This.' She held up the note. 'I'll be there.'

'There's no need. And your work—'

'No, I will.'

He opened his mouth, shut it again. A tug of tension in the set of his lips. Sceptical.

'OK,' she said. 'It may be hard to stay for all of it, depends how long it takes, but I'll be there at the beginning.' She put a hand on his shoulder.

He reached up and squeezed it. 'OK. Thanks.'

A rush of affection took her by surprise. She moved in front of him. 'Hey, I know things have been hard . . . and . . .' The strained atmosphere that had come to characterise their interactions, the lack of pleasure, not just sex but any shared enjoyment, wasn't only because Jim had been injured and needed time to recuperate. It wasn't just the low hum of resentment she felt as she struggled to pack everything in, sole breadwinner, work and family stretching her too thin. Even before that there'd been a distance growing between them. Or was it just in her head? Her heart? Was he oblivious?

'But I do love you,' she said.

'I know,' he said.

She thought about saying more. How they should talk, work out a way of rebuilding the relationship and— Sudden shouts and a raucous cheer came from upstairs. The twins, Rob and Lewis. Matt twitched in his sleep.

'European league,' Jim said.

'Much longer?'

'They're in extra time,' Jim said.

'Is Bryony still out?'

'Yes.'

'OK.' She held up his summons. 'I'll put this in the drawer.'

He nodded. 'Thanks.'

In the kitchen Donna made herself cheese on toast and a tomato and basil salad. She poured a glass of white wine, her mind lighting on moments from the day. The bruising on Rosa's face, Mr Siddique in his doorway, Colette's story, the rape that had led her to feel safer in the squalid bin than out on the street, her sorrow at finding the dead baby.

Then she carried Matt upstairs and put him back into bed.

She cracked open the door to Kirsten's room, holding her breath and hoping she was asleep, like her little brother.

Kirsten had always been hard work and was struggling after the recent move up to high school, complaining about being lonely and how the homework was too hard. Jim bore the brunt of it, dealing with her tears because he was around when she got home from school.

'It'll get better,' Donna had said to her. 'You've only done a few weeks.'

'A few weeks of torture,' Kirsten shot back. Always dramatic. Rarely happy. 'What if it gets worse?'

'We'll talk about it,' Donna had said. 'And Dad and I can help with the homework side of things.'

'Dad doesn't know anything,' she sneered. 'And you're never here.'

'That's not true,' Donna said.

'Do you want proof? Do you want evidence? Cos I can—'

'Kirsten, I'm sorry you're finding it tough but it might help to think about the good bits.'

'What good bits?'

'Your English marks. They've been brilliant. And geography,' Donna said. 'Music.'

'You don't understand. You never understand.'

Donna had taken a steadying breath and then said, 'We can always come in and talk to your form tutor, if you think that would help. And the school have a clear bullying policy so if—'

'It's not bullying,' Kirsten had said. 'They just ignore me. I've no

56

friends.' She cried then and Donna moved to comfort her but Kirsten had pushed her away and run upstairs.

At least she seemed to have inherited her father's ability to get to sleep in spite of all her woes.

Now Donna threw back the duvet and crossed the landing to the toilet. She heard the front door click shut. Midnight. Half an hour after Bryony's curfew. Was that why Donna hadn't been able to sleep, waiting for her eldest to be home safe?

She considered going down to ask Bryony why she was late, then ditched the idea. A confrontation too far.

Back in bed she plumped up her pillow and lay down. A spatter of rain hit the window and she thought of Colette Pritchard. Was she awake too, haunted by discovering the baby? *It wasn't right. So still and cold.* And the baby's mother – had she seen the appeal to come forward? Was she too scared? And tonight, was she lying in the dark somewhere mourning her child?

Chapter 13

Jade was back on Rosa Street, door-knocking with the boss by nine in the morning. The late shift had some degree of success canvassing the occupants of the flats but hadn't spoken to the person renting 3B, the flat that George Peel had singled out.

Jade gave another long push on the buzzer and glanced at the boss, who blew out a breath. *A waste of time.* The boss looked cranky, knackered, Jade thought, as though it was the end of the day, not the start.

Jade was checking where was next when the intercom squawked and a man's voice croaked, 'Who is it?'

'Police,' Jade said. 'DI Bell and DC Bradshaw. We're conducting enquiries in the area.'

'You want to talk to me?'

General idea, mate. 'Yes,' Jade said.

'Any chance we could do it later?'

Jade looked at the boss. *Cheeky get.*

The boss let her mouth hang open, pulled a face. She leaned into the speaker and said, 'We'll only take a few minutes of your time, sir,' in a voice that could have cracked metal.

"Kay,' he said, and there was a blurting sound as he released the door lock.

They took the lift to the third floor.

There was an undeniable stench of skunk as the door to flat 3B opened. The man there was a hipster, complete with beard and side-burns and a high ponytail. Shiny face, sweating. Tense. Probably been clearing up the drugs. He had ear stretchers in, golden ones. And crease marks on one cheek. He might have been in his PJs. Tartan sweatpants and a T-shirt with a Manchester bee symbol on it. Celtic bands tattooed on each arm. And some letters and numbers in a line, a maths formula, or maybe physics. An equation. Jade remembered the term. She'd not been bad at maths, when she was actually in school. Maths made sense. What you got was either right or wrong. It added up or it didn't.

'I was asleep,' he said. Like they couldn't tell. 'Come in.'

The curtains were still drawn and the room was littered with takeaway cartons, an empty vodka bottle, glasses on the coffee-table, two games controllers. A massive smart TV with a console, the main attraction. At first Jade had thought the flats were a step up from her place. Forty years younger for a start. But then she realised how low the ceilings were, and the rooms were smaller. Everything silver grey and maroon.

His name was Clark Whitman. He was thirty-four.

The boss explained why they were there and asked Whitman if he could think of anything to help them. If he knew anything about the baby or her mother.

'No, nothing,' he said.

Had he heard or seen anything on Monday? Anything unusual? Any disturbance?

'The break-in behind, you mean? A policeman called and asked about it. I told him I did hear banging but I thought it was just someone doing building work, or something on the industrial unit down the road.'

'Did you see anything?' the boss said.

'No. We only have frosted glass at the back but I never even looked. Like I say, I'd no idea there was anything wrong. But just before he came there was some noise outside at the front. So I thought the police were here for that at first.'

Jade's interest sharpened.

'What sort of noise?' the boss said.

'People shouting. It sounded heavy, you know?'

'Man or woman?' the boss said.

'A woman, mainly. But I think I heard a man too.'

'What time was it?' Jade said.

'Well, it was dark by then. Maybe a quarter of an hour before the police knocked,' Whitman said.

That fitted with George Peel's time of seven p.m.

'Could you make out anything that was said?' the boss asked.

'It sounded like, "No. No. Don't." I thought maybe someone was in trouble. I looked out and couldn't see anything, just next-door's van driving off.' He hitched a thumb to the right. Towards the last house on that side of the cul-de-sac, next to the railway. Number fourteen.

Jade pulled back the curtains, far enough to see out. No van there now.

'Can you describe the van?' Jade said.

'A Transit type. White.'

The boss asked him some more questions. He'd left for work on the first train on the Tuesday morning, commuting to London.

'London?' Jade said.

'Got to go where the work is,' Whitman said.

Footsteps tremored through the floor.

'Clark?' The bedroom door was flung back. 'I tell you, my head—' A man there, bollock naked. Full morning glory. 'Oh, fuck. Sorry,' he said. His hands flew to cover his crotch. 'Shit. Fuck.' He retreated, closing the door.

Whitman flushed red. The boss, too. Jade's cheeks felt warm.

'Boyfriend?' the boss said.

'Fiancé.' Clark swallowed. 'Leo.' He fiddled with his ear stretcher. Jade wondered if it hurt. Wondered why anyone would want to end up with ears looking like that. Minging. Ears were manky enough already, if you thought about it.

'Does Leo live here too?' the boss said.

'No.'

'Was he here on Monday?' the boss said.

'No. Just me.'

'Let us know if you think of anything else,' the boss said.

When they reached the door the boss turned back to Whitman and said crisply, 'You are aware that cannabis is a Class B drug. Possession can result in a prison sentence of up to five years, an unlimited fine, or both?'

'Right,' he said. He went pale. Bobbed his head, the ponytail bouncing.

'Best to be informed,' the boss added.

Jade knew the boss wouldn't give him an official warning – they'd have to find the drugs for a start (and he might have flushed them), then do the paperwork. It was small scale, personal use. The police were busy enough tackling grow-houses, the spice epidemic, and chasing down county lines without messing with the likes of Whitman.

The boss looked a bit brighter, a smile in her eyes when they got into the lift. As soon as the door closed she winked at Jade. 'Interesting start to the day.'

'The van?' Jade said.

'That as well.' And she gave a little laugh. Bit pervy, if you asked Jade, a woman as old as the boss.

'Has next door been done?' the boss said.

Jade checked. 'No.'

'Shall we?' And she gave another little laugh as they reached the ground floor.

Chapter 14

No answer at number fourteen and Donna had just decided they'd move on when her phone rang.

'Isla?'

'Boss, we've heard back—' The rest was drowned out by the clatter of a train passing on the top of the embankment, only yards from the pavement where they stood. How long would it take to get used to that? Donna thought. How long before you could sleep through it? She watched it thunder by, the sky beyond a dappled grey, carrying the promise of rain.

Turning away, she glimpsed George Peel staring out of his front-room window on the other side of the road. As the train noise faded, she said to Isla, 'Tell us again.'

'The leaflet distributors covered both sides of the A6 corridor from the McVitie factory in the south along Stockport Road as far as the Longsight boundary in the north. But the Labour Party pamphlet was a much smaller round, took in the west side of Stockport Road between Frances Street, where the industrial estate is, as far as Martha Street, including Rosa Street and Grace Street. We're talking in the region of seventy households.'

'And the flats?' Donna said.

'They don't leaflet the flats, can't get access,' Isla said.

'What about businesses, commercial premises?'

'No, only residential,' Isla said. 'And we're still chasing the dog-walker.'

'Good. Let me know when you hear,' Donna said.

She relayed the news to Jade who said, 'Looks like it's someone local then.' And gave Donna a stare. *I told you so.*

'Yes, it looks that way,' Donna said. 'Happy now?'

Jade grinned, dimples in her cheeks, then suddenly stood straighter. 'Incoming,' she said, pushing her hands into the pockets of her leather jacket.

A woman with long blonde hair wearing a bright blue down coat and heeled boots came past the flats, heading in their direction, a carrier-bag in each hand. 'Hello?' she said, as she reached them.

'Do you live here?' Donna said.

'That's right.'

In her forties, Donna guessed. Her hair was styled in soft waves with a blunt fringe, make-up expertly done, and she wore slim rectangular glasses, golden frames.

She gave her name as Gaynor Harrington. Her face softened in pity when Donna explained why they were there. 'It's awful, isn't it?' she said. 'You can't imagine someone leaving a baby like that when you've got kids of your own . . .'

She took them inside, apologising for the mess. 'I always tell them they're not to get their toys out before school but they never take a blind bit of notice.'

The house was bigger than the neighbouring ones: the diagonal angle of the railway track gave extra land at the end of the terrace, space enough for someone to have added a two-storey extension.

Gaynor scooped toys off the sofa and offered them drinks, which they declined. She excused herself to go and put the shopping in the freezer.

Jade picked up a child's drawing, turned it this way and that. 'Which way is up?' she said. 'What's it supposed to be?'

'It's a house.' Donna gestured for her to turn it the other way. 'Fourteen on the door. That's the roof, the triangle, those are the people.' Six shaky circles for heads, hair scrawled in yellow, brown on one, stick limbs. Picasso-style facial features.

'Signed – look. Aidan,' Donna pointed to the wobbly letters in the bottom corner.

Jade raised her eyebrows, dropped the picture back onto the floor.

'Work of art, that,' Donna told her.

The living room was not unlike Donna's. Comfy sofas, two arm-chairs, a cast-iron fireplace with a log burner. Gaynor's hearth had a safety guard: her children would be younger than Donna's. A drinks cabinet, high up out of reach, held cut-glass tumblers and an assort-ment of spirits.

Donna turned and saw the family portrait on the wall behind her. Posed and tastefully lit, a beach scene for a backdrop. She recog-nised the children: the trio they'd met in the corner shop coming in to buy sweets. They looked a little younger in the photo. The whole family were dressed in blue and white, their pale hair almost the same colour as the sand. Eyes and smiles gleaming. Bare feet.

Gaynor returned and sat down. She'd taken off her coat and was wearing a cream roll-neck sweater and skinny jeans. Like her neigh-bours, she couldn't think of anyone who'd been expecting. 'You think she lived round here?' she said.

'It's one line of enquiry,' Donna said. 'Did you notice anything or anyone out of the ordinary on Monday?'

'No, sorry.'

'Any disturbance?' Donna said.

'No,' Gaynor said.

'Any callers?'

'No one.'

Had she forgotten about the PCSO?

When Donna asked if her husband drove a white Transit, Gaynor blinked fast, a shadow clouding her blue eyes. She gave half a laugh. Why had the question unsettled her?

'Yes, he does,' she said.

'Can you tell me if he used it on Friday night?' Donna said.

'He went out for pizza.'

'What time was that?' Jade said.

'About seven?'

'And did you hear anything just before that, an argument, shout-ing in the street?'

64

Gaynor thought for a moment. 'No.'

The growl of a diesel engine grew louder and Gaynor stood. 'That'll be Stewart now. I don't know if he heard anything, he never said. There is sometimes trouble over the way.' She hesitated. 'Number thirteen. I shouldn't gossip, but Karen and Mitch, they row and that. The police have been out to them before now.'

Stewart Harrington came in and looked perplexed to find strangers in the house. Gaynor sat down again.

'It's the police, Stewart. About the baby.'

'Oh, right.'

He sat on the arm of his wife's chair. A handsome man once, Donna would have said, but his cheeks were riddled with broken veins and his nose swollen and purple, like a fig stuck to his face. Drink. She'd put money on it. His hair, streaked with grey, reached to his collar. They must have airbrushed him for the family portrait.

'They want to know if we noticed anything on Monday,' Gaynor told him.

'No, nothing,' he said.

'What about in the evening?' Donna said. 'You went out for pizza around seven. Did you hear any shouting around then, see anyone outside?'

'No,' Harrington said.

'Has that got something to do with the baby?' Gaynor said.

'We don't know,' Donna said. 'We're just following up on any unusual activity.' She asked the Harringtons to go through their movements that day.

'Just normal routine,' Gaynor said. 'I took the kids to school, came back. Did the books, the admin. Emails.'

'You work from home?' Donna said.

'Yes, we've a few properties, rentals. Stewart was out working on one in Rusholme.'

'Till when?' Donna said.

'About five,' he said.

'Then you went out for a takeaway at seven?'

'That's right. Domino's.'

'You drove?' Donna remembered from the map there was a branch not far down the main road.

Gaynor laughed, nudged his knee with the heel of her hand. 'He's a lazy sod, aren't you?'

'And after that?' Jade said.

'Nothing, really. We were just in watching telly,' Gaynor said.

'All evening?' Jade said.

'Yes,' Stewart said.

Still no mention of the attempted burglary and the police follow-up. 'You had a visit from a Police Community Support Officer?' Donna said.

'What?' Stewart frowned. 'No.'

'Oh!' Gaynor shook her head. 'We did. I'd forgotten. They left a note. Someone had tried to break into one of the houses over the back. They asked us to get in touch if we'd seen anything. But we hadn't.'

'You didn't speak to them directly?' Donna said.

'No. I wasn't feeling so good,' she said. 'Migraine. All I can do when I'm like that is lie in a darkened room. It's a nightmare. That's why Stewart had to go for pizza, isn't it?'

'Yeah, that's right,' he said. He didn't sound very sure.

Donna saw the way Gaynor was patting her husband's leg as if he needed reassuring or calming. Something slightly out of kilter. She felt like she was watching a performance. Some couples operated that way, playing up their dynamic for public consumption. She and Jim had once had friends like that: the pair would bicker and carp at each other and make asides, 'She loves me really, can't live without me', and 'Oh, here he goes again, bring out the violins', which had made Donna want to grind her teeth with irritation. It was exhausting to witness and, over time, she'd deliberately let the friendship slide and wither.

'But we'd not heard a thing, had we?' Gaynor looked up at him.

'No,' he said. 'Double glazing, cuts it all out.'

Gaynor was smiling so fiercely, it seemed as though her muscles would lock or her face shatter with the tension. Her knuckles bleached white on the hand that pressed her husband's leg.

Donna stood to leave and looked again at the perfect family photo, glossy and glowing. Then at the scrappy child's drawing, which was probably closer to the truth. Something rankled, itched under her skin.

'What d'you make of that pair?' she asked Jade, when they were outside. The rain had started, a fine misty drizzle that darkened the brick of the railway embankment and the houses.

'They're lying to each other.'

'How d'you work that out?' Donna said.

'He'd no idea about the PCSO calling. She hadn't told him,' Jade said.

'I think you're right. And if they're lying to each other they could be lying to us as well.'

'Maybe it was them doing the shouting, a domestic. He storms off in the van,' Jade said.

'This shouting in the street, doors banging, it's probably a dead end, unrelated to our case, but I'd be happier if we could give it a name and rule it out. Same with the break-in. I think we should talk to PCSO Evans, see if he can shed any more light,' Donna said.

She checked her phone. 'Message from Tessa – something to show us from the CCTV.'

Donna and Jade sat either side of Tessa, who was summarising the coverage from Chuckie Chicken. She'd taken screenshots of customers throughout the working day and printed them out. She'd also sent them through to Isla so she could map them in the geographical timeline.

'Now, everything seems as you'd expect, succession of people buying food, until . . .' Tessa clicked play. The footage fed through to a flat screen up on the wall. Black-and-white film from a single camera covering the area from the shop counter to the doorway.

'Twenty thirty-three.' Jade read out the timestamp.

Donna watched as a young man entered. Was it a man? She thought so from the stance, the breadth of the shoulders. He wore a baseball cap pulled low, a hoodie over that, trackie bottoms and trainers.

He went up to the counter as Mr Siddique came into view. The lad handed him something. A piece of paper? A note?

Mr Siddique moved out of shot and came back a few seconds later with a dark bin liner, the top scrunched together, maybe a quarter full. He passed it over the counter.

The customer headed out. The back of his hoodie was decorated with a print of a flaming torch. He held the door open for a couple coming in, then left.

'What's in the bag?' Jade said.

'Well, it ain't takeaway,' Donna said. 'He never looked at any menu, there wasn't time to cook anything, and even if he'd rung in an order, you don't put it in a big sack like that. Go back, Tessa. Zoom in a bit on the bag.'

The image grew bigger, blurred, but Donna could see the outline, a corner pulling straight edges in the plastic. 'A box, boxes?' she said.

'There were boxes on the top shelves in the back room,' Jade said, 'covered with those bags.'

'What does the guy give him when he comes in?' Donna said.

Tessa jumped to the start of the section and again zoomed in. 'Paper? No writing, no design visible,' she said.

'Is it a bag, a paper bag?' Donna said.

'Or an envelope?' Tessa said.

'He's paying him,' Jade said quickly.

Donna felt a kick of recognition. They couldn't demonstrate that unequivocally from what the film showed but it felt right. 'And not for chicken wings,' Donna said.

Chapter 15

At the Chuckie Chicken, Jade stared at the space where the boxes had been. Mr Siddique was playing dumb. 'Up there? They were just old empty tray cartons.'

'They were covered with bin bags,' Jade said. 'Why bother?'

'What has this to do with the baby?' he said.

'Where are they now?' said the boss.

'In the bin—' He bit off his reply. The bin, of course, had been carted off for forensics.

Try again, mate.

'Waheed must've taken them to the recycling.'

Dobbing his brother in.

'We can ask him when he gets back, can't we?' The boss plonked herself down on one of the chairs. The table rocked as she knocked it. The tube light spat and sizzled.

'Well, he's away now,' Mr Siddique said. 'Gone to Pakistan for a visit.'

'Bit sudden?' the boss said.

Mr Siddique laughed. It was painful.

The boss kept the poker face, lips zipped. Jade did, too, until the man was forced to fill the silence. 'Last-minute deal. Saves a fortune.' He looked at Jade then, like she'd know, like she'd agree with him because she was half Pakistani and must be nipping over there every five minutes to chummy up with the family. *Way off the mark, mate. Never met any of that lot. Not even the one who was liable for me being born.*

'You have his number?' the boss said.

'Yes, but he'll probably get a local phone, pay as you go. It's cheaper.' Again he looked to Jade for agreement.

Jade gave him a dead stare. Eventually he picked up his phone and read out his brother's number.

The boss got out her tablet. 'You'll be pleased to know your CCTV was working perfectly. Perhaps you can clear this up for us, Mr Siddique. The transaction on the film.' She ran the footage.

'It's just . . . erm . . . he was . . .' Mr Siddique was fretting with his beard and giving these quick smiles one after another, like he was stuck buffering and couldn't load the right expression. Then he said, 'He buys cooking oil off us. Discount.' But his eyes wandered, like he could tell it wouldn't fly.

'You sure about that?' the boss said.

'Yes. That's right.' Emphatic. Guns and sticking to them.

'Then he'll be able to corroborate that, will he?' the boss said.

'I don't know where he lives.'

'Contact number, then?' the boss said.

'He just comes in,' Mr Siddique said.

'Name?'

Mr Siddique shook his head.

The boss planted her palms on the table and sighed. The fluorescent light droned on. 'I don't think you're being honest with me, Mr Siddique. And I don't want to be diverting time and resources into whatever little number you've got going on here when I've the death of a baby and the disappearance of a new mother to be looking into. I will, however, pass this over to my colleagues for further investigation unless there's anything you'd like to tell me now.'

'No, nothing,' he said.

'The item in the bag, it wasn't a baby, was it?' the boss said.

It was like she'd plugged him into the electric. He jumped. 'No! No. It's not, it wasn't that . . . I've never!' And he was sweating. Like it had started raining inside, drips on his face, even though it wasn't all that warm in the room. 'It was cooking oil,' he said. 'Just cooking oil.'

The boss stood up. 'Someone will be in touch,' she said. And they left him with the threat hanging in the air.

Chapter 16

Word came through from Isla: Rosa Street was the only location that had been targeted for mailshots by Lady and the Tramp and the other leaflet distributors, further narrowing the area where the wastepaper found with the baby's body had originated.

Donna stood at the top of the street with Jade. 'We can rule out the flats so that leaves us with just three households on the right-hand side.'

Jade pointed. 'The Harringtons, number fourteen, at the very bottom, Odelia, number six, this side of the flats, her neighbours at number four are away, then Chuckie Chicken.'

'And the other side?' Donna counted. 'Seven houses.'

'What about the lottery ticket?' Jade said. 'Mandy Myers – she could tell us who plays that game. If we had that as well . . .'

'Good idea,' Donna said. She recalled the Harrington kids at the shop, Mandy giving them a message for their mother about a roll-over. Gaynor was a habitual player. 'Let's go and see.'

'That's the biggest seller,' Mandy said, when they asked about the Lotto. 'Everyone plays it.'

'What about any customers from Rosa Street?' Donna said.

'Yes. George gets it, Odelia's son Oscar. Oh, and Mitch.'

'Mitch?'

'Mitch Cookson, number thirteen.' The couple that Gaynor Harrington had said argued.

'Anyone else?' Donna said. Her interest in Gaynor Harrington was piqued by the dynamic she'd witnessed earlier. But she didn't want to put words into Mandy's mouth.

'Not that I can think of.'

'What about Gaynor Harrington?' Jade jumped in with both feet.

'No, she does EuroMillions.' Mandy smiled.

Outside, Donna turned to Jade. 'Oscar Johnson is on the high seas and we've spoken to George Peel. What about the Cooksons?'

Jade checked the house-to-house log. 'No one home on either visit.'

'Let's try, eh? Third time lucky.'

Karen Cookson was frowning as she flung back the door. She had a pale face, with deep lines around her eyes and across her forehead. Her chin-length hair looked brittle and dry, a broad stripe of dark roots running down her central parting. 'What?' she said, uncompromising.

Donna told her it was about the baby and her shoulders slumped. 'I don't know anything about it. I can't help you. And I haven't the time. I've got to get to work.' She began closing the door.

'It won't take long,' Donna said, stepping forward.

'Christ's sake,' Karen muttered, and let them in.

There was a boy on the sofa, six or seven, Donna guessed, watching TV. He was pale, like his mother, but chubby. There were holes in his jumper. And his trousers, once black, had now faded to a dark purple, shiny at the knees, and didn't reach his ankles. His socks had holes in them, too.

'He's off sick,' Karen said, putting on an overall over her shirt. 'Asthma. Soon as his dad gets in I have to go. I'll get the sack if I'm late.'

The house was cold and smelt of mildew.

The boy had turned to look at Jade and Donna but had already lost interest and resumed watching television, breathing through his mouth. Donna could hear the wheeze.

'Could we have a word in the kitchen?' Donna said.

The room was cluttered but not dirty, apart from the black mould that speckled the corners of the ceiling. A pile of crockery on the

72

draining board, bags of groceries on the table. It was even colder than the living room and Karen shivered.

'Heat or eat,' she said, when Donna noticed. The vibration in her voice, the tension in her frame spoke of her suppressed anger.

Her replies to their questions were curt, monosyllabic, as she rushed to put the food into the kitchen cupboards, which were otherwise bare.

Donna wanted to tell her to stop, to sit down and take a moment, but sensed the woman might explode if she did.

When Donna asked if she knew anyone who'd been expecting a baby Karen stopped in her tracks. Turned, a tin in each hand. 'Needn't go looking at me,' she said. 'Fall foul of the two-child welfare cap? No, thanks. When did we start punishing kids for being born? Taking food out of their mouths and giving the rich bastards tax breaks? It's vicious, that's what it is.'

Donna didn't disagree. The policy drove poor families who had a third child even deeper into poverty.

'What about Monday night around seven o'clock?' Jade said. 'Did you hear anything then?'

'Wasn't here,' she said. 'I'm never bloody here. I'm cleaning five till eight of a morning, more of the same in the evening, six till nine. In between I'm packing at a warehouse in Stockport unless I get a text cancelling my shift. Zero hours. He's the same, shifts at two different places, opposite sides of town. And what do we get for it?' She held up a can of beans. 'Food bank.' Her eyes glittered with angry tears, her lips pinched white round the edges. 'And it's always bloody baked beans.'

In the other room the child coughed.

Karen glanced at the clock, pulled a coat from the back of a chair and began to put it on.

'The police were called to a disturbance here earlier in the year,' Donna said.

'What? Who told you that?' she said.

'Was that the case?' Donna said.

'It was something and nothing. A mix-up. They thought it was a fight. Well, they got that wrong.'

73

'So what did happen?' Jade said.

'Mitch. He . . . His mum had died and he was due to go in and see his job coach about universal credit. He *failed to notify them.*' She signalled quote marks with her fingers. 'So they sanctioned him, cut his benefit. He was beyond himself. Shouting about that. Can you imagine? Bastards. Fucking bastards. I'm sick of it. He just lost it. And some idiot called the police. It'd drive anyone crazy.'

It was a familiar story. And with services cut to the bone, it was the police who ended up dealing with the damage and the damaged.

There was the sound of a key in the door and a man's voice. 'All right, Tobes? You right now?'

A murmured reply.

Mitch Cookson came to the kitchen door.

'He's just had a dose,' Karen said to her husband, zipping up her coat. 'And I've told Kylie to walk home with Serena and her mum.'

'And you are?' Mitch said, looking first at Donna, then at Jade.

'Police,' Donna said. 'We're looking for the mother of the baby who was found on Monday night.'

'Well, she isn't here,' Mitch said, sitting heavily. He wore chunky work boots, jeans and a woollen jacket with frayed cuffs and a button missing. Hollow-cheeked with a long thin nose, an angry-looking rash covered one side of his face, and stubble stippled his chin. He yawned and winced, put a hand to his jaw. 'Toothache,' he said.

'Awful,' Donna agreed.

'That's me gone,' Karen said, touching Mitch's shoulder briefly as she passed him.

Mitch opened his jacket and pulled out a rolled-up copy of the *Metro*.

'Do you get any other papers?' Donna asked.

'Why?'

When she didn't answer, he said, 'Just this, pick it up free on the bus.'

'You play the lottery, the Lotto,' Jade said.

'What's that got to do with anything? OK, it's two quid, it's two

74

quid we haven't got, but I've won a tenner enough times to break even.' A note of agitation rising in his voice.

'These are routine enquiries, Mr Cookson,' Donna said. 'We're talking to everyone in the area.'

'Yeah? You asking them about the lottery an' all? Look, we don't know anything. Can't help you.' He stood up, the message plain. Scratched at the side of his face while he waited for them to leave.

'They've got kids,' Jade said, once they were back on the street. 'And he could've been lying about the newspaper. They weren't mad keen on talking to us, were they?'

'Too bloody stressed,' Donna said. 'We can come back again if we find anything that warrants it. Five jobs between them and they're living off the food bank. It's not right, is it, Jade?'

Jade looked at her. *The way it is.*

'My generation,' Donna went on, 'you got a job, even a shit job, and you could pay the bills. You might not have anything left over for cars or holidays or new clothes. Haircuts.' She thought of Karen's hair. 'But you could manage. And there were rules, basic decency. Sick pay and holiday pay and some security.'

'We still get all that,' Jade said.

'*We* do, those of us still on the payroll. But for a lot of people, that's gone.'

Donna wasn't sure what she'd expected from Jade, a shared sense of outrage, perhaps, but all her DC did was zip up her jacket and say, 'PCSO Evans is free now. Shall we have a word?'

Chapter 17

PCSO Evans reminded Jade of a seal. Same body shape, plump shiny face, thick neck and big dark eyes, like snooker balls. Slicked-back hair. No whiskers, though.

He leafed through his notebook making sure he didn't miss anything out. Jade told him it was his enquiries on Rosa Street they were especially interested in.

He flicked forward a page. He'd called at the Harringtons' and got no answer, though he was sure people were in. 'I could hear movement, lights were on, the TV.' He'd rung the bell again, and nothing. 'Can't force someone to answer the door.' So he'd left a note.

'Was there a van parked outside? A white Transit?' Jade said.

He thought for a moment. 'No. No van. After that I spoke directly to . . .' head bobbing, adding up the numbers, '. . . four of the flats. Only one of them had been aware of a disturbance, but that was out front on Rosa Street, not on Grace Street.'

'Clark Whitman?' Jade said.

'That's right. So we left it at that.' He gave a nod and closed his book.

'Cheeky,' the boss said. 'Trying to break in at that time, still daylight.'

'But no one heard anything, saw anything,' he said. 'And I've not had any follow-up information. No one's been in touch. Apart from the poor girl on Grace Street, who's seeing bogeymen left, right and centre. Hearing noises and frightened of her own shadow.'

'Shame,' the boss said.

'She rings us up again later that evening, in a right state. Heard someone in the alley and should she call nine-nine-nine?'

The back of Jade's neck prickled.

'Totally stressed out, she was. I was off duty but I said I'd call round to check it out. I felt bad for her.'

'What time was this?' the boss said.

He checked his book. 'Twenty-two twenty-five. So I've just set off and she phones me back. It was only a neighbour, sorry to bother me and all that.'

'What neighbour?' Jade said, her wrists tingling, looking at the boss, who shared the stare.

'She didn't say.' PCSO Evans shook his head.

'Do you have her number?' Jade said.

He watched while Jade dialled and went through the intros as fast as she could to get to the point. 'You thought you heard someone out the back later that evening?'

'I did, yes. I heard a clatter, like a back gate. Mine's padlocked but they'd still climbed over it earlier anyway. I thought they might be coming back. I didn't know if I was imagining it. I was paranoid. Still am. So I looked out the back bedroom and I rang the police. They said they'd come.' She took a breath. 'I kept watching out and then I saw someone coming down the ginnel and going into their yard. The man from the bottom house.'

Stewart Harrington.

Jade wanted to cheer. 'You know him?' she said.

'Just by sight. Seen him sometimes in the back, fetching the bins in and out, and the kids' bikes. Enough to nod to, you know? It's horrible . . . every little sound. We need gates on the ginnels, you know.'

'Yes,' Jade said. 'Thanks for your help.' Eager to get off the line.

'Stewart Harrington,' she said to the boss. 'Going up and down the alley at half past ten.'

'And he said he'd been in all evening,' the boss said, her eyes brightening.

'And if you wanted to get to the commercial bin without being seen . . .' Jade said.

PCSO Evans was looking from one of them to the other, bulbous black eyes shining.

'One foot in front of the other, Jade. No pole vaults,' the boss said. But there was a smile in her voice.

'It's a big fucking question mark, though, isn't it?' Jade said. 'Why'd he keep that from us?'

'And he'll have to answer it.' The boss checked the time. 'But tomorrow will do. Thanks.' She nodded at PCSO Evans, who grinned.

'Not a complete waste of time, then?' he said.

'I'm going to be off in the morning,' the boss said, when they reached their cars. 'Personal time.'

'Fine,' Jade said quickly. She didn't need the details. Personal was personal and she was happier not knowing about people's hospital appointments and dying relatives and domestics. But the boss carried on regardless: 'It's the start of the inquest into Aaron Drummond's death, Jim's accident.'

Jade nodded. 'I can go back to Stewart Harrington,' she said.

'We do it together, Jade. Decide on our angle before we go in. Could you ask Isla to collate everything she's got on Harrington's movements for us, from the timeline map? We can focus in on Rosa Street too, revisit the house-to-house statements, make sure we haven't missed anything, pick out the anomalies.'

'Boss, if it was Harrington who dumped the bag, then is that their baby?' Jade said. 'Did she look like she'd just had a baby?'

'Whoa!' The boss held her hands up. 'That's a massive *if* right there. Let's just start with what we know, see whether a bit more poking and prodding opens anything up.'

Jade shuffled, impatient. They'd a lead on Harrington. 'He lied.'

'And there could be a dozen reasons. We need to be smart, strategic. Not go in half cocked. You know this, Jade.' She had her lecture face on now, mix of concerned and cranky. 'If he's responsible we'll get him, but we won't do that by wading in without thorough preparation. So I'll find you when I'm back, you brief me with what Isla's established, and we'll make a plan. OK?'

'Fine,' Jade said, not that she felt fine. She hated being told to wait.

It was one of the worst things about the boss: she was so bloody cautious. Meticulous, she called it. 'We have to be meticulous,' she said. 'So everything we bring forward for prosecution is rock solid.'

Jade moved to her car.

'Jade?'

'Yes, I know,' Jade said, pissed off. 'I get it.' *Doesn't mean I have to like it.*

Chapter 18

On her way home, Donna dropped into the station. She made a call to colleagues who had picked up the ball on Waheed Siddique and were following up on their suspicions of some sort of illicit activity connected to the takeaway. Waheed had eluded them for now. His phone was either off or he'd ditched it.

Calvin was at his desk. 'Boss, I just had word back from Asda. There was a sale of the jumpsuit and nappies at the Levenshulme store on Thursday, along with baby wipes, vests, feeding bottles and formula.'

'Excellent!' Donna said.

'Like a starter kit,' he added.

'If those were for Rosa,' Donna said, 'why leave it so late?'

'Maybe the mother didn't want to jinx it. My sister didn't want any baby gear until late on with hers,' Calvin said.

'Me too,' Donna said. 'But by seven or eight months you know that even if the baby's premature they've a good chance of survival. You sort stuff out then.'

'She got loads of things at the baby shower anyway,' Calvin said.

'We never had all that,' Donna said, thinking back to the layette she'd assembled for her firstborn. The matinee jackets and bootees her mother had knitted. The tiny vests and romper suits she'd bought in Mothercare. They'd borrowed a Moses basket and cot from a friend and were looking for a second-hand pram when Jim's parents had splashed out and bought one for them, brand new.

'Look, can we get CCTV for that transaction?' she said to Calvin.

'I've put in the request,' he said.

'Good man.' She told him about the sighting of Stewart Harrington. 'Maybe we're finally getting somewhere.'

Calvin laughed, eyes sparkling.

'What?' she said.

'We only caught the case at midnight on Monday. It could be weeks yet, months even.'

'I know. It often is,' Donna said. 'But there's a woman out there who's given birth and in all probability has smothered her child. The longer it takes us to identify her, the less chance we have of actually tracking her down. Just imagine the state she's in.'

'Fair play,' Calvin said. He rolled his shoulders and rubbed the back of his neck.

Donna said, 'Go home.'

He saluted.

Donna's phone buzzed. 'Front desk, ma'am. We've a Colette Pritchard asking for you.'

'I'm coming down,' Donna said. 'Put her in a visitor's room if there's one free.'

'Yes, ma'am.'

Colette was huddled in a chair when Donna found her. Clothes and hair bedraggled.

'I heard her,' Colette said. 'I heard her.'

'Colette, let me get you a cup of tea and you can tell me all about it.'

'I'm fine. If I'd known. I heard her and I—' The woman looked haunted, her eyes vivid with pain. 'I heard her. But I didn't know.'

Donna reached out a hand and touched Colette's shoulder, then went to the cooler, filled a cup with water and took it over.

Donna sat beside her, angled to face her. She held out the water.

Colette shook her head. 'I thought it was a cat.'

Donna remembered times she'd heard that sound, the wailing outside, and had been sure it was a baby. She'd even gone out to check in the garden once. It was when the twins were teething and she was stupid with lack of sleep.

Jim had teased her. 'Even if there is a baby,' he'd said, 'it can stay there. We've already got three of them bawling their eyes out. We don't need another.'

'You thought it was Rosa?' Donna said.

'That noise, the crying. It must have been her. I didn't know.'

'Where did you hear it, Colette?'

'On Rosa Street, I didn't know it was . . . If only I'd known . . .' She covered her face with her hands. Her nails were split, peeling, her knuckles still raw and chapped.

Donna put a hand on her arm. 'You didn't know,' she said. 'How could you? Perhaps it was a cat.'

'No.' Colette's hands fell. 'That's why I'm here – because I *thought* it was a cat. But I was wrong.'

'It might have been a baby crying,' Donna said carefully. 'But what could you have done?'

'Found her. Found her and saved her.' Colette's face flickered, spasms of hope and then sorrow.

'You did find her,' Donna said.

'But it was too late.' Tears sprang into her eyes.

'You found her and you came to us. You did the right thing. And we're going to try to find her mother, too.'

'I thought it was a cat. I just wanted you to know, to let you know. I'll go now.'

'Colette, wait a minute. Tell me, when did you hear the crying?'

'Saturday. There was a gang of men chanting Saturday and I didn't want to be there.' She was almost inarticulate compared to how she'd been before.

'Where?'

'With the men, on the main road, I had to go . . . and then the cat . . .'

'You went down Rosa Street on Saturday and that's where you heard it?' Donna said.

'The football.' Colette frowned, as though working it out. 'The chanting, football fans.'

There had been a match on Saturday night. Donna had no idea

who had been playing but Rob and Lewis had gone to watch it at a friend's house.

'What time was it?' Donna said.

'I can't remember.'

'Do you know where the crying was coming from? Which house?'

'I don't know,' Colette said. 'I'm sorry.'

'There's no need to be sorry,' Donna said. 'Look, how about we go and get something to eat? Would you like that?'

'I've got to go.'

'Where are you going? Have you got somewhere to stay?'

'I'll be fine.' But she looked wretched. 'I thought it was a cat,' she said, pleading with Donna to understand. 'I just thought you should know.'

'Thank you. Perhaps it was,' Donna said. 'Listen, where are you heading? I could give you a lift.'

'No, thanks, I'm fine.'

Donna walked her out, offered food or drink again, to rest awhile. Colette politely refused. She couldn't, or wouldn't, look at Donna. Donna didn't want her to go, which was daft. She could hardly offer her a bed for the night.

'Take care,' Donna said, at the entrance. 'Here.' She passed her a card. 'My number's there. If you need anything, if there's anything I can do, please call me. Yes?'

Colette took the card and muttered a thank-you.

Donna watched her until she was out of sight, lost among the stream of pedestrians.

Chapter 19

Jade had just got her key into the door, lamb bhuna, rice and parathas in the bag in her other hand, mouth watering and stomach gurgling in anticipation, when she heard Mina's door scrape open and Mina call out, 'Jade? Jade?'

Fuck! 'It's me, Mina. It's just me,' Jade shouted.

'I know it's you. Come here.'

Jade stepped back far enough to see Mina peering out from her own doorway.

'I'm getting my tea.' Jade hoisted the bag up. Proof.

'Come, come,' Mina said. 'You have a visitor.'

Jade went cold. There was a thudding in her throat.

The last time Jade had had a visitor, the man was out to kill her. He'd spun Mina a pack of lies about fire safety checks and blagged his way into Jade's flat where he ambushed her.

She didn't do visitors. DD knew where she lived but he wouldn't come off his own bat, not unless she asked him to. They didn't socialise, these days.

Jade glared at Mina but the old woman just nodded fast, smiling. She beckoned to Jade. 'Come, come.'

Jade wanted to run. Back down the stairs and into the car, head off anywhere, put miles between her and this. Because whoever it was in there it wasn't going to be good. How could it be when they'd sneaked in like this? Anyone from work would have rung her, not just pitched up. They didn't socialise either – or if they did it was impersonal, the boozer round the corner from the station.

Jade walked closer to Mina. 'Who is it?' she said.

'A surprise.'

Fuck surprises. 'Mina?' she hissed.

'Come.' Mina grabbed Jade's free hand and tugged. 'It's OK, it's good,' she was saying, as they crossed the threshold.

Jade wrested her hand free.

'It's your sister,' Mina said.

'I don't have a s—'

The girl stood up. She was fat and pink-cheeked, with sleek brown hair and sparkly make-up. She wore a short yellow and black check skirt, a gauzy yellow blouse, black ankle boots. She looked nothing like Jade.

'Hiya, Jade.' The girl beamed and launched herself at Jade, flung her arms round her.

Jade went rigid, suppressed the urge to kick her away. The girl smelt of perfume, a sweet woody scent, and bananas. She finally let Jade go.

'You look amazing,' she said. 'You don't remember me, do you?'

Barely. They'd met once, twice maybe. Some sort of miserable access visit. Shannon was eight years younger. She'd been born after Jade had gone into care. She'd be seventeen by now.

Now and again, over the years, Jade had had updates from a social worker. Shannon was living with Mam again. Shannon was in temporary foster care. Shannon was back at home.

Jade didn't give a toss. Hadn't then, didn't now.

'I got to eat,' Jade said. Raised her bag, though she felt like chucking up.

'Eat here,' Mina said. 'Shannon had some casserole.'

How long has she been here?

'It was lovely,' Shannon said, sitting down again on the other armchair, leaving Jade with the footstool.

'I'll take it next door,' Jade said.

'No, no, no,' Mina chuntered. 'Sit, eat.'

Fuck.

Jade sat, concentrated on opening the cartons.

Shannon was wittering on about her angel pendant and bur-bling about wishes and how angels were different from saints and you didn't have to be Catholic, or like Christian, even, to believe in angels. Angels would help anybody. Mina was drinking in every word.

Jade gobbled the food, dimly registering the rich, spicy sauce and the tang of cardamom in the rice. She crushed the containers in the plastic bag and went through to Mina's kitchen, dumped them and rinsed her fingers, wiped her mouth.

Mina was laughing. She'd taken a shine to Shannon. Well, she was welcome to her. Jade hadn't asked her to come. She wasn't about to play long-lost families, like the TV show that reunited relatives.

Why was Shannon here?

Had their mother died? Was that it? And, for some reason, she'd thought Jade would want to know?

Would she be joking with Mina and twittering about angels if that was the case?

'You must have so much to talk about,' Mina said, when Jade went back in. 'You go now, have a good chat. But, Shannon, you come see me again soon.'

'Course I will,' Shannon said.

'Promise? When you come see Jade. I'll make you more food.'

'You could teach me how to do it,' Shannon said. 'To cook it, like.'

'It's a family recipe,' Mina said. 'But maybe I'll share it with you.' Then she gurgled a laugh. Shannon joined in. Jade wanted to puke.

There was a burst of music from Shannon's phone, Beyoncé sing-ing about being crazy. Shannon glanced at it and cut it off as she got to her feet. 'See you later,' she said to Mina.

Jade didn't speak. She was trapped. OK, she'd take Shannon next door, find out what she wanted and send her packing.

'It's really nice,' Shannon said in Jade's flat. Then she laughed. 'You've got a nana blanket.' She waved a hand at the crocheted throw. Her fingernails matched her clothes, patterned yellow and black, long and curved. They reminded Jade of wasps.

'Mina made it,' Jade said. 'How did you find me?'

'Played detective,' Shannon said, pleased with herself.

Oh, Christ.

'Well . . .' Shannon sat down, put her phone on the sofa beside her. Jade stayed standing. 'I saw you on the telly. Mam had said you'd joined the police.'

How the fuck did she know?

'I saw you on the news with that murder, that trans girl, so I got to thinking, like, I'd come and say hello. I knew where you worked. So one day last week I watched for you going home.'

'You followed me?' Jade was furious.

'It wasn't hard – it was easy.'

It was a fucking liberty.

'But Ryan needed the car back so I couldn't stop.'

'Ryan?'

'My boyfriend. I'm living with him at the moment. So I came again today and Mina said you were still at work and I could wait with her. She's dead nice, isn't she? She says she—'

'Have you passed your test?' Jade said.

Shannon gave a little chuckle.

'You got a licence?' Jade said, stony-faced.

'I'm really careful,' Shannon said. 'I'm a good driver. Ryan says I'm a natural.'

Jade sat down. Beyoncé burst into action again and Shannon killed the call. It rang again and she did the same.

'You gonna report me?' Shannon laughed.

Hardly. Jade wanted shot of her, nothing else. 'I've got an early start,' she said, 'so if you could just—'

'Is it another murder?' Shannon said. 'Is that what you're doing?'

'Can't talk about work,' Jade said.

'Is it that baby?' Shannon said. 'Is it? Or is it that lad that got knifed?' Her lips parted, eager. She was dying to know more.

Shut up.

Another blast of R&B from the phone.

'You'd better answer that,' Jade said.

87

Shannon gave her a snarky look but picked up the phone and plastered on a smile as she said, 'Hey, babe? . . . Yeah, my sister's . . . Well, I can bring it now, if you like . . . I didn't know, you never told me . . . It's off the main road, the flats near the bridge. Five minutes tops . . . But I can bring it . . . OK, don't stress, babe. Chill.' She swiped the screen with her thumb. 'He wants the car,' she said to Jade.

'Has he got a licence?' Jade said.

'Course, he's twenty-three. Been driving for years. He's got a few points but everyone has them, don't they? Anyway, now I know where you are, you give us your number and I'll come again. We can have a proper catch-up, quality time.'

No. Fucking. Way.

Jade was spared a reply when Shannon's phone rang.

'I'm here,' she said, aeriated. 'Chill. I'm coming now.'

Thank Christ.

'I'll let you out,' Jade said. Not that Shannon needed help to leave the building but Jade wanted to escort her, make sure she had definitely left the premises.

Walking downstairs behind Shannon, who was talking now about starting a job-search course next week in town and how she really wanted to work in hotel management but it was hard to get into if you hadn't been to uni, Jade wondered again what had brought her here. What did Shannon expect? That there would be some bond because they shared a bit of DNA? That's all they shared. There were no joint memories, no common history, nothing to reminisce about. They'd grown up apart and keeping it that way suited Jade just fine.

Shannon opened the door to the car park and a voice rang out. 'Keys. Now.' An Uber was driving away. Presumably the one Ryan had hired to bring him here.

Shannon went towards him, keys in hand. A keyring with a big enamel bee on it. The Manchester symbol had been everywhere since the Arena bombing.

'This is my sister, Jade,' Shannon said. His eyes flicked towards Jade but he didn't speak. Shannon handed him the keys.

He pointed the fob at the white Toyota Yaris, released the locks. 'You can fucking stay with her, then, you crazy bitch,' Ryan said. 'You're all mental.'

'Ryan! Babe!'

'I've had it, Shannon. It's done. You're doing my head in. You can get your stuff and do one.'

Oh, fuck. Please no.

'Just cos I borrowed the car.' Shannon's voice squealed with tears.

'You *took* it. Good as robbed it. I told you before but you just took it. You take everything. You're a fucking leech.'

'Ryan, please don't.' Shannon ran to the passenger door but before she could open it he'd jumped into the driver's seat and hit central locking.

'Ryan!' Shannon screamed. She pounded on the window. 'Ryan, don't. Don't leave me like this. Don't. You fucking— Don't.'

He started the engine.

Shannon slung her bag at the window. Then slammed the heels of her hands against the glass.

The car wheels spun, the exhaust roared and it skidded away. Shannon stood screaming after it. 'You fucking bastard, you fucking shitty, fucking bastard. You wanker.'

Then it was pretty quiet. Jade could hear background noise in the distance, traffic swooshing on the main road and the low hum of an HGV somewhere closer, but in the car park there was just the sound of Shannon gasping and crying and some bird squawking in the big tree near the entrance.

I'll call you a cab. Jade practised the sentence in her head.

Shannon turned back to her, wiping her face. She raised her chin, gave a quick wobble of a smile, then a sharp nod, and said, 'Well, sis, looks like I'm staying at yours, then.'

Chapter 20

Jade woke really early, wondering why, and then it hit her like a truck: Shannon.

Jade had to get out, out of the flat, away from this.

Last night she'd made it plain as day that Shannon could stay for one night. Then she'd have to sort something else out.

Shannon had glossed over it: 'Yeah, course.' She was sure Ryan would come round. 'He's just being a dick. I'll talk to him tomorrow.' And then she'd started on a string of stories about Ryan and her falling out and how he always took her back and was sorry.

Sorry he took you back, more like.

Jade had stuck it for a bit, Shannon slavering over *Love Island* and giving a running commentary on all the contestants. Then Jade said she had to sleep. Shannon could use the sofa. Shannon asked for a pillow and Jade gave her one off her bed but she told her to use Mina's blanket. She didn't have any spare bedding.

'Leave the lights on when you go tomorrow,' Jade had said.

'How come?' Shannon said.

'Insurance,' Jade said.

'I haven't got your number,' Shannon said, waggling her own phone.

'I'm in the middle of switching,' Jade said. 'Write yours down and—'

'Have you got a pen?'

FFS. Jade found one and a notepad. Left it with her.

'I'll be gone early,' Jade had said.

She just hadn't expected it to be this early. Still dark, half six, as she went to the car. The air was cold and smelt of wet stone. The sky was clear, a star shining bright behind the flats.

The streets were quiet as she drove to the café. She ate a full English, no mushrooms, had two cups of coffee and swallowed her medication.

Same mix of people as before, bouncers and cleaners, joking quietly together. Karen Cookson would be stuck into her first job of the day. Jade wondered whether the Cooksons were hiding anything behind their hostility or if the boss was right – that they were just too strung out with stress to care. Gaynor had made out like the Cooksons were a regular nuisance, but the way Karen put it, it'd been one spectacular meltdown that brought the police round.

You crazy bitch. You're all mental.

All? Had Shannon told Ryan about Jade's condition? *Bit of a psycho. Had to be sectioned. Locked ward.* The thought made her feel sick. The taste of coffee in her mouth turned bitter, metallic.

How could Shannon even know? She couldn't. It was all confidential. Doctors, social workers, they couldn't tell anyone about it without Jade's express permission. Jade felt her pulse quicken and a tightening in her throat. *Stop it!*

'Anyone sitting here?' A man, clothes clouded with plaster dust, face chalk lined, stood with a tray in his hands.

'No,' Jade said. 'But I'm off, anyway.'

He stood back and let her out.

She felt shaky, cold in spite of the hot food.

She pinned her mind on work. Had Gaynor been trying to deflect attention, pointing her finger at the Cooksons, or had she just heard rumours about the couple and repeated them? No smoke without fire. Mud sticks.

Someone on that street had left Rosa in the bin. They knew that much. She thought of Stewart Harrington creeping down the alley with a bag, coming back without it. Not that the woman from Grace Street had actually seen him with a bag . . . But all the same.

Methodical, Jade. Meticulous. The boss in her head. She had told

Jade not to talk to Harrington on her own but that didn't mean she couldn't keep her eyes on him. See what he was up to. Was his life going on as usual? 'Act normal': that was what people did when they were trying to hide their guilt. Was he really working in Rusholme, for example?

Besides it was still early – no one would be in the incident room yet. No harm in Jade taking a detour on her way.

She drove the two miles to Levenshulme, a blue-grey wash seeping through the skies as day broke. The streetlamps went out.

She couldn't park on the main road but found a space on Grace Street and walked back from there. She crossed to the bus stop on the far side where the slope gave her a clear view down Rosa Street to the railway across the bottom. Stewart Harrington's van was in place outside his house.

A bus pulled in, air brakes hissing, and a woman with a kid in a buggy got off, calling a thank-you over her shoulder to the driver. The kid stared at Jade. It had a dummy, fat cheeks and a red nose, tufts of pink netting splaying out of the bottom of its coat. Wearing a tutu or something. It reminded Jade of Shannon, fuck knew why, and her heart gave an extra thump.

The bus drove away and Jade focused back on Rosa Street.

Odelia walked up with the dogs, straining on their leashes, and turned right towards the park. Her attention was on the animals and she didn't look in Jade's direction.

The traffic was picking up now, building towards rush-hour.

Nothing else happened for a while. Then she saw a woman come out of number eleven, the house between George Peel's and the Cooksons', and get into a Mini, then another resident emerging from the flats to start a car. Both drove up and away towards Manchester. Jade didn't recognise either of them.

Mandy Myers appeared. She rolled up the shutter at Super Saver, then hauled out a sandwich board. She went inside and the lights came on.

A cyclist in a high-vis vest and helmet left the flats, carrying his bike through the door. Rode off.

Jade's interest sharpened when she saw Stewart Harrington leave his house, climb into the white Transit and drive towards her. Would he notice her? Would it spook him?

She saw his face clearly as he reached the junction. Papers and old coffee cups cluttered the dashboard, a toy Spider-Man fixed in the centre waving around. The traffic was nose to tail now and he had to wait for a break before he could pull out.

Jade checked the time: eight twenty. How long till Gaynor took the kids to school? Half an hour? Less? Did they start at nine? Jade didn't know. It had been just after ten when they'd spoken to Gaynor on the previous day and she'd had time to get some shopping after dropping the kids.

With the traffic moving at a crawl, if Jade got a move on she'd be able to reach her car and trail Harrington. See where he went.

She was halfway across the road when she saw someone leaving Super Saver and felt a kick of recognition. It took her a split second to place him, the black hoodie with a flaming torch printed on the back, jeans and trainers. The customer from Mr Siddique's CCTV. Today a striped plastic carrier bag dangled from his hand, a litre of milk inside.

Jade ran after him.

Chapter 21

Donna dropped Matt at school and in the course of the journey learned all about his latest exploits on Fortnite. Or she pretended to. She tried really hard to concentrate, to listen carefully to what he was telling her about skins and a bush wookie, but time and again she caught her attention sliding away. It was another language he was talking, one she didn't understand. She had shown willingness, in as much as she'd asked some questions, but that had only led to more opaque explanations. I mean, *looking like a default?*

Back at the house, Jim was shouting up the stairs, 'Get down here now. I'm not telling you again.'

'What?' Donna said, putting the keys on the hall table.

'Kirsten. Says she doesn't feel well.'

'Today of all days,' Donna said. 'Perfect timing.'

'She's doing it on purpose, I swear to God.' He was wound up. He didn't usually get so stressed with the kids. Most of the time he could laugh off the dramas and disagreements. Face the challenges they spat out on a frequent basis with more equilibrium than Donna.

'I'll talk to her.' Donna ran upstairs. 'Kirsten?' Her room was empty.

Donna knocked on the bathroom door. 'Kirsten?'

'Go away.'

'I'm not going anywhere. What's wrong?' Donna said.

'I've got stomach-ache.'

'Have you been sick?' Donna said.

'No.'

'Diarrhoea?'

'No. Mum!' Horrified.

Oh, get over yourself. 'Look, open the door so I can see you.'

A mumble.

'What?'

Another mumble.

'I can't hear you.' Donna struggled to keep her tone calm. 'You need to get to school. You can have some Calpol, or paracetamol, if it's really bad.'

'I'm not going,' Kirsten said.

'Yes, you are.'

A muttered scream. Then the door flew back. 'I started my period,' Kirsten snarled.

Donna almost laughed. 'Oh, love. It'll hurt for a bit. It's just cramps, that's all.'

'I can't go, Mum. It's horrible. It's agony.'

Donna hesitated. 'Come here.' She held her arms open. Kirsten stepped forward. Donna hugged her. 'I know it hurts but you can take something for that. It's all part of growing up. Becoming a woman.'

'I don't want to be a woman,' Kirsten said. 'It sucks.'

'It's natural. The first day or two are the worst,' Donna said.

'How long will it go on?' Kirsten pulled back, face appalled.

'Four days, five. It varies from person to person. I thought you knew all this. We have talked about it.'

Kirsten's face creased and she doubled over. 'It really hurts.'

'You've got pads?'

'Yes,' she said irritably.

'Donna?' Jim called. 'We need to go.'

'OK. OK.' Donna rubbed Kirsten's back. 'Listen, I'll ring in and say you're sick but that's just for today. Life can't stop every time you have a period. So, you're going in tomorrow.'

'What will you say?'

'I'll say you've got menstrual cramps.'

'No. Mum!' Kirsten said.

'It's nothing to be embarrassed about,' Donna said.

'You don't know,' Kirsten said.

'We need to go now,' Jim shouted.

'Coming!' Donna knocked on Bryony's door. 'Are you home this afternoon?'

'Yes.'

'OK. Kirsten's going to be here – she's off school. So you come straight back.'

She turned to Kirsten. 'Get paracetamol from the cabinet, take one now and one in four hours' time. Try a hot-water bottle too. Do some coursework or something, OK?'

Kirsten gave a nod. Face a picture of misery.

As Donna drove, she told Jim about her conversation with Kirsten.

'I warned her it's just today. If she does end up having particularly painful periods we'll get the GP to check it out. Make sure there's nothing else going on. I think she's just not used to the cramps.'

'Yes,' Jim said, and that was all. He was distracted.

Donna put the radio on, caught the news. A march in London to demand a people's vote on any Brexit deal was planned for the weekend. She turned it off again, depressed at the prospect of the UK leaving the EU, at the rank stupidity of it, the isolationism – and the sort of future it would bring.

'Look, you just drop me off. I'll be fine,' Jim said, as they drew closer.

'No, I said I'd come – and I am.' What was he worried about – that he'd make a fool of himself? Or he didn't want the fuss? Exactly the same attitudes that had put him off seeing a doctor when Donna had asked him to. What was at the root of that? Leftover machismo, him not wanting to admit weakness of any sort? Or fear – he'd rather stay in denial and not know about any frailty?

The multi-storey car park was packed and the only place she could find to park was on the roof. They walked to the lifts. Jim's limp was pronounced even without the cast. He was still undergoing tests on his heart and no decision had been made yet whether he'd need a procedure. The prospect of him returning to work as a driving instructor any time soon felt remote. Once, he'd have been stir crazy at the enforced rest but he seemed resigned to it. That worried Donna. She could carry the family finances for now, paying the way for seven of them. As an experienced detective she was on a good salary. But in the longer term they'd start to struggle, especially with university on the horizon for Bryony, and for the twins a couple of years after. She felt the burn of resentment at having to carry that burden herself. Then she thought of Toby Cookson, holes in his jumper, the cold and mouldy home, food parcels donated by strangers, his father driven half mad by the malicious benefits system, and she chided herself for worrying. They'd manage.

They went through security, putting their bags and coats in the X-ray machines, and walking through the archway scanner. They were ten minutes early so sat outside the courtroom, where an usher checked Jim in as a witness.

It was easy to see who the family were: their demeanour said it all. A group of eight or so. Donna heard the usher greet the woman in the centre of the group, Mrs Drummond. Aaron's wife. She looked so young, was so young, to be widowed.

At ten o'clock they were all called in.

The legal team took their places on benches facing the front of the court; the family had seats directly behind. Jim and Donna sat at the end of a row near the back. There was a smattering of other people. Witnesses, Donna assumed. Two men in suits, a woman with short red hair and freckles, another man in chinos and a casual jacket. Doctors, perhaps, paramedics. She didn't recognise anyone from the team who'd treated Jim at the hospital but several departments had been involved. And some of these people might have been caring for Aaron Drummond.

The court officer asked them to stand for the coroner, who came in wearing a gown and wig. When she sat down the rest of them followed.

The coroner addressed them: 'Our purpose at this inquest is to establish the facts about who the deceased was, when and where they died, and how. By what means did they come by their death? To be clear, as coroner I do not consider criminal or civil liability, apportion guilt or attribute blame. I'll begin by inviting Mrs Drummond, the deceased's wife, to take the stand. If you'd like to read out your statement.'

The woman hesitated and the coroner said, 'You may read it from your seat if you'd prefer.'

Mrs Drummond nodded. The usher came to her and she swore to tell the truth, then read out her statement. Donna listened to the story of a life compressed into a few paragraphs. The bare bones of a life cut short. The loving husband and father, who enjoyed mountain biking and wild swimming. Who had left for work that morning as usual. Who had never come home. His wife's life shattered, her children bereft.

The room was quiet, the full consequences of that awful twist of Fate reflected in sombre faces.

Jim ran a finger under his shirt collar. Was he too hot, feeling faint? Donna clasped his hand. His palm was unpleasantly damp, but she resisted the impulse to let go.

A second statement was made by Aaron Drummond's father. Aaron was their only child. He had spoken on the phone to him on the morning of the accident, making arrangements for a family get-together the following weekend. The whole family were devastated. His voice cracked as he spoke. Not wanting to betray her emotion, Donna gritted her teeth.

The coroner was making notes, and when she had finished, she thanked the family.

She read out a witness statement from a colleague, Ian Rose, explaining how Aaron had left to run an errand and had not returned. Aaron hadn't answered his mobile when Ian rang him. Ian also left the office and had seen police recovering a vehicle from the side of the road nearby, not realising that Aaron had been involved in the incident. Ian learned what had happened late that afternoon when someone at the hospital contacted them.

The coroner asked for Mr James Bell to take the stand.

As Jim got to his feet, a copy of his witness statement in hand,

Donna wanted to reassure him with a look, a nod. *You'll be OK.* But he didn't make eye contact as he left their row of seats.

'Mr Bell will be able to answer any questions put to him by the barrister, or by the deceased's family, after we have heard his statement,' the coroner explained.

Donna listened to Jim speak, taking the oath, then reciting the formal details: name, age, residency, married with five children, working as a driving instructor.

Jim cleared his throat and again tugged at his collar. His hand trembled as he read from his paper. 'On the morning of Wednesday, the fifth of June 2018, I was on my way to the supermarket at Parrswood to do some shopping. I felt fit and well and I had not been receiving treatment for any medical condition.'

But a couple of nights before you were white with pain. And you wouldn't get it checked out, no matter how much I nagged you.

Mrs Drummond's head was bowed, a tissue in her hand. Mr Drummond's father kept pinching the bridge of his nose.

'I remember approaching the traffic lights at Didsbury Park but I have no memory of the actual accident. When I regained awareness I was in an ambulance being taken to Accident and Emergency at Manchester Royal Infirmary. I learned later that I had suffered a heart attack and lost control of the car. My leg was broken in the collision. I was shocked and very sad when I was told that Mr Drummond had died as a result of the accident.'

Jim folded the paper in half. He looked so alone, vulnerable there. Face drawn, sorrow in his eyes. Donna felt tears block her throat.

'Are there any questions?' the coroner said.

The barrister stood. 'Mr Bell, you told the coroner that you were fit and well that day. What about previous days?'

Jim stumbled over his words: 'Well . . . I . . . well, generally fine.'

'No ailments at all?'

'Well, a bit of indigestion one night,' Jim said.

It was more than indigestion.

'You didn't seek medical help?' the barrister said.

'It was gone by the morning.'

'And you felt well enough to drive?'

'Yes. I'd never have got into the car if I hadn't.'

Not true, Donna thought. He never let anything stop him driving, apart from when he'd been drinking. Not tiredness or coughs and colds or minor injuries.

'Are there any questions from the family?' the coroner said.

The barrister turned and signalled to Mrs Drummond.

She spoke: 'Did you see Aaron? When the car went on to the pavement, do you remember him?' Her voice shook terribly as she spoke.

'No. I'm sorry. I don't remember losing control. I don't remember anything about it.'

'Any further questions?' the coroner asked. When no one responded she thanked Jim, and once he was back in his seat, she said, 'We will now move on to a written statement from a member of the public who was at the scene and had a clear view of the accident as it happened.'

Jim sat rigid beside Donna as the coroner relayed the account.

A sob escaped from Mrs Drummond when she heard the witness talk about Aaron being unresponsive and not being able to find a pulse.

Once the statement was finished Mrs Drummond's stifled crying echoed round the room.

'Ma'am, can we have a short break?' the barrister asked the coroner.

'By all means.'

'Court stand,' instructed the court officer.

The coroner withdrew.

Jim turned to Donna. 'You get back to work.'

'I'll stay till lunch,' she said.

'Really. I've done my bit.'

Donna could hear Mrs Drummond saying, 'Sorry. I'm sorry,' apologising for her tears.

'You'll get a cab?' Donna said.

'Yes,' Jim said.

'If you're sure?'

'Really, you go. I'll be fine,' he said.

Donna squeezed his hand and said she'd see him later.

She walked to the door and stood aside to let Mr Drummond senior go ahead of her. She caught the smell of tobacco – he'd be going for a smoke. Donna glanced back and saw that people were either looking at Mrs Drummond and the family or determinedly staring the other way. Everyone except the red-haired doctor, or whatever she was, who was looking at Jim. Jim, sitting bowed over, his hands bracing his head.

On the roof of the car park, Donna paused to view the city centre. Cranes rose like an invasive species, dozens of them building new additions to the skyline. The wind blew hard but still couldn't eradicate the smell of oil, exhaust fumes and concrete.

A question had lodged in Donna's head, one she couldn't shake off. Like a tick, mouth buried deep under the skin, sucking blood.

Jim and Donna always shopped at their local supermarket, invariably once a week. So what the hell had Jim been doing driving to one six miles away? It didn't make sense.

Chapter 22

Jade tailed the man along the main road, past the mosque and the industrial estate.

He took a left into a street that led under the railway bridge.

The road and pavement below the bridge were paint-bombed with bird shit, pigeons roosting in the supports underneath it in spite of the wire netting and rows of spikes.

Beyond the bridge he turned right into a side street and went into the second house along, one with a black door. These were terraces but smaller than those on Rosa Street. Two-up-two-down, Jade thought. Outside toilet in the old days.

She made a note of the address, and had a quick recce. Nothing much to see from the outside. Curtains were closed at all the windows and looked like they had been that way for ever, blue fabric bleached to grey stripes where the sun caught them. Windows thick with dust. Paint peeling on the drainpipe. Old wooden window frames, the sill of the door crumbled away, chewed by the elements to expose honeycombed wood.

A pneumatic drill started up, cutting through the ambient traffic sounds and the slower rhythmic banging of someone thumping metal. There was a panel-beater's on the industrial estate, she'd seen from Isla's map. And a scrap-metal dealer. Lots of small firms renting prefabricated units and Portakabins for manufacture or storage. Noise dawn to dusk.

Jade crossed to the door and banged hard.

The man opened the door, just a crack. He didn't speak. Eyes wary. He still wore the hoodie and baseball cap.

'Police.' Jade showed him her warrant card. A blaze of fear in his eyes. 'I'll come in.' Jade gestured.

He shook his head. 'No.'

Not an option, mate.

'Open the door,' Jade said.

'No.' He was holding its edge.

'Police,' Jade said. 'I want to talk to you. Now.'

'No English,' he said.

'Passport, papers?' Jade said.

He swung his head away, defeated, it seemed. He stepped back and she went inside.

The smell hit her, a reek like rotting cheese and blocked drains mixed with stale cigarette smoke.

The floor was covered with four thin foam sleeping mats and sleeping bags. Two young men were waking, alarmed. A rapid exchange of words between them was answered by the man she'd followed.

A third man sat cross-legged on his bed near the door into the kitchen. He had a large pot of Vaseline. His feet were badly swollen, fish-white, marked by vivid open sores, patches of raw pink, seeping snotty yellow. It explained the stench.

Jade saw tattered holdalls, which must have served as storage. The only furniture in the room was a coffee-table between two sleeping mats holding a full ashtray, a pack of cards, and three small mugs.

Her attention was caught by two bin bags, one black and lumpy, possibly full of clothing. But the other, folded round straight-edged boxes, was exactly like the ones she'd seen on Siddique's shelves. And the one this man had collected at the takeaway.

The others all sat watching, silent.

'Passport?' Jade said again, to the man she'd followed.

He shook his head. 'Work,' he said.

'Where? Work where?'

'Car wash.'

Jade pointed to the man tending his rotten feet. 'Car wash?' she said.

He gave a nod.

'Paid?' She rubbed her fingers and thumb together. It was a simple enough question but they all played dumb.

'English? Speak English?' she said, looking from one to another. Lots of head-shaking.

Fucking perfect.

'What's in the bag?' She pointed. No one spoke but there were glances flying around between them like darts.

She pulled on a pair of protective gloves and used her phone to take pictures of the bag in place. When she turned to photograph the room and the men they shielded their faces.

It didn't take a degree to work out that they were either indentured labour or modern slaves. Car washes, nail bars, sweatshops were notorious for employing illegal workers, many of them trafficked and obliged to pay off their debt through labour. Any resistance brought the threat of danger for their families back home.

Jade pulled open the plastic sack and there they were. Cartons of cigarettes. Marlboro Reds. 200s. One torn open, two packs missing. She took more photographs.

Smuggling. Lucrative. A mainstay of organised crime.

'Name?' Jade said to the man.

He didn't answer.

She said it again, sharper, eyes hard on him.

'Vasile Mirga.'

'Ukraine?' Jade took a wild guess. 'Speak Ukrainian?'

He looked at the floor.

No answers there, mate.

'Polish?'

He shook his head.

'Speak Romanian?' His eyes flickered but he said no.

The man with the ragged feet was putting his trainers on. 'Work?' he said.

The other two got up, shoving their feet into trainers too. Sensing an escape.

She wasn't going to argue with them. She could pass on the

intelligence about them to the gang-master and labour-abuse authority to investigate.

'OK,' she said. She held up her hand to the cigarette guy. 'Not
you. Romani?' she asked. 'You Roma?'

He looked up and crossed his arms over his head.

'Vasile?' Jade said.

'Roma.' He looked at her directly. Eyes flat.

The other men were ready to leave.

'Names?' Jade said.

They were unpronounceable. Two wrote them down. They could
well have lied. The third shook his head. Jade thought maybe he was
illiterate, then saw that his hands were twisted, claw-shaped. She
wondered how he managed at the car wash. His friend wrote his
name down for him.

She let them go.

'Work?' Vasile said.

'No. Talk,' Jade said, making a glove-puppet gesture with her
hand. She'd have to get an interpreter. It'd take for ever. Unless . . .

She rang DD's number, let it ring three times, then stopped.
Repeated the process. And waited for him to reply.

'J?'

'Got a job for you,' she said.

'Who says I want a job?'

'Easy money,' Jade said.

'As in?'

'Translating,' Jade said.

'What?'

'Someone I need to talk to. He's Roma like you.'

'J, nah, man. No way. Me and police stations. You even ask.'

'Home visit. His home,' she added. 'Levenshulme. Just you, me
and him.'

'I don't know, J.'

'Make a change, won't it?' she said. 'From dealing and stealing
and all that.'

'You dissing me?'

'Telling it straight,' Jade said. 'And I could really do with a hand here.'

There was a wall in Jade's head between her old life, when she and DD were kids running riot on the wrong side of the tracks, and her life now. DD was still over that side, small-time crime, living in the shadows. Jade could ignore that because she owed him. Always would. And he owed her. Closest thing to a friend DD was, even though they barely saw each other now. And when things got really dark, the old bond of loyalty still held. It was DD she'd called when she'd been in danger earlier in the year. DD who'd been by her side, confronting the bastard out for her blood.

'I can't remember much of the lingo,' DD said.

'Better than nothing,' Jade said.

'How long will it take?'

'An hour tops. Less if you get a shift on.'

'Three hundred,' he said.

Sod off.

She gave him the address. Fuck knows how she'd pay him.

'Cosy,' DD said first off, when he arrived. 'We open a window?'

'Painted shut.' Jade had already tried.

'Where's he from?' DD said.

'Romania.'

'You know we've all got different dialects, different words even,' DD said. 'You can get ten different ways of saying the same thing.'

'I just need the gist. Vasile – DD.' She introduced them.

They exchanged some greeting. Then Jade said to DD, 'Tell him we have CCTV footage of him collecting these cigarettes from Mr Siddique at Chuckie Chicken.'

'Chuckie Chicken?' DD said. 'Get a lot of food poisoning, do they? Needs a rebrand.'

Jade waited for him to stop talking. He was enjoying this already, she could see, even with the hard-man front. A light in his green eyes, smile playing around his mouth.

'I know he was buying,' Jade said. 'I want to know who put him in touch with Siddique.'

It took a lot of to-ing and fro-ing, the conversation sounding Asian: Urdu or Punjabi maybe, not that Jade could understand or speak either. But there were similar sounds and rhythms.

DD gestured when he couldn't make himself understood, and at last he turned to Jade and said, 'He went looking for work, evenings after his car-wash job. Mr Siddique, the one with no beard . . .'

Must mean Waheed.

'. . . told him they'd no need for staff but he could make some money selling duty-free cigs.'

'How did they communicate if he doesn't speak English?' Jade said.

'Fuck, Jade, I don't know. Sign language?'

'Ask him,' Jade said.

DD had to ask three times before Vasile understood the question, which sort of proved her point, but Vasile said it'd been clear what the deal was. Waheed had shown him the merchandise and written down the price.

'What did he pay?'

'Thirty quid for two hundred,' DD said.

'And sells them for what?'

Another exchange. 'Twice that.'

'What does he get paid at the car wash?' Jade said.

'Five pound an hour.'

Less than the minimum wage. 'Does he owe money?'

'Eh?'

'To the people who brought him over?' Jade said.

When DD asked that, Vasile shook his head. He spoke for a while. DD interrupted a couple of times, to clear up confusion, then said, 'The guy's happy here. He wasn't trafficked like you mean. He paid a fee to travel and that's cleared. He makes enough to send money home. That's why he's doing it. And that's why he's shifting fags an' all. His boss has his passport for safe-keeping.'

'You believe him?' Jade said.

'Why not? Good a story as any.'

Vasile spoke quickly, looking at Jade.

107

DD said, 'He's asking what you're going to do. His kids won't manage if he can't keep working.'

'He's got kids?' Jade said. 'How old is he?'

DD asked. 'Twenty-three,' he told her.

'We've got him on camera collecting the cigs,' Jade said.

'Yes, but he's small fry, isn't he? You going to waste your time on that?' DD said.

'You care?'

'Matter of priorities, I'd have thought. Not like he killed anyone.'

'Only slowly,' Jade said. 'Lung disease, cancer.'

'Fuck off.' DD grinned.

Jade wondered how she could spin it for the boss. Tried to separate out the two things, the contraband goods and the illegal working practices. There were guidelines to protect vulnerable workers from exploitation, and stuff about offering alternative, safe forms of employment, if they were entitled to work here. But there was a gap between the talk and the walk.

With practically no English, what hope would Vasile have? Zero-hours contract like the ones Karen Cookson was on and he'd be even worse off. Not my problem, Jade thought. But it'd be easier all round if she just turned a blind eye to that side of things. Tell the man his employer was ripping him off and leave it up to him to carry on washing cars if he wanted. She said as much to DD, who translated it for Vasile.

And the fags? Their team had already passed intel on to Organised Crime as they suspected some sort of illicit activity but didn't know what was being traded. But maybe there was a way to go through the Siddiques to the suppliers higher up the chain without charging Vasile.

'Tell him he stops the cigarettes. Now. End of. He doesn't go near the Siddiques. He doesn't say a word. If he talks we'll pick him up.'

Vasile looked solemn as he agreed.

'And this . . .' she hefted up the bag of cigarettes, held it out towards DD, '. . . is for you. Payment in kind. There's a thousand smokes there, near enough. You can turn that into your interpreter's fee. Make more if you charge extra.'

DD looked like he was going to argue. Head rearing back for a moment. 'And if I'd rather have the cash?'

'Leaves me with this little lot to get rid of,' Jade said. 'Not a good look. This way the contraband disappears and I can tell my boss that Vasile here *had* bought some fags, but by the time I found him, he'd sold them on. Promises not to do it again. It gives us the information we need to investigate the smugglers.'

'You speak Romani now, do you?' DD said.

'They won't know how bad his English is. Not unless they meet him. Which I'm hoping need never happen,' Jade said.

'Word,' DD said.

'You were never here,' Jade said. 'Tell him that too, in case.'

DD spoke to Vasile, repeating the same phrase, pointing to his own chest and making a dismissive motion with his hands. Then DD put a finger to his lips and leaned in close to the other man. No translation needed.

'*Da*,' Vasile said, which Jade guessed meant yes. He was nodding earnestly and his fist went to his chest, like he was swearing on his heart.

'Work?' Vasile said.

'Keen, in't he?' DD observed.

Vasile spoke again. 'He said thank you,' DD translated.

They stepped outside.

Vasile pulled the door shut and hurried away.

'Ta,' Jade said. 'You remembered quite a bit, after all.'

DD lifted the bin bag over his shoulder. 'Shithole, innit?' He tipped his head at the house.

'Seen worse.'

'Lived in worse. Mind, that stink . . .' DD said.

'Trench foot.'

'What?'

'From the car wash, wet feet all the time. Not got the proper gear,' Jade said.

'Well rank. You move jobs?'

'Eh?'

109

'Thought you were murders?' DD said, green eyes on her.

'Still am. The baby found abandoned.'

'Right.'

'This cropped up along the way.'

Jade didn't ask how DD was doing, what he was up to. Less she knew the better. But she did take in the car parked opposite, a white 4x4 the size of a small tank. 'That yours?'

'Sweet, innit?'

'You say so.'

He looked at her, head tilted. For a fraction of a second she thought of telling him about Shannon. DD was the only person who might understand, but he said, 'We done?'

'See you.' Jade walked away.

She reached the bridge where the pigeons were cooing and crapping and heard the deep roar of an engine, which she assumed was DD's car accelerating away in the other direction.

She didn't look back.

Chapter 23

Arriving at the police station, Donna met Jade who was on her way out.

'Boss, want anything fetching?' Jade said.

'You eating again?' Jade could pack it away and never seemed to gain weight. Fast metabolism, maybe, nervous energy.

'She worries the weight off' – something Donna's mother used to say about people like that.

Donna was hungry. 'I'll come with you. Working lunch. Bring the files from Isla.'

'Downloaded.' Jade patted her bag.

'Good. Where were you thinking?' Donna said.

'Lemi's,' Jade said. The Turkish café had changed its name several times since Lemi opened it back in the nineties. It was always popular, generous portions and low prices.

Donna bagged a booth that had just been vacated. She skimmed through the menu and asked Jade to order her a chicken and chorizo salad and an Americano.

While Jade went to the counter, Donna looked at the family photos on the walls. Some were old, black-and-white, of an unsmiling couple in formal poses and traditional dress. Another, sepia-tinted, showed a house on a hillside, the sea visible down below. A large colour photo had three brothers, looking just like their mother, who stood in their midst. Donna thought of her own kids, how similar they were to each other, apart from Kirsten. How she often couldn't tell in the baby photos whether she was looking at Bryony, Matt or one of the twins. Only by their clothes. Unlike the four of them, Kirsten had shown up with curly hair and a tip-tilted nose that nobody recognised.

Donna rang her. 'You OK?'

'Yes.'

'What have you been doing?'

'History,' Kirsten said.

'Are you warm enough? Put the heating on if you're cold.'

'How?' Sounding sullen.

'There's a button on the front of the boiler, it says "Advance". Press that once.'

'The boiler?' Kirsten said.

Donna bit her tongue. She would not get into a row over the phone. 'Big white box next to the back door. Can't miss it.'

Silence.

'I'll see you later. Did you get a hot-water bottle?'

'Don't know where they are.'

Struth!

'Bathroom cupboard,' Donna said, failing to keep the snap from her voice. She saw Jade coming back. 'OK. I've got to go. See you later.'

Jade sat opposite. 'I found our mystery shopper,' she said. 'Mr Siddique's pal.'

'Go on.' Donna was all ears.

'Recognised his hoodie. He was out buying milk. So I followed him home and had a chat.' Jade was fiddling with the salt cellar then the vinegar bottle. 'The stuff in the boxes was black-market cigarettes. He'd sold them on already.' She straightened the napkin rack. 'I told him to steer clear, not a peep to the Siddiques, and I've passed the intel on to Organised Crime.'

'Nice work,' Donna said.

Jade flushed. She bit at a nail. Donna tried to ignore it.

'Any sign of Waheed?' Donna said.

'No, nothing from Border Force,' Jade said. 'I don't reckon he's gone to Pakistan, though. He's probably in Wolverhampton or Stoke or somewhere. The officer I spoke to says the black market in fags is rocketing. The smugglers can buy a pack for less than a quid somewhere like Ukraine.'

'What do they cost here?' Donna said. Years since she'd smoked.

'Eleven, twelve. A lot of money to be made.'

The server called over that their food was ready and Jade went to fetch it.

There was little conversation while they began to eat. Jade was demolishing a cheeseburger with rice and salad, the meal crowding the large oval platter. She'd sprayed everything with ketchup and vinegar and liberally doused it with salt.

The sort of food Jim loved but which was no longer on the menu since his heart attack.

Jade stopped mid-chew, looked at Donna and said something. Still had a mouthful of food. 'Mmmfff etta ffuf?' Donna couldn't understand a word.

Donna mimicked a reply in similar style and laughed. Jade too. A small snort. Then swallowed.

'What was that about Colette Pritchard coming in?' Jade said.

Donna told her the story. 'She was really distressed. I don't know – maybe she did hear a baby, maybe it was a cat. I'm not sure it really gets us anywhere.' Donna hated not having been able to help her. Not even to get her a hot meal or a lift somewhere.

'It fits, though, doesn't it?' Jade said. 'The baby clothes and nappies were bought on Friday. Rosa was two to four days old on Monday.' She took another bite of her burger, holding the stack between both hands. Tomato sauce squirted out, daubing the corners of her mouth.

Donna resisted the temptation to point it out. Not yet. Jade would wipe her mouth when she'd finished. She wasn't a child. It was peculiar how Donna morphed into a parent sometimes when she was with her.

Donna finished her salad and drank some coffee. She felt sleepy after the meal, her mind thicker.

Jade had cleared her plate and now she wiped her mouth, screwed up the napkin and dropped it onto the plate.

'So,' Donna said. 'Let's see what we've got.'

Jade moved round to sit beside her. The tall wooden walls of the booth would afford them plenty of privacy from other diners. Jade took out her tablet and set it in rest position so they could both see the screen. She pulled up the file and pressed play.

Donna drained the rest of her coffee.

The software Isla used looked like a stripped-back computer game. The 2D figure representing Stewart Harrington moved around the grid of streets among his neighbours who remembered seeing him when they were out and about on Monday. A car symbol stood in for his vehicle so when he drove anywhere that moved too.

To indicate information that was corroborated by others, Isla had included a neon green tick next to the figure. Where it was only Stewart's account or that of his wife, a black question mark accompanied the avatar. Likewise, if it was a sighting of him where he'd not admitted to any movement, like going down the alley, a red question mark was used.

Donna and Jade watched the program all the way through, then Jade switched to a document that contained the data Isla had entered for the modelling. Donna read through it.

'So he leaves for work in the van at eight thirty and that's corroborated, as is his return at five fifteen,' Donna said. 'We also pick him up on traffic cameras heading west to Rusholme and coming back at those times. He is seen leaving home, allegedly to get a pizza, by Clark Whitman but no one corroborates his return. Then we have him in the alley at twenty-two thirty.'

Donna picked up her phone and rang Calvin. 'Go to Domino's on Stockport Road and see if they have any CCTV of Stewart Harrington dropping in on Monday evening around seven. Get back to me as soon as you know. Thanks, Calvin.'

Next Donna and Jade ran the model of Gaynor Harrington's movements. Odelia had remembered her taking the kids to school and George Peel had seen her bringing them back. As had Mandy Myers, when the family had called in for their sweets. No one had reported seeing Gaynor in the area between those times, or in the evening.

'Stewart Harrington's not likely to be at home yet,' Donna said. 'I don't want to call on spec and alert Gaynor, just in case. So we get whatever else we can this afternoon and aim to arrive at teatime. Tell him we have a couple of points to clarify and talk to him on his own.'

Matt was at after-school club until six thirty. Donna could text Jim and ask him to do the pick-up on his way home. She wasn't sure when she'd finish but she knew the inquest would never run late.

Jade's phone rang. A flash of irritation when she saw who it was and she declined to answer. Turned it over.

Not work, then. Something personal? Donna hadn't a clue about Jade's personal life. She never referred to it. She might be living in a commune or planning her wedding or caring for her parents and Donna would be none the wiser.

The void, the lack of any chitchat or details, made Donna think that Jade was quite monastic. She lived for work and not much else. Perhaps focusing her energies on work was enough for her. She didn't have space for a social life too. But it wasn't healthy. Not for most people, anyway.

Donna didn't want to pry but if she never attempted to open channels of communication she'd never find out anything. 'You OK?' She nodded towards Jade's phone.

'Yes,' Jade said quickly. Too quickly. As though caught out. 'Cold caller. My recent traffic accident.' She ran a hand through her hair, the jagged cut falling back into place. 'Like bleeding ferrets.'

She was lying. Donna didn't know why she was so certain about that. But she was. One hundred per cent. Whatever it was, whoever was ringing, Jade was lying about it.

Calvin phoned Donna back while she and Jade waited to cross the road to the station. Buses and vans were thundering past.

'Boss, Stewart Harrington arrived at Domino's at seven thirty-one and left nine minutes later.'

'So where was he from seven till half past?' Donna said. 'It's only five hundred metres away.'

'Taking the scenic route?' Calvin said.

'We've not got him on any traffic cams in that time frame,' Donna said. A truck laden with a skip went past, the wind snatching up dust as it passed. Some blew into Donna's eyes. She blinked fast.

'No, boss. Only earlier going to and from work. But—'

Donna was deafened by a car screaming past with a hole in its exhaust. She asked Calvin to repeat what he'd said.

'There's one route he could have taken where he'd go under the railway bridge near the industrial estate. We could check ANPR, see if his number-plate comes up around there?'

'Do that,' Donna said. 'Let me know if you get anything.'

The traffic came to a halt and they were able to cross.

Donna walked quickly, any after-lunch slump had gone. Her mind was clear and she was eager to start planning their tactics for challenging Stewart Harrington.

Chapter 24

'Boss? You need to see this.' Isla limped over to the desk where Donna and Jade were working. Isla looked worried, her fresh face marred by frown lines, lower lip caught by her teeth. She pulled out a chair and sat. Swung her tablet round to face Donna and Jade, who leaned forward over their notes.

The screen showed George Peel outside his front gate. 'The police have been back here every day,' he was saying. 'To the flats opposite, to both lots of neighbours at the end of the street.' Silence as the camera panned to show the flats, then the Harringtons' and the Cooksons' houses, with the high wall of the railway embankment running between the two.

'They must know something, the police.' He nodded emphatically. 'But they're taking their time about it. Meanwhile the rest of us have got to carry on and we're told nothing. Like we're the enemy.'

'Fuck,' Jade breathed.

'What the hell is this?' said Donna.

'YouTube channel, called FrankManc. Citizen journalism,' Isla said.

'Oh, Christ. Tell the press office,' Donna said. 'See if we can get it taken down.'

'Yes, boss,' Isla said.

'We'll have a word with Mr Peel when we—' Donna broke off. Her phone ringing. *Chief constable*. Her guts twisted. 'Sir?' she answered.

'Are you in the building?'

'Yes, sir.'

'My office. Now.'

'Sir.' Donna closed her eyes and took a breath. 'I've been summoned,' she said.

Jade rolled her eyes and Isla pulled a face.

'You carry on here,' Donna said. 'I may be some time.' The reference was wasted on Jade, but Isla smiled and mouthed, 'Good luck.'

The chief constable's office had the hallowed atmosphere of old money. Ingrained authority in everything from the jewel-like colours of the Indian carpet to the gleam of the oak panelling and the commanding view from the huge arched windows towards Manchester Central Library and the town hall.

'DI Bell.' He greeted her coldly. There was a time he'd called her Donna, offered encouragement, but she'd dropped off his Christmas-card list pretty quick as he sought to distance himself from the taint of corruption in her team.

'Take a seat.' An order more than an invitation.

He was a tall man with iron-grey hair and a slab-shaped face. He'd only a few months left until retirement.

'I don't normally involve myself in the detail of an investigation . . .'

But . . .

'. . . but if I have cause for concern . . .' He paused. Waiting for acknowledgement?

'Sir,' Donna said.

'You've seen this video?' His lip curled with distaste. He might have been talking about extreme pornography.

'Yes, sir, and I'm hoping the press office—'

'Noise fills a vacuum. Misinformation. Disinformation. You know we need to keep the community onside if we're to do the job properly.'

'Of course, and I believe—'

'The last official statement was Tuesday, the launch and appeal. Is that right?' he said.

Donna saw the row of classic cars on his desk, the neat line, bumper-to-bumper. She wondered what on earth he would do afterwards, when he no longer had all this to get up for in the morning. Was he a golfer, a sailor, or was his only passion old Bentleys and Jags? Maybe he and the wife had a decade of cruises booked in.

'Yes, Tuesday,' Donna said.

'Time to take the focus back. Release a fresh statement, confirm it is now a murder inquiry, urgent appeal for help and so on.'

Donna wanted to protest – heat flushed her neck. 'Sir, the reason for not publicising it as murder—'

'I'm well aware,' he said. 'But we're three days in and the mother has *not* come forward. She's had her chance. So I want to see the gravity of the crime communicated. Confirm the cause of death as suffocation. Nothing grabs the attention, and the desire for punishment, like a child murder.'

'Sir, if we disclose the cause of death at this point we may lose an advantage when questioning suspects.'

'You have suspects?' He was sarcastic. Belittling her. Patronising twat.

Her cheeks burned. 'We do. A local resident, Stewart Harrington, is a person of interest. I'm preparing an interview with him for later today.'

'Under caution?' He wanted to know how strong their evidence was.

'We're not there yet. But if he can't satisfactorily answer the anomalies we put to him we'll be looking at interview under caution as the next step. I can provide you with a report laying out what we have.'

'Do that,' he said, though so dismissively that she wondered if he would even read it. 'But sort out the PR first. We've already got half the city up in arms banging on about no-go areas because of the stabbing. We've got to reassure the public, make them believe we're still providing an excellent service, never mind that we've been haemorrhaging staff.'

Donna felt a twinge of sympathy in spite of herself. The double-speak of management. The Federation, representing police officers, had been shouting about the crisis for months, warning about the rise of violent crime and the force's inability to respond to more minor offences. But senior officers had to 'maintain confidence'. Put a positive gloss on the work of the service. Politics.

'And this person of interest,' he said, 'if he's not a goer, is there anyone else?'

'No, sir. Apart from the mother.'

'Press office are preparing a statement now. Talk to them about filming the appeal,' he said.

'Sir, we don't gain anything from releasing cause of death,' she said. 'I'd strongly recommend we hold back on that.'

He gave a sharp sigh, turned his large head to the windows, then back. 'Very well, for the interim.' Telling her she was on borrowed time and he could change tack when it suited him.

'Sir.'

He stood. Donna did the same. Dismissed.

The press officer, Kenton, was a fast-talking Irishman who had been promoted to the post recently. Donna had always found him likeable. He'd a quick sense of humour, and while enthusiastic and energetic, he'd a healthy sense of irony, too, about the ongoing dance between the media, the police and the public.

'Come in, come in.' He waved her through into the press office. 'Do you want a brew?' He took his glasses off, rubbing at them with a polishing cloth.

'I'd love one,' Donna said. 'Coffee, black no sugar.'

'Claire?' He asked his assistant to get it. 'Nothing for me, thanks,' he added. 'And can we get a printout of the draft statement for Donna?'

Kenton gestured to a chair for Donna and sat beside her. His phone was switched to silent but kept flashing. Each time, he glanced at the content on the screen to see if it merited his attention.

'So, I'm suggesting that we take the circus back to Levenshulme. We see you in the heart of the neighbourhood, rather than some missive delivered from the station steps.'

Claire brought Donna's coffee and the printout.

'If you're happy with that, we'll go live at four,' Kenton said to Donna. 'Website, social-media platforms and MSM.' Which Donna knew meant 'mainstream media'. 'Along with visuals from your appeal.'

Donna read the text, formal language, crisp and objective. 'Police investigating the death of newborn baby Rosa, found in Levenshulme on Monday evening, have announced that following the results of post-mortem tests the investigation has been upgraded to murder. Police are appealing for anyone with information to contact them at any police station, through the police helpline or via Crimestoppers UK. The officer in charge of the investigation, DI Donna Bell, made a public appeal today.'

'Then we have your section.' Kenton nodded. The small rectangular glasses he wore glistened neon blue.

'I'd like to include an invitation to the mother, as before,' Donna said. 'If she has been thinking about coming forward, then a murder charge could just freak her out.'

'She must be crippled with guilt,' Kenton said.

'I'm sure she is, if she's responsible, but she may be in denial, or mentally ill and at risk of self-harm. I need to give her a lifeline.'

'Fine. You take a few minutes to work on that and have your coffee. I've some calls to make, then we can head down there.'

Donna called Jade and told her to warn the team about the statement. 'Send someone to tell George Peel to button it, and you meet me in Levenshulme. I'm filming the appeal at Rosa Street so we can talk to Stewart Harrington after. No point in me coming back in between with all the traffic.'

'Will do, boss.'

Donna took a sip of her coffee, prepared to wince, but it was surprisingly good. The press office must have their own machine.

She began to write: *We need help identifying this baby, in establishing what happened to her. The death of a child, of someone so vulnerable, is always shocking and I know that people will do all they can to help us in our enquiries. There are people who know who*

Rosa is and who can tell us what happened to her. Please talk to us. We still wish to speak to Rosa's mother. Your baby deserves a decent burial or cremation. Whatever happened to Rosa, we need your help now so she can be laid to rest. You can do that for her. Please get in touch. We understand that you yourself will also need help. You need support and that will be made available to you.

Donna read it back and changed the final line: *We understand that you may need help and support, and that is here for you, now.*

Chapter 25

The boss had done her bit for the cameras and was parked on Rosa Street outside Odelia's when Jade reached her.

'How'd it go?' Jade said, as the boss stepped out of the car.

'Fine, apart from the bloody racket. We had to do three takes before the level was right.' Soon as she mentioned it, Jade noticed the hammering and clattering sounds, the drilling and the chug of machinery that rose louder than the traffic.

'He's back.' Jade nodded to the Harringtons' house, the white Transit outside.

'Fifteen minutes since,' the boss said. 'You take the lead. I'll chip in if I see an opportunity.'

Finally!

Jade felt a kick of energy, a quickening in her blood. They walked down the street. Jade saw the figure in the window at number nine. A sour look on his face.

'Peel's at his station,' she said.

'Has anyone had a word?' the boss said.

'Calvin paid him a visit. But Isla says they're having trouble getting the content removed from the website. Free speech, blah blah.'

Gaynor Harrington opened the door to them. 'Hello?' She'd half a smile on her lips but a scowl around her eyes. The sort of look you get from strangers when you stop them and they don't know if you're gonna mug them or ask for directions. Sort of 'You talking to me?' mixed with indulgence.

'We'd like to speak to Mr Harrington,' Jade said.

'Oh, right. You'd better come in,' Gaynor said. She nudged the bridge of her glasses, moving them up her nose a fraction.

Jade clocked the television on through the doorway off the hall, two of the kids in there.

'Stewart?' Gaynor called up the stairs. She moved to close the living-room door. Then raised her voice. 'The police are here.'

Giving him the heads-up? Jade wondered if the couple had prepared for a follow-up visit, agreed what to say if the police came back. Or had they imagined they were off the hook? That they wouldn't be hassled any more?

Stewart Harrington came downstairs, feet bare and greying hair wet from the shower. Jade remembered the rancid feet of the car-wash worker, the raw ulcers shining with Vaseline.

'Is there somewhere we can talk in private?' Jade said.

'We can go through to the office,' Gaynor said.

'It's just your husband we want to talk to,' Jade said.

Gaynor's face twitched. 'Oh.' Not a happy bunny.

'It's this way.' Stewart Harrington moved past them in the hall. He smelt of lemons.

The office was reached through a door behind the stairs, which led into the extension on the side of the house. The room had been fitted out in blond wood, with walls painted a muddy blue, one of those retro colours that were all the rage. There were windows to the front and side, covered with white-wood venetian blinds, like the ones at Odelia's. The space contained a desk and a filing cabinet, a swivel office chair and an easy chair with a footstool. A printer was set up on a table next to the desk and beside that was a swing bin. Shelves held lever-arch folders, and several bottles of Scotch. Pictures on the walls, one of a forest and one of a tropical beach, were like something from a travel brochure. A flat-screen TV had been fixed up in one corner.

Maybe Stewart or Gaynor came in here when they couldn't agree what programme to watch. Jade flashed back to yesterday. *Shannon giggling at* Love Island. *Her waspy nails. Screaming at Ryan and swinging her bag against the car window.* And today's stream of calls. How had Shannon got Jade's phone number? Mina must have given it to her. How long before Shannon realised Jade wasn't going to pick up? Ever.

'I can get another chair,' Harrington offered.

'This is fine.' Jade lifted the footstool, moved it to the side of the easy chair and sat down.

The boss took her coat off and lowered herself into the easy chair, leaving Harrington perched on the office chair. He fiddled with the lever, trying to lower it. 'Think it's stuck.' He gave an awkward laugh.

Jade began: 'Mr Harrington, we wanted to follow up on our last visit. There are some points we need you to clarify.'

'Sure,' he said. His hands tapped the armrests.

'You told us you had been to collect a pizza from Domino's on Monday evening.'

'That's right,' he said.

'What time was that?' Jade said.

'About seven.'

'Can you be more specific?' Jade said.

'Seven,' he said. He locked his eyes on Jade's. *Look, I'm telling the truth.* She waited a moment to see if he would break eye contact but he stuck at it. When she looked away she saw his toes were curled tight, pressing white onto the laminate floor.

'And how long were you out of the house?' Jade said.

'Ten or fifteen minutes,' he said.

'You went directly to the takeaway?' Jade said.

'Yes.'

'And came straight back?'

'Yes,' he said. He smiled.

Jade nodded slowly. To her left the boss was writing. Jade waited for her to finish. They were in no rush. Walking him slowly into the trap.

'So you would have returned here by quarter past seven at the latest?'

'Yes.'

'Could you be mistaken about those times?' Jade said.

His face worked. He wasn't sure how to answer. Should he stick to his guns or admit uncertainty?

'No,' he said at last, tapping the armrest again. 'It was seven o'clock because Charlie and Aidan had just gone to bed. We keep to a routine.'

Jade didn't respond but switched to the second of the issues that concerned them. His other lie.

'You came back with the pizza, you say, at seven fifteen, and you were in the house for the rest of the evening. Is that correct?'

'Yes, that's right.'

'You didn't go out at all?' Jade said.

The boss sat back in her chair, adjusting the paper on her knee. *No worries here, mate.*

'No.' He cleared his throat. His toes relaxed, the colour returning to the knuckles.

'Not to the corner shop, or to the bins, or to a neighbour?' Jade saw a flash of alarm pass through his eyes when she mentioned the bins.

'No,' he said quickly. He dragged a hand through his hair.

'Perhaps you went out to the van for something.' The boss spoke up.

'No,' he said, shaking his head. 'I was in all evening. I didn't need to go out for anything.' He flushed, at least Jade thought he did but it was hard to know with his face already puce to start with.

The toes were scrunched up again.

The boss turned to look at Jade.

'Thank you,' Jade said. 'I think that's all we need for now.' Buzzing with the knowledge that the guy was lying every which way and had dug a very nice hole for himself.

His eyes flickered between the two of them. Bewildered. *Is that it? Do you believe me?*

The boss did her Columbo routine as they reached the door through to the hall. 'You've heard the inquiry has been upgraded to murder?'

Harrington gave a breathy gasp. 'Terrible that,' he said. 'But, like I told you, we didn't see anything or hear anything. Just wish I could help.'

Oh, you have, mate, Jade thought. And this is only the start. In fact we'll be back first thing, before you get a chance to neck your toast and jam. That won't be a chat in your home office but an interview under caution at the police station.

Chapter 26

Jade's good mood curdled as she drove home, dreading what she might find. Who she might find.

She'd been clear, though. Crystal. *One night.* One night only.

Parking behind the flats she saw her lights were on, as she'd instructed. Was anyone home?

Jade rapped the code on Mina's door as she passed.

She reached her own.

The door was slightly ajar. Jade's spine prickled. She pulled out the pepper spray she kept in her bag, then slid the bag from her shoulder and lowered it to the floor so she'd be able to move more easily.

Maybe Shannon had not pulled the door shut when she'd left.

There was only silence from Jade's flat but she could make out the murmur of sound from the other flats on the landing. Perhaps Bert was watching his History Channel or listening to Radio 4, Mina glued to reruns on Gold, bag of wool at her side.

Jade nudged the door with her foot and it swung open.

No one in the living room. No noise from the kitchen, no running water from the bathroom. Mina's blanket was folded neatly on the sofa beside the pillow.

Jade's back was locked rigid as she walked quietly to check each room. Everything looked just as she'd left it.

She let out a long breath and leaned back against the wall.

With a bubbling sense of relief she brought her bag in from the corridor then bolted the door.

A yawn brought tears to her eyes. She was knackered but a meal and an hour or so's telly and she'd be able to get some kip.

She chose a Chinese dish from the freezer and put it into the microwave, then switched on the convector heater.

The food was good, a perfect mix of sweet and sour, a gingery aftertaste. She must remember to get more of that.

Jade had changed into her pyjamas and was brushing her teeth when she thought she heard banging. Shutting off the tap, she listened and the noise came again. Knocking at her front door.

Jade spat out the toothpaste and wiped her mouth. At the door she looked through the spyhole. Bert, his face gaunt, eyes bloodshot, hair sticking out every which way.

Something wrong? Not a fall. But what?

Jade flung open the door. 'Bert?' Saw, too late, too fucking late, Shannon at his side.

'What do you want?' Jade said to Shannon.

'You locked me out,' Shannon said.

'You left my fucking door open,' Jade said.

'Only a bit,' Shannon said.

'A bit? It's either open or it's locked.'

'I didn't have a key to get back inside, that's why.'

You weren't supposed to get back inside. You were supposed to be gone.

'What are you doing bothering Bert?' Jade said.

'It's all right, Jade,' Bert said. 'Shannon's been helping me out.'

'What?' Now Jade wanted to smack him as well.

'The bulb went in the main light. I thought you were back. I could hear you but . . . well, it wasn't you, it was Shannon.'

'I changed the bulb,' Shannon said, grinning. 'And I took the rubbish down.'

Want a fucking medal?

Bert started backing away. He could obviously sense the atmosphere. 'I'll say goodnight then.'

'I've not changed a bulb before but Bert told me what to do. It's dead easy.'

As soon as Bert's door closed, Jade said, 'I told you one night. One.'

Shannon's lips clenched, like she was getting ready to spit or bite. Then she shook it off, hair fluttering, and said, 'I know and I tried, but Abbie's away and Sam's got her brother's kids at hers and my other friend's not picking up. I don't want to trek all the way over to Crumpsall if she isn't there.'

'What about Ryan?' Jade said.

'He's a wanker,' Shannon said.

'Yeah, but he's your wanker. You said he'd take you back.'

'He will.' Shannon shook her head. 'He's just playing games. He'll come round. Might need a day or two.'

'You can't stay here, Shannon. I told you.'

'Well, where do you expect me to go, then?'

'It's not my problem,' Jade said. 'Why don't you get those angels to sort you out?'

A blade of hatred flashed in Shannon's glare. She blinked. 'You're my sister. Family.'

'Family? Why don't you go to Mam's, then?' The name unfamiliar, dangerous, on her tongue.

'You're joking,' Shannon said. 'Have you met Ricky? She's bad enough but him . . . You know how she's always—'

'I don't want to know. I've not seen her for years. And if I never see her again it'll be too soon.' Heat rose up her back, through her cheeks. The floor rippled.

'Yeah? Well, you got out, didn't you?' Shannon said.

'Got out?' Jade's head was going to explode. 'I didn't *get out*, I was taken. Emergency court order, at risk, removed to a place of safety.' *Supposedly.* A swirl of dread spun through her, wrapping tendrils round her arms, her chest, her neck.

'She talked about you, you know. Said you was difficult. Like her, I guess,' Shannon said.

'I was five,' Jade said. 'And she was a fucking monster.'

Jade felt her throat close, her mouth water, the pressure filling her head, the drumbeat in her temples. Vision darkening. She couldn't breathe. Pictures danced round, a freakshow tableau: Jade tugging to get free, her wrists bound; Jade flinching, trying to dodge the open palm, the crack banging through the bones of her skull, deafening her; eyes burning, refusing to cry, inviting another slap. Her mother screaming at the social worker. *'You can't fucking take her! You can't!'* Jade shivering, cold everywhere. Her belly aching. Licking her fingers, pretending they were sausages, tasting salt.

Jade was drowning. She reeled back into the flat, sat on the sofa, hands cupped over her nose. Sick. Suffocating.

Shannon's voice bounced overhead.

Jade sipped little hiccups of air, the room spinning. She was dying.

The wild panic was throttling her. She fought to sip more air. Choked. Clamoured for escape. Something she must do. Grounding. A way back. The lessons, the psychologist. *Find the present. Root yourself. Feet planted.* Jade dragged half a breath. *In the moment. What can you feel?*

Woven fabric under my fingers. She opened her eyes. Brown woven fabric, little arrows in the pattern.

Shannon was talking, shouting at Jade, but Jade was unable to respond. Even if the words had made any sense.

Focus. Five things. What can you see?

Brown arrows, a line of piping. She ran the edge of her thumb over it. *What can you smell? Soy sauce and ginger. What can you hear? A plane overhead, jet engines.* Brown arrows, soy sauce, a jet. Shannon's nails, talons, shiny hornets.

Shannon was touching her shoulders. Jade pushed her away. Saw their reflections on the TV screen. *No screens. Screens could be portholes, people listening, watchers, secret messages, death threats.*

Five things: brown arrows – she pressed her fingers into the fabric – soy sauce, a jet, hornets. One more. A taste in Jade's mouth: toothpaste. Minty. *Brown arrows, soy sauce, a jet, hornets, mint.*

She could breathe.

I am here in my flat. It is Thursday. I am safe. I am sane.

'Jade,' Shannon still talking, 'what's wrong? Are you gonna be sick?'

Jade shivered. She was drained, bloodless, weak.

'What the fuck was that?' Shannon said. 'Was it a fit or something? Shall I call an ambulance? Do you want to go to hospital?'

'I just need to sleep,' Jade said.

There was something she had to tell Shannon but she couldn't think of it. Her brain was mush.

Her eyes stung. She was so very tired. Shuddering.

She went into her bedroom and shut the door. Took tablets from her bedside table. She climbed into bed and pulled the covers over her head. She ran through the list until the words and images, and the senses that came with them, melted into a thick, dark sleep.

Chapter 27

'You can't arrest him.' Gaynor Harrington stood beside her husband, hand on his arm. 'He hasn't done anything wrong. He doesn't know anything about all that.'

Donna had read out the caution, then asked Stewart Harrington to hold out his arms for the handcuffs.

'Is this down to George Peel?' Gaynor said, spittle at the corners of her carefully painted mouth. 'Because he'll do anything for attention, you know. He's just stirring it.'

Donna ignored the question. She addressed Stewart again. 'You have the right to a solicitor and if you don't have one of your own then one can be provided for you.'

'Mummy?' The middle child came out into the hall.

'Aidan, get back in there now!' Gaynor snapped. The child's face crumpled. 'Now!' Gaynor said. 'I'll be in in a minute.'

The boy disappeared.

Stewart Harrington was poleaxed, swaying in place. Donna wondered if he'd keel over before they could get him into the patrol car.

'Have you got your phone?' Gaynor said to him. 'Let me know what's happening.'

'It's charging,' Harrington said.

'You need to bring that with you,' Donna said. 'You won't be able to make calls when being interviewed. And we may need to retain it for examination.'

'It's in the living room,' Harrington said.

'I'll get it,' Jade said. Standard practice. Not giving them a chance to delete anything.

'It'll be fine,' Harrington said to Gaynor, while Jade was gone. 'Just some stupid mistake.' But his voice sounded thready and uncertain.

'Officers will be searching the property and you'll be given a list of anything we remove for examination,' Donna said.

'Search here?' Gaynor said, flint in her tone.

'That's right.' Specifically they were looking for evidence of Rosa or her mother at the property. The couple owned other houses, rental properties, but none of them was close to where Rosa had been found so, at this stage, Donna hadn't applied for other warrants.

As they went out to the car, Donna noticed Mitch Cookson opposite, watching from his front door. And next-door-but-one George Peel at his post.

No doubt Mandy's shop would be humming with gossip all day.

What was Harrington's exact involvement? Could Gaynor possibly be Rosa's mother? Looking at her, it was hard to believe. She didn't show any physical signs of being post-partum. No rounded belly or swollen breasts. And if she had been pregnant surely some of the neighbours would have noticed it.

Donna and Jade waited while the patrol car drove away.

Jade looked wan, her brown skin ashy, a dullness in her eyes. Even her hair was dull. 'Rough night?' Donna teased her.

'No.' Jade was defensive.

'You look a bit under the weather, that's all,' Donna said.

Jade glared at her. Then rolled her eyes. Stuffed her hands into her jacket.

Bloody rude.

Determined not to respond in kind, Donna turned the conversation back to her own life. 'The inquest was concluded, death by road-traffic collision. Jim's – well, he's glad it's over.'

He'd been giddy with relief when he'd told her, sighing and smiling, saying, 'Thank God it's over,' several times.

Donna thought again about the anomaly in Jim's story. The trip to

134

an unfamiliar supermarket. She'd not raised it last night, not wanted to unsettle him. And something about the prospect of asking the question made her feel needy. Surely there must be a simple explanation – so why was she so reluctant to ask?

Something had changed. Donna had less . . . not strength but courage. Was it courage? Or less certainty? Less sure of herself, and her judgement. Though certainty could lead to someone being blinkered. Perhaps a bit of doubt, even self-doubt, could be helpful.

'Right,' Jade said, uninterested. 'Shall we get on, then?'

At the station, while Jade went to book Stewart Harrington into the custody suite, Donna met with the team.

'He's no criminal record,' Calvin said. 'Clean sheet.'

'And Gaynor?' Donna said.

'Same,' Calvin said.

'I find it hard to believe it was her baby,' Donna said, and explained why.

'We'll soon know if it's his,' Isla said. Harrington would be giving a DNA sample along with his fingerprints.

'Yes.'

'Nothing's come back on the ANPR system for his van leaving the area between seven and half past,' Calvin said.

'So he was AWOL but we don't know where,' Donna said. 'Or whether it connects to what he was doing three hours later in the alley.'

'It must be linked,' Tessa said.

At least they had something newsworthy now. The bulletin would go out as soon as he was in custody: 'A thirty-eight-year-old man has been arrested in connection with the investigation into the suspected murder of baby Rosa and is helping police with their enquiries.'

The clock was ticking. They could hold Stewart Harrington for twenty-four hours without charging him, and he must be given an eight-hour sleep break in that time. Donna thought it might be best to work through until seven p.m. Then resume at three in the morning. Get into their stride by four, the darkest hour, when people were at their most vulnerable. It would mean a horribly early start for the team, but if it wrong-footed Stewart Harrington and bought them more leverage it might be worth it. She'd monitor their progress and make a firm decision later.

Of course Harrington might turn out to be an angel, his lies built on some minor misdemeanour, which he'd mistakenly concealed from the police. Time would tell but she bloody hoped not.

Chapter 28

Dumbstruck, Jade reckoned, when she looked at Stewart Harrington. Whatever he'd been up to he hadn't expected to end up here, in a police interview room as a murder suspect.

Jade had seen the duty solicitor before. She was a happy-clappy sort, which must be a hard act to pull off, given the toe-rags and scumbags she had to work with. She was also pregnant. And the size of a minibus.

Jade couldn't believe how huge the woman's belly was. Like someone had stuck a massive beachball on her front. Cartoonish. And the chairs in the room were bolted down, which meant she wouldn't fit. The boss had sent Jade to fetch a folding chair and the solicitor used that placed at the end of the table.

Jade repeated back to Stewart Harrington his account of his movements on Monday. He spoke very little, saying only, 'Yes, that's right,' each time she asked for confirmation.

'And you went to bed at?'

'Eleven o'clock.'

'Given how serious the situation is, do you want to change anything you have said so far?'

'No.' He swallowed. The cords in his neck tightened like ropes.

'We have more than one witness who heard a commotion outside your property at seven p.m. on Monday evening. What can you tell us about that?'

'Nothing. I don't know what it was. I didn't hear anything.' He spoke quietly, eyes on the desk, greying hair falling forward, partly shielding his face.

'Are you sure? Shouting? An argument? You say you went out to your van at that time.'

'No, it was all quiet.'

'You've stated that you went to collect a pizza from Domino's on Stockport Road at seven p.m. and that you returned at seven fifteen. Is that correct?'

'Yes.' Jade heard the tick in his throat as he swallowed. For a moment her own throat contracted in response. The aftertaste from last night's meltdown, the hollow pit seething with unease in her stomach.

She gripped the folder in front of her, opened it and spoke for the recording. 'I'm now showing the suspect a still photograph taken from CCTV at Domino's on Stockport Road. The photograph shows the suspect arriving at the premises. Please, will you read out the timestamp for us?' Jade pointed to the figures.

'Nineteen thirty-one oh seven,' his voice was husky.

'*After* you claim to have returned home.'

'I might have been a few minutes later,' he said, giving a weak laugh.

Jade looked at him for a moment. *Nothing to laugh about, mate.* 'You agree this is you in the photograph?'

'Yes.'

'And that you reached the takeaway at nineteen thirty-one?'

'Yes,' he said.

'Where were you immediately before that?' Jade said.

'At home,' he said.

'We have witnesses who saw you drive away at seven p.m., that gives us thirty-one minutes unaccounted for. Where did you go, Mr Harrington?'

'Nowhere. They must be mixed up, about seeing me go, about—' He stopped dead. Swallowed again, tucked his hair behind his ears.

Feeling the pressure now, pal? Things can only get harder.

'You told us repeatedly that you left the house at seven p.m. but now you're saying that's not the case?'

He swung his head. His solicitor leaned forward. 'You are not obliged to answer.'

138

'It must have been later,' he said. 'Maybe quarter past.'

'We have an eyewitness says differently. How do you explain the discrepancy?'

'I can't.'

'Your youngest sons, Charlie and Aidan, had just gone to bed, you told us. You . . .' Jade flicked through the pages. She knew exactly what she was going to say but it wouldn't hurt him to realise it was all down there in black-and-white. Every word he'd said. Every little lie. ' . . . you said you keep to a routine.'

'Not to the minute.' Agitation in his voice. Or was it irritation?

'To be clear, do you wish to alter your account of your movements? Are you now saying you must have left the house at seven fifteen?'

'Yes, I must have.'

Jade paused for a couple of seconds. 'Mr Harrington, at seven fifteen PCSO Evans called at your home in connection with an attempted break-in on Grace Street. No one answered the door.'

'Yes, because Gaynor had a headache,' he said. 'We don't let the kids do it.'

'Officer Evans reported that there was no van parked at the property.'

'Then I must have just gone.' His face was shiny, sweat glistening, like oil, on his forehead, around his bulbous nose.

'In which case you left before seven fifteen,' Jade said.

'I don't know. I don't know.' His hands flew up. His nails were split, horny. Knuckles swollen. Working hands. He sat back and made an obvious effort to wind his neck in, adopting a reasonable tone. 'Look, I wasn't paying attention to the time. You're right, I can't remember exactly. Either way, I could be a few minutes out.'

'So you can't tell us with any certainty when you drove away?' Jade said.

'It must have been just before seven fifteen,' he said.

'Are you telling me that it took you seventeen minutes to travel the five hundred metres from your home to the takeaway? Isn't that excessive?'

He put his fist to his forehead. 'I don't know.'

Jade waited a few beats. Beside her the boss drew a line under her notes. A signal for her to move on.

Jade removed the photo and replaced it in her folder. 'After you returned with pizza you've told us you were in all evening.'

'Yes.'

This time Jade went in quickly. 'We have a witness who saw you in the alley at the back of your property at ten thirty. What were you doing there?'

His mouth hung open momentarily. 'They couldn't have.'

'They saw you coming down the alley and going in your back gate,' she said.

'No. I was in the house. I didn't go out. They've got it wrong.' His lips were pale – even the purple of his nose seemed to fade. There was a naked look on his face. He was rattled. Well rattled.

Jade's tablet flashed an alert. His fingerprint comparison was back. She scanned it. Yes! The evidence they'd been hoping for.

'We believe the body of baby Rosa was placed in the commercial bin at the end of the alley sometime during Monday. Can you tell us anything about that?'

'No.' The muscles around his jawline clenched. 'I swear,' he said.

'Please take a look at these photographs.' Jade pulled out two A4 prints from her folder and turned them so Harrington could see. The contents of the bin were laid out on a white background. Newspapers, drinks cartons, packaging, the lottery ticket, fish-fingers cartons, the flyers that had narrowed the search to a handful of homes on Rosa Street.

'These items of paper waste were found with Rosa's body. Do you recognise any of them?'

'How do you mean?' he said.

'Have you seen them before?' Jade said.

'Well, I know what they are,' he said, 'but whether I've seen these actual ones, I've no idea.'

'Have any of these items been in your house in the last week?' Jade asked.

140

'I don't know.'

'Which newspaper do you get?' she said.

'The *Mirror*.'

'Like these in the photo. What about the drinks, the fish fingers? Do you buy those brands?'

'Maybe . . . I . . . Some like those,' he said. 'But not those exact ones. Not if they were in the bin at the shops.'

Jade turned her tablet to face him. 'Mr Harrington, these are the results of a test comparing your fingerprints to fingerprints recovered from the paper waste and from the refuse sack that contained the paper waste, and also Rosa's body. The comparison shows us these are your fingerprints. Can you explain how your fingerprints got onto these items?'

'No.' He covered his nose and mouth.

Jade stumbled. Sweat broke out across her scalp, her neck and forehead. Her mouth flooded with spit.

Sitting on her sofa, Shannon shouting. Dread surged through her, twisting her organs, flooding every cell. *Brown arrows and hornets.* She struggled to swallow. *Not here. Not now. Keep it together.*

Beside her the boss tensed, ready to prompt and Jade forced herself to recapture her line of argument. She cleared her throat, held her voice as level as she could. 'We think we can explain them. The evidence suggests that you were involved in disposing of Rosa's body and concealing her death.'

'No,' he said, more of a groan than a word.

'Mr Harrington, your account of your movements earlier in the evening contradicts the statements of several independent witnesses. You've denied that you were in the alleyway when we have an eyewitness who saw you there at half past ten. Your fingerprints are all over the pieces of evidence found with Rosa's body. Isn't it true that you were in the alley because you were taking the bin bag with Rosa's body in it to the bin on the main road to dispose of it?'

He just shook his head on and on, like a puppet, like the dancing Spider-Man in his van, until the solicitor requested a short break and Jade, still sick with fear, agreed.

Chapter 29

'He's not the baby's father.' Donna licked icing sugar from her fingers. Isla had bought pastries and cakes and they were all tucking in. 'The DNA says not – so where does that leave us?'

Calvin stroked the bridge of his nose, seemingly lost in thought.

'Up Shit Creek,' Jade muttered.

'Possibilities?' Donna looked round the group. 'Come on. This isn't Harrington's child so how come he's disposing of the body? What's the connection?'

'Gaynor's the mother,' Jade said, 'but he's not the father. Maybe he doesn't know.'

'She's playing away?' Donna said. 'But how did she hide the pregnancy? Why would she hide the pregnancy?'

'She didn't realise?' Isla sounded tentative.

'I'd buy that if it was her first time, or if she'd been ill, which could confuse the symptoms but . . .' Donna shook her head. 'It doesn't work for me.'

'We need her DNA,' Jade said.

'Which we can get if we find grounds to arrest her,' Donna said.

'Illegal adoption,' Calvin said, picking up a slab of rocky road. 'They want a baby, so they pay for a baby.'

'Trafficking?' Donna said.

There was a minute's silence, everyone imagining that scenario.

'They've already got three kids,' Jade said. 'Come on, three's more than enough for anyone. Who in their right mind? Yeah?'

Donna stiffened, waiting to see if Jade would realise what she'd just said and try to qualify it. She didn't. Isla met Donna's gaze, a bead of amusement in her eye. Donna drew a breath. 'Three boys,' she said. 'Perhaps they wanted a girl.'

Jade tilted her head, scowling, as though listening for something. 'What?' Donna said.

'Nothing, just . . .' Jade raised her hands '. . . there's something about—' Again she broke off. 'It's gone,' she said.

'Well, let me know if it comes back and you can put a name to it,' Donna said.

'Or they stole the baby?' Calvin said. 'And the mother is incapacitated. That's why she's not come forward.' He took a bite of his cake.

'OK,' Donna said. 'Incapacitated how?'

Calvin chewed, made an effort to swallow. 'Mentally ill?'

Opposite, Jade had tipped back her chair, one hand rubbing her wrist, looking over to the door. Distancing herself, it felt like. Jade had blanked out towards the end of the Harrington interview, just dried up. Donna had been about to step in when Jade had finally come to her senses. She'd not done that before, and Donna didn't want it to happen again. Was it likely to?

'Maybe the mother's too afraid of the police, the authorities,' Isla said.

'Because she's illegal or done something illegal?' Calvin said.

Jade rocked forward. 'Or she's dead. Harrington killed her.'

'Or she dies having the baby,' Isla said.

Donna wiped her hands on a napkin. 'Right, field's wide open,' she said. 'I'm confident we can get an extension to question Harrington for longer. The forensics we've got are strong. He's still denying all knowledge. I want to pin him down on that missing half-hour. Isla, you've got the phone log from his mobile?'

'Texts and calls. There was a message from Gaynor at ten past seven on the Monday night, "Get pizza", short and sweet.'

'Good. Let's see how he explains that for starters,' Donna said.

Calvin's phone pinged. 'Store CCTV from Asda,' he said.

He swivelled round in his chair and used the remote to turn on the large screen, then uploaded the file from his phone. Something that would have taken Donna half the afternoon. He started the video.

The camera covered three checkouts and Donna scanned the queues twice before Jade said, 'In the middle.'

'Holy shit,' said Calvin.

'Holy shit, indeed,' said Donna.

The picture wasn't sharply focused, covering such a wide area, but there was no mistaking the slim figure with the long, wavy blonde hair and glasses, loading nappies, formula, feeding bottles and baby clothes onto the checkout. *Gaynor Harrington.*

Donna felt a rush of excitement, of validation. They were on the right track and they were drawing closer.

'We going to nick her, boss?' Jade said.

'Too bloody right, we are. Tell Harrington's solicitor we'll break for another two hours. And not a word to them about Gaynor. We'll tell Harrington we've picked her up when we're good and ready.'

Everyone was grinning, Calvin shaking his head at the break-through, Isla waving a thumbs-up. Even Jade, who had looked miserable as sin most of the day, had a spark back in her eyes.

'Good work,' Donna said. 'It's going to be a late finish tonight. That a problem for anyone?'

It wasn't.

Chapter 30

The search was still under way at the Harringtons' when Jade and the boss arrived. The door jambs were dirty grey, gritty with fingerprint powder.

Gaynor had gone to collect the children from school.

'I told her we're nearly done but she needs to sign the forms when she's back,' said Anthea, who they found in the utility room, bagging the contents of the vacuum cleaner.

The room was behind the home office and was probably ten feet square. Large enough for a washer-dryer, a chest freezer, a Belfast sink. Drying racks and an ironing board were set up next to a trestle table. Mop and brush in the corner. Waterproofs in assorted sizes hung from a row of hooks, below them boots and wellies.

'Find any baby things?' the boss asked.

'Nothing. But this room's been washed with bleach.'

Jade's stomach turned over. 'I can smell it,' she said. It made her think of cold toilets, doors with broken locks, walls painted thick cream or institutional green and obscenities scrawled in felt tip or lipstick, blood or shit.

The floor was terracotta-coloured vinyl, patterned like fake tiling. Blotchy now. From use or from the bleach? Blood would stain, wouldn't it? Unless it was cleaned up quickly. Or bleached away.

'I know it's where they do the laundry,' Anthea said. 'But *everything* has been wiped down. Floor, skirting boards, doors, the machines.'

'So you looked for blood?' the boss said.

'Course we did, be rude not to when they've gone to all that trouble. We've found traces down here.' Pointing to a section of skirting board. 'And under the washing-machine.' Triumph in her voice.

'Did you check the freezer?' the boss said.

'Yes, nothing.'

'What about the garden?'

'Mainly flagged, no sign of recent disturbance. Nothing to say we should start digging it up.'

There were questions hovering on everyone's lips but they weren't close to being answered and no one spoke them out loud. At least not until the boss said, 'No blood loss involved with the baby's death, so is this from the mother? What on earth would possess them to . . .' She checked her watch. 'Gaynor should be back by now.'

'Unless . . .' Jade said. *What if she's bolted? Picked up the kids and run?* She hurried to the door, the boss behind her.

Outside, Jade could see Gaynor halfway up the street, a child holding her hands on either side, the older one, William, trailing after.

Gaynor stopped dead when she saw them and Jade noticed her glance round as if searching for a way out. But then she carried on walking. One of the kids was talking and Gaynor was nodding but her eyes kept returning to Jade and the boss, and her face was set, hostile.

'Where's Stewart?' she said, reaching them.

'Let's go inside,' the boss said.

The smallest child, Charlie, was sucking a lolly, a lump in his cheek, the stick poking out from between his lips. The middle one, Aidan, was mithering for a drink.

'Jesus.' Gaynor had spotted the fingerprint powder. 'Don't touch the doors,' she said to the kids.

'What's all that?' William said.

'Doesn't matter, just don't touch it. Are they going to clean that up?' she said to Jade, taking off her glasses and rubbing at them with a tissue.

'No,' Jade said, because they never did and people always whined on about it. They'd rather bitch about the mess than think about why the police were crawling all over the house in the first place.

'You lot – in there.' Gaynor sent the kids to the living room.

'But, Mum—' Aidan began.

'Now! William, get them a drink.'

'Why do I have to?'

'Because I say so. Christ!' She glared at him and he stomped past Jade into the kitchen.

'We can go into the office,' the boss said. 'The team have finished in there.'

Gaynor went through and stood, arms crossed. 'So – Stewart?'

'Your husband is still at the police station. He'll be there overnight. Perhaps longer. We need you to come with us as well,' the boss said.

'What?' Dismay twisted her features.

'Is there someone you can get to stay with the children? A relative or friend?' the boss said.

'No,' she said.

'A babysitter?' Jade suggested.

'No. Can't it just wait until Stewart comes home?'

'We can arrange for emergency foster care,' the boss said.

'You can't take my kids!' Outraged.

'We can't leave them unsupervised so unless you can think of anyone to help – a neighbour perhaps?' the boss said.

'No,' Gaynor said. 'They don't know anyone. This is insane. Why do I have to come? Just talk to me here.'

'We can't do that,' the boss said. 'Gaynor Harrington, I am arresting you on suspicion of murder . . .'

Gaynor kept shouting, 'No!' and 'You're crazy!' as the boss read the caution. The boss just kept going. 'Do you understand what I've told you?'

'No, because it doesn't make any bloody sense,' Gaynor said. 'It's mad. You're off your trolley.'

'Call the emergency social-work team, Jade.'

'Don't do that. You can't take them. You fucking bitch.' Gaynor's face was ugly, distorted with rage.

'They will do their best to find someone in the area,' the boss said, ignoring the language and the aggro, 'so the children can carry on in the same school. Try to minimise the disruption.'

'You can't. You can't do this.' But the fight was draining away, reality sinking in. She was fucked, every which way.

Once the child-protection social worker arrived and was briefed, he explained to Gaynor that his priority was safeguarding and that everything would be done to make sure the children were well looked after. As he asked for the boys' names, dates of birth and medical information, Jade could see the shock taking hold. Gaynor's voice wavered as she talked about William's nut allergy and Charlie's car sickness.

'Are we all right to pack some clothes and toys? It helps if they can have their own things with them,' the social worker said.

'Aidan needs his teddy—' Gaynor broke off.

'You show me where things are and I can sort that out while we wait for confirmation of a place. I've a lovely foster mum in Gorton. She'd be just perfect. They're OK with cats?'

'Yes.'

'Great. Let's go and speak to the boys now.'

At last the kids were ready to leave and saying their goodbyes in the living room. Jade was shaky. Everything seemed to be slipping out of sync, the words of the social worker reaching her a beat behind him saying them, like bad dubbing. Jump cuts in the scene before her, frames missing so it was juddering.

William, eyes big and scared, his mouth twitching, close to tears. Aidan crying, shoulders jerking. His mum rubbing his back. Charlie, still with a lolly in his mouth, patting his brother's knee. Jade's throat ached, mouth dry as dust. Heat burned at the back of her knees, the base of her skull. She had to get out. She lifted her hand, caught the attention of the boss, signalled her out to the hall.

'Boss, I'm gagging. I'll get a drink from the corner.' Jade's neck felt peculiar, a fizzing like pins and needles, a buzzing in her head, and she was nauseous. The pastry from Isla. She could still taste the almond paste, sickly now. 'You good?'

148

'I'm fine, thanks,' the boss said.

The team were packing up, carrying equipment, cases and bags out to their vans. Nothing else significant had come to light.

It had begun to rain, a soft drizzle that smelt of earth and rock and engine oil. Jade breathed in as she walked, trying to clear her head, cool her nerves.

Mandy Myers didn't say anything when Jade bought a Pepsi but her eyes, fringed with navy lashes, were alive with curiosity.

Only as Jade picked up her change and turned to go, did Mandy say, 'They've been searching at the Harringtons'?'

'Yes,' Jade said. She could hardly deny it.

'And you've arrested him?'

Stewart Harrington's name hadn't been released yet and Jade wasn't going to spill the beans.

'You really think they . . . that little baby . . .'

'We still want to talk to the mother. Rosa's mother,' she added, in case Mandy thought she meant Gaynor. Though the mother could be one and the same person. 'If you hear anything . . .'

'Of course.' She sighed. 'I don't know.' Mandy's eyes swam, close to tears over someone she'd never even met.

Jade opened her can, the fizz of foam like the buzzing in her blood.

If Mandy looked out of the window in the next few minutes she would see Gaynor being driven away by the police, just like her husband had been.

Back at the house Gaynor was being put into the patrol car. This time there was no cavalcade of neighbours watching. Presumably the action of the search had been going on for so long that they'd grown bored, drifted away and missed out on the main act.

They'd know soon enough, Jade thought. *Police have arrested a forty-year-old woman in connection with the murder of baby Rosa.*

Jade drained her Coke and squashed the can. She thought she heard one of the kids crying from inside. It set her teeth on edge. She needed to leave. 'You ready, boss?'

149

The boss smiled at her. 'I am.'

Her mind kept yanking her back to last night, like a half-crazed dog that can smell carrion, straining on the leash. Shannon, of all people, to see her lose it like that. Shame drenched her each time she remembered, thick and sticky as tar. Shannon should never have seen that. And she wouldn't have if she'd done as she'd fucking well been told and pissed off to someone else's sofa.

The boss had said tonight would be a late one so Jade might as well sleep at the office. There was no point in driving all the way home, even if Shannon had slung her hook, like Jade had told her to.

That's a plan, she said to herself. And the twist in her guts unwound a notch.

Chapter 31

Jade shuddered, hunched her shoulders, as they walked back to where they'd left the cars. It wasn't even particularly cold.

'You OK?' Donna asked her.

'I'm good,' Jade said. Rote response. But she didn't look at Donna, which made it hard to judge if she was being honest.

You're so young, Donna thought, picturing herself at the same age. She'd been a beat cop at twenty-five, responding to whatever the shift threw at her. Trying to make good, to prove herself. But terrified inside. Of getting it wrong, of making a mistake.

Was Jade anxious about this particular investigation? She'd always been keen, diving in and apparently impervious to the disturbing elements of the murders they dealt with. Was something different now?

A lorry backed out of a side street, automated voice warning, *Vehicle reversing*. Puffs of grey exhaust billowed in the air.

'A case like this can be hard,' Donna said.

Jade flicked her a glance, dark eyes cautious.

'Emotionally, not just practically. We're pulling long hours but we all still need to find a way to stay sane. To decompress. You understand what I'm saying?'

'Yeah, but I'm fine.' An empty laugh. A shrug. On the defensive.

'Are you? Only you seem pretty stressed out and that worries me. Talk to me, Jade.'

Jade bit her lip. Donna was shocked to see a glint of tears in her eyes before she blinked them away.

'If this investigation is too much for any reason. If I'm asking too much—'

'Work's fine,' Jade said. She cleared her throat.

The sun broke through: the golden light, low in the sky, was dazzling. Donna shielded her eyes with her hand. 'Personal stuff?' she said.

Jade gave a nod.

Jade was tough, Donna knew that, street smart, hard-edged, but she sensed the vulnerability behind the mask. She understood that Jade presented a cool veneer as a form of protection.

Donna stopped walking. 'You want to talk about it?'

'No,' Jade said flatly.

'Guess you'd rather drink bleach?'

Jade laughed, wiped her nose on the back of her hand.

'Seriously, do you need any time off?' Donna said. 'Space to deal with it.'

'No.'

'Anything else I can do?' Donna said.

Jade shook her head.

'If that changes, just ask. Yeah? Anything.' Donna touched Jade's shoulder, a quick tap.

Jade turned her head away, gave a vigorous nod.

Above, a passenger jet climbed through the sky, the roar of the engines drowning out all other sound, cutting off the light for a second as it crossed in front of the sun.

Chapter 32

Gaynor's eyes glittered behind her gold-framed glasses, part desperation, part rage as Donna repeated the caution in the interview room.

'When can I see my kids?' Gaynor said.

'That's not going to be possible. Not while you're here,' Donna said.

'Call them, then?'

'No,' Donna said.

'You can't just— I'll bloody sue you. I'll put in a complaint and I'll sue for compensation. It's a bloody joke.'

'If that's what you wish to do, we can provide you with the relevant information,' Donna said. 'Now, I'd like to show you these items.' Donna placed photos of the paper waste and bin liner in front of Gaynor.

Gaynor blinked twice when she set eyes on them but otherwise her face betrayed only a wary hostility.

'On Monday night a plastic bag was removed from the rubbish bins by the shops at the end of Rosa Street. The bag contained the body of an infant girl known as Rosa. These things were also recovered from the bag. Do you recognise them?' Donna said.

'No,' Gaynor said tersely.

'Please take a good look. Do you recognise them?'

'No.'

'Are you sure of that?' Donna said.

'Yes, I'm sure.'

'Then how do you explain the fact that your fingerprints were found on several of those articles?' Donna said.

'What?' Gaynor's brow furrowed.

'Detective, please be specific, which items?' The duty solicitor was an old hand, a man in his sixties with a grey tonsure and varifocal glasses. He spoke with a precise Edinburgh accent.

'This is an inventory of the wastepaper and card.' Donna showed them the list. 'Your prints were found on three of the drinks cartons, also on the fish-fingers packaging and on the lottery ticket. You handled these items, didn't you?'

'If you say so.'

Her solicitor cleared his throat: he didn't like his client agreeing.

Gaynor said, 'But our wastepaper goes in our blue wheelie bin so someone must have taken it from there.'

'Taken your old papers?' Donna said.

'Yes. That's all I can think of.'

Far-fetched but not a totally implausible explanation. The killer, searching for something to hide the baby in, steals into the Harringtons' backyard and finds a sack of rubbish. Except . . . paper waste was deposited loose into the blue recycling bins – no plastic sacks.

Gaynor looked directly at Donna, emboldened perhaps, thinking she had scored a point and deflected the attack.

Donna gave her a brief smile. 'Mrs Harrington, I'd like you to look at this photograph now.'

Donna placed a photograph of Gaynor buying the baby supplies on the table.

Gaynor didn't speak. The muscles in her cheeks contracted and she clasped her hands together.

'This is you in the photograph?' Donna said.

Gaynor didn't reply.

'Mrs Harrington, is this you?'

'Yes.'

'And this is a copy of the receipt for the goods you bought a week ago, on Friday, the twelfth of October. It lists newborn nappies and baby wipes, baby sleepsuits and vests. Also feeding formula, bottles and sterilising equipment. Why were you buying these?'

Gaynor blinked.

'Why did you buy these baby goods? Who were they for?'

'For the food bank,' she said. Her eyes took a moment to settle on Donna's.

A lie, Donna was sure, but it couldn't be proven so immediately.

'I don't think that's the case,' Donna said. 'And when we request CCTV records for that area of the store I think they'll show that you left with those items.'

Gaynor cast her eyes up to a corner of the ceiling. Looking for answers?

'Mrs Harrington, you're here under caution on suspicion of the most heinous charges. I would urge you to consider what you say very, very carefully. It is all being recorded and should this matter come to court—'

'My client understands the situation,' said the solicitor. 'And that no duress will be brought to bear,' he added, with emphasis. Warning Donna to tread carefully. Had she sounded threatening? Donna felt Jade's eyes on her. Any hint of coercion or undue pressure and a defence barrister would milk it for all it was worth. Imply that Gaynor's answers were not sound, that they'd been obtained unfairly. And use that to undermine the prosecution case.

'Where are those items now?' Donna said levelly.

'I told you, I donated them to the food bank,' Gaynor said. 'Not the box in Asda's,' she added. 'The church place. I dropped them there.'

Oh, very clever. Thinking on her feet. Her fictions would surely unravel in time but for now they served to delay their progress.

'A moment, please.' Donna suspended the interview and stood. 'DC Bradshaw?' She nodded towards the door.

Out in the corridor Donna told Jade to send Calvin to the food bank and establish if they'd had any such donation.

'It's bullshit,' Jade said hotly.

'I know it's bullshit, you know it's bullshit, but we have to prove it, Jade.' Donna reined in her frustration. 'Go now. We'll start again as soon as you get back. I'm going to call the lab and chase the DNA.'

'It's not ready,' the technician told Donna.

155

'Have you any idea how long?' Donna said.

'It depends on how many interruptions we have to deal with. All these people ringing up wanting results, wanting to know how long it will be till theirs are ready. You wouldn't believe how much it slows us down.'

Christ! Donna hung up. She could have done without a lecture.

'Just heard from Border Force,' Jade said, when she got back. 'They've apprehended Waheed Siddique in Sheffield. So much for going to Pakistan.'

'Nice one. Right,' Donna said, moving to the interview room. 'Let's crack on.'

'I'd like you to take me through events as you remember them on Monday evening, Mrs Harrington. Starting with you fetching the children home from school,' Donna said.

Gaynor flinched at the mention of the children. She tossed back her hair and said, 'I brought them home. Stewart got in about five. I had a migraine and went to bed. And he went for pizza. That was it.' She shrugged her shoulders. 'Oh, and the police left a note. I didn't know that till later.'

'What time did your husband leave to get the pizza?'

'Seven,' Gaynor said.

'Who decided on buying takeaway?'

'What?' Gaynor said irritably.

'Did he suggest it or did you?' Donna said.

'I asked him to get it,' Gaynor said.

'Before he left?' Donna said.

'Yes.'

'Only we've seen a text message from you to Mr Harrington sent at ten past seven asking him to get pizza. But you just told me you spoke to him about it before he left.'

'It was a reminder,' she said. Her pupils dilated, the blue of her irises seeming to intensify.

'Why did he leave the house?'

'To get the pizza,' she snapped.

156

'Why a reminder then? Only ten minutes after?' Donna felt like she was grilling one of her kids, knowing the lie was there, only a matter of moments before it was exposed and the half-truths and misdirections fell away.

'In case he picked something else, garlic bread or wedges or chicken wings,' Gaynor said. She was slippery, quick-thinking, better under pressure than her husband. So far, at least.

'And what time did he return home?' Donna said.

'About ten minutes after that.'

'Ten minutes after you sent the text?' Donna said.

'Yes.'

'Were you still in bed?' Donna said.

'What?' Gaynor said.

'When Stewart came back? You were still in bed. So you wouldn't have seen him?'

'I heard him.'

'You said earlier that you were in the house together the rest of the evening.'

'Yes,' Gaynor said.

'But you were in bed, isn't that right? With a migraine?' Donna said.

'Yes.'

'So you wouldn't know if he left the house again?' Donna said.

'He didn't,' Gaynor said.

'You can't know that.'

'He wouldn't leave the kids.' She lifted her chin as she spoke. 'I know he didn't,' she said tightly.

Donna saw what it cost her to mention the children, and her determination not to let it derail the conviction of her answers.

'But if you were upstairs in your room and your husband was downstairs, you can't confirm to us that he remained in the property throughout the entire evening.'

'They'd all be in bed, wouldn't they?' Jade broke in. 'The kids. By when?'

'Half eight,' Gaynor said.

157

'So if you were all asleep upstairs, he might have gone out,' Jade said.

'He didn't,' Gaynor insisted.

'We have information that suggests otherwise,' Donna said.

Gaynor didn't respond, but Donna saw her throat tighten as she swallowed and was sure they'd unnerved her. Before Gaynor had a chance to regroup, Donna said, 'Do you have a cleaner, Mrs Harrington?'

'What?'

'Someone who cleans, a home help?'

'No,' Gaynor said.

'You do it yourself?' Donna said.

Gaynor made a sound, half snort, half sigh. 'Yes.'

'You have a routine?' Donna said.

'No. Just do what needs doing as and when,' Gaynor said.

'Can you tell me when you last cleaned the kitchen?'

'Every day, wiping up, clearing away. With three kids . . .'

'And the kitchen floor? How often do you clean that?' Donna said.

Gaynor blew air out of her cheeks. Donna sensed her grasping for an answer. 'Once or twice a week.'

'What about the utility room?' Donna said.

'Don't know,' she said, shaking her head. 'Probably a while back.'

'Not this week, then?'

'Could be,' Gaynor said.

'Which is it?' Donna said.

'I can't remember,' Gaynor said. She held Donna's eyes with her vivid blue gaze.

'Are you sure? It looked like it had been given a real spring clean. Everything washed with bleach. And recently.'

'Can't remember.' The muscles in her cheeks bunched again. The tension in the woman was like a high-pitched whine in the atmosphere.

'Was it very dirty in there?' Donna said.

'Not especially,' Gaynor said.

'So why bleach everything?' Donna said.

158

'Best way to kill germs,' Gaynor said.

'Did something happen in the utility room, Gaynor?'

'Mrs Harrington,' the solicitor corrected Donna.

'Mrs Harrington?' Donna said.

'I don't know what you're talking about,' Gaynor said.

'We found traces of blood in the room. Can you tell me whose blood that is?'

'No idea.'

'People think bleach kills everything, washes away everything, blood, DNA, other bodily fluids. It's true that it does degrade those substances but the thing about blood and the work we do here is that we only need to find one speck, a tiny drop. That's enough for our forensics people. And we found some in your utility room. The lab is examining it now. We can wait for those tests to be completed or you can save us all some time and tell me whose blood you were trying to wash away.'

'I don't know what you're on about,' Gaynor said. 'There was no *blood.*'

'But there was,' said Donna.

'Well, I never saw any. Probably one of the kids, a nosebleed or something. Ages ago.'

'We'll soon be able to tell,' Donna said. And now that Gaynor Harrington had some measure of the amount of evidence that was stacking up against her, Donna decided to conclude the interview and let her stew in her own juices for a while.

Chapter 33

Donna had received initial reports and photographs from the search at the Harringtons'. Now she summarised the findings for the team. 'As well as traces of blood recovered from the utility room we have fingerprints on the door jamb in the kitchen, which match prints from the paper waste, from two of the drinks cartons and one of the newspapers. The prints are not Gaynor's or Stewart's but they are a match to the partials from Rosa's jaw and temple.'

'One of the kids?' Jade said.

'They'd be smaller. The other items of interest are several long hairs, brown ones, in the vacuum cleaner. But Gaynor is blonde. And Stewart Harrington is blond going grey. The search found no baby things, no nappies, wipes, formula. Nothing. Photos from the house are here. Pass them round,' Donna said.

Calvin reported he hadn't had any luck at the food bank. The hall was closed. A sign gave food-bank opening times as Monday and Friday mornings, ten till twelve. Otherwise donations could be left in the public library during office hours. Calvin had rung the food-bank contact number and left a message asking them to return his call as soon as possible.

He had also followed up with Asda: he'd asked for CCTV tracking Gaynor's movements after she'd bought the baby clothes. 'She went to the counter, bought a Lotto ticket,' he said.

'Found in the rubbish with her dibs on.' Donna smiled.

'Mandy Myers told us Gaynor only plays EuroMillions,' Jade said.

'Perhaps she fancied her chances on something else,' Isla said.

'Hoping for a change of luck? That didn't pan out, did it?' Donna said. 'So what background have we got on Gaynor and Stewart Harrington?' she asked Isla and Calvin.

'Harrington's previous address was in West Yorkshire, Huddersfield,' Calvin said. 'Moved here in 2012, six years ago.'

'He or they?' Donna said.

'He,' Calvin answered.

'Gaynor has been at various addresses in Manchester and Salford for the last twenty years,' Isla said.

'They married in 2014,' Calvin said. 'He'd been married before to an Alison Cartwright.'

'No previous marriages for Gaynor,' Isla said.

'So he's divorced?' Donna said.

'I'm checking on that now,' Calvin said.

'The business appears to be above board, registered with the city council. They have three rental properties, two in Fallowfield, one in Rusholme.' Isla picked up a photograph, studied it briefly, then passed it to Jade on her left.

Donna's phone rang, the screen lit, *Forensics*. 'DI Bell,' she answered.

'DNA profile is through for Mrs Gaynor Harrington. We're preparing the documents to email over now but I thought you'd want to know there is no match with the victim Rosa.' An improvement on his snippy tone with her earlier.

'Thank you. I appreciate it,' Donna said.

'It's not Gaynor's baby,' she told the team. 'I knew as much. So who is Rosa? Who is her mother? Where is she? I think it's fair to assume Gaynor is blagging about most things, if not all of them. We have her buying baby food and clothes and nappies last Friday. Three days later we have Rosa discovered along with articles we can prove were handled by both Gaynor and Stewart. All the baby items were gone from their property when we searched, and we also know that attempts were made to remove any biological material from the utility room. If we trust the combined testimony of the eyewitnesses, what do we have? A confrontation outside the Harringtons' at seven o'clock that evening. A woman and a man shouting and screaming. Harrington drives off in the van.'

'He's dumping the body, the mother,' Jade said.

Donna stared at her.

'What?' Jade said. 'We're all thinking it.' She tapped on the photos of the room, the fake-quarry-tile floor, the white goods, the ironing station. 'They kill her in the utility room and clean up. Gaynor must have been shitting herself when she saw the PCSO at the door just after.'

'So who is she, the mother?' Donna said. 'We've already considered trafficking and illegal adoption.'

'There's nothing to suggest they had links with people involved in criminal activity,' Calvin said.

'You wouldn't need to, not till you get to the point where you decide you're desperate enough to break the law. Then you cross the line,' Donna said.

'What about a surrogate?' Isla suggested. 'Someone who was having a baby for them.'

Jade shifted, sighed. She tugged at a nail with her teeth.

'We boring you?' Donna demanded.

'No. I still don't get why they'd want another kid,' Jade said, picking up another photograph.

'OK. Have we come across anything to suggest they'd want another child when they've already got three?' Donna said.

'Not three, four!' Jade shouted. She slapped her hand on the photograph. 'They've got four kids. Look at the drawing! She was there all along.'

Chapter 34

Jade's head was banging, heart thumping. The photo of the children's room in her hand. The drawing, the little kid's drawing.

The kid's picture. *Six* figures, not five. Two big ones, three smaller and one in between. One with long strings of brown hair, a triangle for a skirt.

Jade recalled the sick feeling in the pit of her stomach when they had to draw a picture of their family at school. She'd make it up: mum, dad, brother, sister. When she was a bit older she refused. Covered the paper with scribbles, drew animals, a monster, wrote *shit* and then scribbled over it. Caught out for that, she was sent to stand in the corridor. She'd walked out. Kept walking.

Other days too, making cards for Mother's Day or Father's Day. A ritual in humiliation.

'Look!' she said now. Isla and the boss, faces gawking at her. 'The drawing on the top bunk. Pull that up and zoom in.'

Isla got the drawing on screen, enlarged it, sharpened the focus.

'It's their house, right? See the number on the door – fourteen. We saw it that first time at the house, in the living room,' she told the boss. 'And look – mum, dad, three little boys, different sizes, and a girl. A *bigger* girl.'

'Christ,' the boss said. 'It's a stretch but—'

'This is her,' Jade said, hitting at the photo.

'There's been no mention of a daughter,' the boss said. 'Not a peep.'

'And no one's reported seeing a pregnant girl at the house, or coming and going,' Calvin said.

163

'Maybe she's a babysitter, Jade, a friend of the family, a cousin,' the boss said.

Jade was unwilling to consider that explanation. 'The brown hair, the prints that matched the partials on the baby. This is her.' Jade's heart was thudding in her chest, so hard it ached. 'Maybe Gaynor already had a kid when she met Stewart,' she said. 'He moved in in 2012. How old are the boys?'

'Ten, four and three,' Isla said.

'So the younger two are likely to be theirs, but what about William? Birth records?' the boss said to Isla.

Have you any brothers or sisters?

Jade had learned to say no. Easier all round. Made herself out to be an orphan as well. Parents dead. Might as well be. Now Shannon was blowing that apart, like a rhino in a suicide vest. *Fuck!*

'Jade?'

She'd zoned out. 'We should check Harrington too, him and the first wife, Alison Cartwright,' she said quickly.

'I'll start with the census,' Isla said. Her fingers flew over the keyboard and before long she read out what she'd found. '2011, we have Gaynor living at the Rosa Street address on her own.'

Calvin's phone rang. 'Food bank,' he told them.

He rose, saying, 'Yes, I could come down now. We'd need to see the inventory. Yes. Good.' He looked over at the boss, checking. She nodded to him to leave. He picked up his jacket, waved a goodbye.

'What about Harrington, Huddersfield?' Jade said.

She held her breath while Isla navigated the records.

'Yes,' Isla said. 'Stewart Harrington, Alison Harrington, William Harrington aged two, and Evie Potter aged seven. Different surname.'

'She's there!' Jade said. 'I found her. I fucking found her!'

'We *think*.' The boss had her eyebrows up, wary.

'I know,' Jade said. 'It explains everything, the forensics. It's obvious.'

'Not quite. It's a lead, Jade. We follow it like any other, see where it takes us.'

164

They should have been popping corks and giving Jade a chair lift. *I've found her.*

'So William isn't Gaynor's,' the boss said.

'Give me ten minutes on the general registry,' Isla said, eyes fixed on the screen.

'Brew?' the boss said.

'Cool,' Isla said. 'Where're you going?'

'I'm sending Jade.'

They all laughed. Jade didn't. Still smarting.

'Do you want anything, boss?' Jade said. *Cyanide? Ricin?*

'Go to the new place,' the boss said. She had a thing about fresh coffee. Jade never touched the stuff. 'Double espresso.'

'Isla?'

'Macchiato,' Isla said, not looking up.

'Tessa?'

'Hot chocolate, please.'

Jade's fingers were tingling, pulse galloping, and she welcomed the chance to get out of the building even for a few minutes.

It was still spitting, everything covered with an oily sheen, the pavements, and roofs, the red-brick walls. Like the city was sweating. Traffic fumes trapped in the air.

At the coffee shop a girl sat on a sleeping bag, holding out a battered paper cup, a dog curled at her side. Tattoos marked her face and neck. Home-made by the look of them. Hair shaved at the sides, the rest twisted into half a dozen braids. How old? Sixteen, seventeen? Same age as Shannon. *Stop thinking about Shannon.*

'Get out of my head!' Jade must have spoken out loud. The girl looked up quickly and the dog lifted its head and turned, ears pricked, to see what the fuss was about.

Jade ignored them and went in. She queued for drinks, got a can of Red Bull for herself. She eyed the sandwiches. The pies and pots of instant porridge and noodles. The thought of food in her mouth made her stomach turn but she knew she needed to take care. *Take your meds. Avoid stress. Regular sleep. Regular meals.* Ballast to counteract the sensation that she might lose touch and float away, mad as a fucking kite.

165

Chapter 35

Jade got back to the office at the same time as Calvin.

'No donation of those items in their records,' he said, shrugging off his jacket. 'They did get some nappies and formula but not the same brand.'

He looked around, catching on to the way the atmosphere had ratcheted up a gear.

'What?' he said. 'What did I miss?'

'Jade?' The boss handed her the floor.

Jade pointed to the kid's drawing. 'There was an older sister, Evie Potter, Stewart Harrington's stepdaughter.'

'Whoa!' Calvin said.

'Look.' Isla had sketched out a family tree with dates. 'In 2003 a woman called Alison Cartwright married a man called James Potter. They had a daughter, Evie, born the following year. When Evie was two, James Potter was killed in a crash. He was on a motorcycle, tangled with an HGV. In 2007 Alison marries Stewart. And in the census of 2011 Alison and Stewart are living in Huddersfield with Evie and their son William. Six months after, Alison dies from cancer. Stewart then moves the family to Manchester and meets Gaynor.'

'Stewart Harrington is Evie's stepfather,' Jade said. 'William is her half-brother – same mother. And he's half-brother to Aidan and Charlie – same father.'

'And where was Evie all that time?' Calvin's dark eyes drilled into Jade's.

'Vanished. But see . . .' Jade gestured to the drawing, '. . . she was there.'

'But off the grid?' Calvin said. 'And she's the mother?'

'It'd fit,' Jade said.

'She's only fourteen,' Isla said.

'Yes.' The boss looked saddened by that. 'Look, maybe she stayed over in Huddersfield. She wasn't Stewart's child – he was landed with her when Alison died. She could have gone into care. Or to another member of the mother's family.'

'But she's in the drawing,' Jade said.

'You *think*. We don't know who that is. Could be an imaginary friend. Elsa from *Frozen*. The Tooth Fairy.' The boss glanced at the clock. 'Listen, I want to prep for Stewart Harrington. I'd like to put this on the table. But we need to check the facts. Jade, can you talk to our child-protection unit, find out the quickest way we can get information out of West Yorkshire? We want to know if Stewart Harrington ever came to the attention of social services. We know he's not got a criminal record but has he ever had any involvement with the local authority concerning his kids?'

'It's five o'clock on a Friday,' Jade said. 'They'll all have packed up.'

'So you may have to talk to their out-of-hours service. Stress that it's urgent. Drive over there, if you have to. I want that information before I go in there and challenge Stewart Harrington about his missing stepdaughter.'

'Can't Calvin go?' Jade said. 'I'd really like to carry on with the interviews.' Jade did not want to be stuck dealing with a load of social-work wankers. They brought out the worst in her.

The boss gave Jade one of her death stares. 'We'll see about that when you get back,' she said. 'But time is precious. So, Jade, instead of arguing the toss, just do what you're told and get on with it, will you?'

In a right strop. And after Jade had found the mother, an' all. Jade had fucking found her!

***

167

If the police were swamped with paperwork, constrained by rules and regulations and red tape, then social workers were bound, gagged and sealed in a lead coffin with it.

The officer in the child-protection unit, Sam Mistry, was clocking off when Jade found him, briefcase in hand, smart coat over one arm. He was a small-framed man with delicate features and sharp eyes. He looked more like a stockbroker than a copper. What did you call them? Hedge-fund managers. Jade always pictured privet when she heard the term, men in pinstripes trimming privet.

'If I can find someone still at work in Kirklees, someone at their desk, I'll need a good reason to request the immediate disclosure of the information you want,' Sam Mistry said.

'Immediate risk to life do you?' Jade said. 'We've a dead baby and a missing teenager, suspected to be the mother, traces of blood at the family home, and there appear to be attempts to conceal a crime scene. Both parents are in custody under investigation.'

'You think Evie might have been killed?'

'It's one of the lines we're pursuing.' Jade trotted out the standard response.

'Rotherham, Rochdale.' He named the child-grooming scandals where police and social services had serially failed young girls, allowing sexual abuse to continue for years on a colossal scale. 'People are trying to up their game. Or at least not sink any lower,' he added, almost to himself. 'So she's missing and post-partum. What years are we looking at?'

'2007 until 2012. Her mother died then and her stepfather moved to Manchester.' Jade had given him the Huddersfield address. She listened as he rang various extension numbers.

'I have an urgent query, immediate risk of harm,' he repeated to each gatekeeper.

Jade would be in a file like that somewhere. And Shannon. She squeezed her wrist and bit her cheek. Watched Sam Mistry work, phone on speaker, fingers typing, keeping notes of exactly who he'd spoken to.

His voice changed, relaxing, as at last he found someone who could help. 'Thanks a lot, Marianne, but we are extremely concerned for this girl's welfare. She's missing post-partum, only fourteen, may have been involved in the death of baby Rosa. If there's anything on file . . .' He passed on the pertinent details.

'OK, let me see what I can do,' Marianne said.

Sam Mistry and Jade listened to the click and clack of Marianne's keyboard, to her breathing, and the names she murmured as she navigated the records.

'Nothing on the at-risk register,' she said. 'I'll check the rest. You're lucky we got the bulk of this computerised. Any earlier and . . .'

'I know,' Sam Mistry said.

'OK, I have a note. April 2012 Evie was absent from school . . . A visit was made by the education-compliance team to the family home. Hang on . . . not much to go on. "Father recently bereaved, struggling to cope. Rent arrears. Children safe and well." That's all.'

'No follow-up?' Sam Mistry said. 'So what? She went back to school?'

'Possibly. But when the family left the area it would become Manchester's responsibility. If the kids had been registered at risk, the expectation is that information would have been exchanged between regions but, even then, you know how many slip under the radar. Just disappear. So for something this minor, with no safe-guarding issues, there wouldn't have been any contact.'

'Thanks for your help,' Sam Mistry said.

He ended the call and looked at Jade, eyes intense. 'Unless there was some informal fostering arrangement, it looks like Evie came to Manchester with her stepdad and her brother.'

'She's a ghost,' Jade said. 'No one's seen her, no one's mentioned her.'

Jade had an idea. 'I'll just make a call,' she said.

Odelia picked up on the third ring, dogs barking and snarking in the background.

Get them fucking trained.

'Odelia, it's DC Bradshaw.'

169

'Hello?'

'You taught at Oaks Primary?'

'I did.'

'Were you still there in 2012 and 2013?' Jade said.

'Yes.'

'Do you remember a girl called Evie? She'd have been eight or nine at the time?'

'No. No Evies. We had an Edith and several Ellas but never an Evie.'

'What about William Harrington?'

'Yes. Of course, he came later. He's still there. His younger brothers are there too now. Nursery. They all live just down the road. Oh dear,' she said, voice sinking. She would know about the arrests, the search.

'Did William have a sister at school? An older sister, or perhaps a cousin?' Jade said.

'No, no one like that.'

'Thank you.' Jade hung up before Odelia got nebby and tried asking any questions of her own.

'Evie never went to school once they got to Manchester,' Jade said. 'It's like she didn't exist any more.'

And now? Blood. Bleach. Maybe we're too late.

Chapter 36

'We know about Evie.' Donna's opening salvo.

Harrington stilled, face rigid. He didn't speak.

'Where is she, Stewart?'

Nothing.

'What's happened to her?'

He closed his eyes. Donna exchanged a look with Calvin. *Will he cooperate?*

'You're her stepfather. You were responsible for her welfare. Where is she?' Donna said.

He shook his head once, eyes still shut.

'Stewart, I need to inform you that your wife, Gaynor Harrington, was arrested earlier today.'

'No!' His eyes flew open. He stared at her. 'Why? What about the boys?'

'They've been placed in emergency foster care.'

'Christ! You can't— You don't know—' His mouth worked. Donna could see he was struggling with himself: whether to talk, whether to drop the pretence of ignorance.

'Stewart, where's Evie?'

He blew a breath out sharply, reared back, then forward. Distressed. Trapped. But he didn't answer her question.

'I'm concerned for her safety,' Donna said. 'She's fourteen years old. Do you know where she is?'

His gaze was unfocused now, vision turned inwards. Donna let the silence stretch, and at last he said quietly, 'It wasn't murder.'

171

The hairs on the back of Donna's neck prickled. She saw Calvin's grip tighten on the pen he held.

Had he killed Evie? An argument? A fight? An accident? Had she died in childbirth?

'The baby,' he said, 'it wasn't murder.'

The baby – not Evie.

'Go on,' Donna said softly.

'It was a cot death. She was asleep and . . . erm . . . she was asleep and then she didn't wake up. She wouldn't wake up. That's all. All this . . .' He looked about the room, bewilderment on his face. 'There's no need. It was a cot death.' He held his hands out, trembling.

The most important thing now was to keep him talking, let him say whatever he would, as though she accepted everything he said as the gospel truth. Any challenges, rebuttals, arguments about his testimony contradicting the evidence could come later.

'When was this?'

'Monday. She was just . . . she wasn't breathing any more.' Then he repeated it quickly, almost dismissively, 'She just wasn't breathing. I never hurt her.'

'OK,' Donna said. 'Where was she, the baby?'

He gave a shake of his head, unwilling. So Donna rowed back. 'She wasn't breathing.' She echoed his words. 'That must have been hard. A shock.'

He was quiet, hands steepled on his forehead.

'There was nothing could be done,' he said then. 'It was too late.'

Behind the sentiment she divined his justification for not calling an ambulance, not alerting the authorities, not giving the baby a decent funeral. *Too late. Nothing could be done.* If he really believed it was a cot death, as he professed, didn't it hurt him, shame him, that he discarded the child in a rubbish bag in a bin full of takeaway refuse and rotting chicken carcasses?

She knew her next questions might rupture the conversation. There was a risk that he'd clam up and close down but she had to ask.

'Was the baby Evie's child?'

He nodded slowly, eyes hooded. He looked as though he'd aged ten years in the last half-hour.

'You're nodding. Where was Evie when you found the baby on Monday?'

'Gone.'

Donna's throat tightened. 'Gone where?'

'I don't know. She ran away. She could be anywhere. Gaynor, she didn't have anything to do with it. Like I told you. So, look, please, you can send her home. Fetch the kids back, right? And you can just sort it all out with me.'

Seriously? In your dreams, mate.

'When did Evie run away?' Donna said.

'Monday.'

'Before you found the baby?'

'Yes,' he said.

'What time?' Donna said.

'At seven,' he said heavily. 'That's where I went, in the van. I was looking for her. But she'd gone.'

'Why did she leave?'

'I don't know. I think she couldn't cope. The baby and that – she was all over the place.' His head sank. He rubbed at his eyes. 'I don't want to. I can't.' He looked at his solicitor.

'We need a break,' the solicitor said.

'Of course. We can stop for a comfort break,' Donna said. 'But before that I need you to tell me where I can get a photograph of Evie so we can ask the public to help in finding her. And anything you can tell me about what she was wearing when she ran away.'

'I don't think we've got one, a photo.'

'A snap will do.'

'No. We . . . erm . . . There isn't anything.'

'You never took her photograph?' That seemed unbearably sad. Donna remembered the artfully posed studio portrait that hung on the living-room wall. The idyllic family and the tropical-island back-ground. Three boys with bare feet.

'Can you describe her, then?'

173

He cleared his throat, voice gruff when he spoke. 'Long brown hair, small – about . . .' He lined his hand up below his chest bone. 'I don't know what she was wearing.' He raised his head sharply, memory clearing his face. 'There's some old photos. An album, in the loft, if . . .'

'Thank you,' Donna said. Using an actual photo and ageing software would get them a better likeness than an artist's drawing based on Harrington's description.

As she went to task someone with bringing the photograph from the house, she couldn't shake the image she had of Evie, a little girl hidden away in a terraced house, excluded from the world and from the family circle. If Evie had run away, had it been a bid for freedom? Or had she been so traumatised by the birth that she had lost her mind, killed her child and run to escape the horror of it all?

Chapter 37

The boss sent them all on a meal break before prepping to go back in to talk to Gaynor Harrington. 'Just half an hour,' she said.

Jade had bought noodles at the coffee shop earlier. Now she added boiling water in the poky staff kitchen and ate them standing up. She still felt a bit sick but hollow too. Noodles were easy to eat and would give her some energy for the rest of the evening.

They'd found Evie. Well, not found-her-found-her, but they knew who she was and that she was Rosa's mother. But now Jade didn't feel half as good as she should.

Perhaps because Evie was dead, stuffed in different bin bags and dumped somewhere. Or because, if Evie had smothered her baby and legged it, she'd be dossing in some doorway and begging, or turning tricks, life one nightmare after another, drink or drugs the only way to oblivion.

'Jade!'

She jumped. Calvin was at the door. 'I said, you're wanted.'

'Which room are we in?' Jade said.

'No, not that. Downstairs. Front desk rang. Your sister's looking for you.'

I don't have a sister.

Jade thought about sending Calvin with a message: Jade's in a meeting, can't come down. But then he'd meet Shannon and it would all be ten times more real than she wanted it to be.

She could feel the heat building in her as she ran down the stairs. Not content with invading her home, her own personal space, now

175

Shannon had the balls to interrupt her at work. Where no one knew about the old Jade Bradshaw, care-leaver, psycho and general fuck-up. Here, Jade had a title, a role, a badge, respect, a form of anonymity. Freedom.

Everything Jade was ready to say died on her tongue when she saw Shannon, her yellow top drenched in blood, a daub on her neck, rusting red in the creases of her knuckles.

'Shit. What happened to you?' Jade said.

Shannon stood up.

'Sit down,' Jade barked. Luckily the waiting area was quiet: a man in combats nodding off in one corner, and a Chinese or Japanese couple sitting sombrely side by side. It was dark outside but not late enough for the rush when the pubs and clubs were chucking out.

'Was this Ryan?' Jade said.

'No!' Shannon glared. 'He's still not picking up. Like you.' Her eyes flashed. 'It was Bert.'

'Bert? What the fuck did you do to Bert?' Jade said.

'I didn't *do* anything,' Shannon said. 'He's in the hospital.'

'He hates the hospital. He never goes in.'

'Yeah, well, he bashed his head, cut it open so it was either that or bleed to death on his living-room floor.'

'Which hospital?' Jade said.

'Wythenshawe. A and E. They said to ring in the morning. They wanted his date of birth, GP and medication. I didn't know. I tried calling you.' She shot Jade a look of accusation.

'I'm at work,' Jade said. 'I can't have my phone on all the time. You should have left a message.'

Shannon looked away, lips pressed together.

'Was he conscious?' Jade said.

'On and off. Woozy, like. They were worried about concussion and if anything's damaged, like, internal. Look, I need to get cleaned up, borrow something to wear.'

Nothing of mine'll fit you.

'I haven't got a key,' Shannon said.

'You're supposed to be gone.'

176

'And if I was, what about Bert, eh? It's a good job I was still there. But I just need to get sorted out, Jade.' Her eyes filled.

Fuck's sake. 'Wait there.'

Jade hurried upstairs to fetch her bag.

Back at Reception, she worked the key off the ring and gave it to Shannon. 'Lock up when you go and leave it with Mina.'

'What about you?' Shannon said.

'I'm working through,' Jade said.

Shannon twisted the key in her hands. 'Look, my money's not in yet. Can I cadge a bit for a taxi? I'll pay you back, I promise.'

Christ! Jade took a twenty-pound note from her purse. 'Here.'

'I thought maybe you were ill, an' all,' Shannon said. 'After last night and that?'

Jade's cheeks burned. 'I'm fine,' she said, turning to go back to work. *And I'll be a whole lot better if you'd just piss off and leave me alone.*

Chapter 38

Donna had notified the chief constable by email of the break in the case, the confirmation of Evie Potter as Rosa's mother, the launch of a fresh appeal and poster campaign.

She hadn't had any acknowledgement but at least he hadn't seen fit to summon her for another exercise in humiliation.

But when she ran into him on the corridor near the press office she couldn't resist blowing her trumpet. 'Good news on the baby Rosa case, sir. Identifying the mother.'

'Yes,' he said curtly. His eyes were wandering somewhere over her head. Translation – you are not worthy of my attention.

'The family went to great lengths to conceal her from us. From everyone,' Donna said.

His eyes flicked to her, then away again. 'You're still looking for her,' he said, criticism in every syllable.

'We are. And at this point we don't know if she killed the child. Or whether she has come to harm herself.'

'I won't keep you, then,' he said, forcing Donna to turn away.

Why couldn't he be pleased for her, for them? Recognise the achievement, offer some encouragement, praise even?

He was never going to let it go, she realised. No matter how many cases she brought to trial, how many murders she solved, she would always be damaged goods, a fuck-up. Blamed for being played, for not knowing she had a Judas on her team.

You'll be gone soon, she thought, with your carriage clock and your classic cars and your big slab of a face and nobody will miss you. You miserable old git.

When she saw Jade, she was still smarting.

'I'll bloody kill him,' Donna said.

'Who?'

'Chief chuffing constable. I've just had a word. I expected a little pat on the back for the fact that we've ID'd the mother. Not a sausage. He's acting like some demon headmaster with a stick up his arse.' She gave a shake of her head. Exasperated. He should be bolstering staff morale, not undermining it.

'You know they call him Count Rushmore?' Jade said.

'What?'

'Face like a rock. Those presidents.' Jade framed her face with her hands, drawing a square, her looks elfin, the polar opposite of the chief's.

'Funny,' Donna said. 'I just wish I'd known that sooner.'

'Whatever helps,' Jade said.

In the interview room Donna informed Gaynor Harrington that the food bank had been unable to identify any donation of the sort she claimed to have made.

'Human error.' Gaynor shrugged. 'I've told you what happened.'

'Really?' Donna said. 'Because we've been hearing from your husband and there are radical differences in his account of events.'

Gaynor stared at her. She still wore the day's make-up but the bronze shadow on her eyelids had melted into the creases, and grease shone on her nose and chin. Specks of dirt dusted the lenses of her glasses and her long hair had lost its wave, hung lank.

'I know what I did,' Gaynor said. She sounded secure but Donna noticed that she picked at her cuticle with her thumbnail. She had nice nails, French manicure.

'Concealing the birth of a child? Prevention of the lawful and decent burial of a dead body?'

Gaynor was shaking her head in denial.

'What part did you have in the death of baby Rosa?'

'I don't know anything about that.'

'Was it Rosa, or did Evie call her something else?'

Gaynor flinched as though Donna had slapped her. Colour flooded her cheeks. But she kept eye contact.

'Take your time, Mrs Harrington. But we're going to sit here until you've answered these questions to my satisfaction.'

'My client will require a sleep break,' the solicitor said.

'And she'll get one,' Donna said. 'Now, we have established that Evie Potter lived with you and that the baby was her child. So, what can you tell me about baby Rosa's death?'

Gaynor fixed her with a stare, flint in her eyes but a shade of something else too – shrewdness, assessing her options. She must have realised by now that Stewart had admitted to those facts.

'She died in her sleep,' Gaynor said.

'Was she ill?'

'No. There was nothing wrong with her.'

Her new version of events matched the story told by Stewart. Evie running away. Stewart going out in the van looking for her. The baby asleep in bed.

'Where was the bed?' Donna asked.

'In the utility room.'

'Evie slept in the utility room?' Donna thought about the spacious home office.

A beat. 'Well, she couldn't share with William.' Not a shred of shame or humility about her treatment of the girl.

'Where's Evie's bed now?' Donna said.

'We had to get rid of it.'

'Why?' Donna said.

'It was a mess.'

'What do you mean?' Donna said.

'It's where she had the baby.'

'Why didn't you take her to hospital?'

Gaynor glared, defiant. 'We didn't *know* she was pregnant. She didn't know. All of a sudden she's screaming the place down and there's a baby there.'

Donna tried to imagine it, one of her own daughters, Bryony or Kirsten, giving birth alone, unaided, petrified.

'And you didn't take them both to get checked out?' Donna said.

'They were fine,' Gaynor said.

Until they weren't.

'Where is Evie now?'

'I don't know. She ran away,' Gaynor said.

'How did you know she'd run away?'

'Because she was gone.'

'Who realised she was gone – you or your husband?' Donna said.

'I did.'

'Because?'

'She wasn't in her room,' Gaynor said, as though Donna was stupid.

'Why had you gone to her room?'

'To see if she wanted another feed making up,' Gaynor said.

'When was this?'

'Just before seven.'

'And when had you last seen Evie?'

'Three-ish.' Shrugging her shoulders as if it was a guess.

'So you don't know exactly when she left the house?' Donna said.

'No,' Gaynor said bluntly.

'Why didn't you call an ambulance for the baby when you found her dead?'

'I didn't find her, Stewart did.'

'And he told you?' Donna said.

'Yes.'

'So why not call an ambulance?' Donna said.

Gaynor hesitated. 'There didn't seem to be any point.'

'No point?' Donna said eventually. 'Or you didn't want to be held accountable for what you'd done? For murder.'

'It wasn't murder,' Gaynor said. 'It was a cot death. She just didn't wake up.'

'That's not what our forensics have established.'

'It was a cot death,' Gaynor insisted, pinning Donna with her brittle gaze, glassy blue eyes.

181

They made no more progress. Jade went to get an escort to take Gaynor back to her cell.

Gaynor held her head high as she walked out of the room but Donna could feel the stress coming off her in waves.

She might have given some partial truth in the tale she'd told them but Donna knew it was still stitched together with lies.

Chapter 39

On the drive home Donna saw posters of Evie, one in a shop window, another on a sandwich board outside a newsagent's. The age-progression software revealed a girl with long dark brown hair and brown eyes, an oval face, a pointed nose. They were already up at all police stations in the region and being shown on local TV news channels. Public interest in the case was so high that Kenton was hopeful they might even get a slot on national news unless something else knocked them off.

Jim was in the middle of a call when Donna got in.

'I'll talk to you later,' she heard him saying, as she hung her coat in the hall.

The TV was on, the sound muted, *The Walking Dead*. A crowd of zombies approaching a damaged bridge. A pile of tree trunks readied for repairs.

'Anyone I know?' Donna said, slumping onto the sofa.

'What?'

'You were on the phone.'

'Oh. Bradley.'

His brother. 'They're all fine,' Jim said.

'And ours?' Donna tilted her head upwards.

'Still breathing, last I saw. Oh, and Matt wanted to see you. Even if it was midnight.'

'OK.' She felt bone tired, her skin itchy, dirty from the long day. Shower first or food? Crumpets, maybe, if there were any left.

'Was Kirsten OK at school?' she said.

'Apart from it being like Auschwitz?'

'She didn't say that.' Donna groaned. 'She needs to get a grip.'

On the TV a log fell, trapping one of the people.

'What if she doesn't settle?' Donna said. 'Another four and a half years of this?'

'Oh, God,' he said.

'You could home-school her,' Donna said. She thought of Evie missing school. Had Gaynor and Stewart given her any education at home? It didn't seem very likely.

'Yeah, right.' Jim laughed. It seemed like a long time since she'd heard him laugh. It made her feel warmer.

'OK.' She got up. 'Crumpets. You want anything?'

'I'm fine.'

'Jim, you know the accident, you were going to the supermarket at Parrswood. How come you were going there?'

A look on his face, uncertainty, quickly hidden. He gave a chuckle, a mirthless laugh. 'Oh,' he said. 'Some offer they had on, petrol. They were filling the tanks at ours.'

There wasn't a filling station at the Parrswood store. He'd know that, surely. Didn't he realise she would too?

She'd spent all day locked in interview rooms watching people lie to her, trying to save their own skins and evade discovery. And here he was now, her husband, doing the exact same thing.

She couldn't think of anything to say, didn't trust herself to say anything civil or coherent. Anything that wouldn't mushroom, like an explosion. So she made a noise, a little noise of understanding, at the back of her throat, and left. Tears pressing at the back of her eyes.

A sign on Matt's door read, *Mum!!! See me imeediatly.*

He stirred as she went in.

'You should be asleep, little man.'

'Not little!' he protested.

'Big boy, then. What's so important?'

'You know you're called Donna?'

'Yes, I did, actually,' she said.

'Mum, don't be sarcastic. Well, Donna in German means "thunder". Like the reindeers Donna and Blitzen.'

Donner not Donna.

'So you're really called Thunder Bell.' He giggled. 'Like Thunder-pants. It sounds like a fart. You could be Thunder Smell. Ha-ha.'

'Hilarious,' she said. 'Was that why you wanted to see me?'

'Yes.' He yawned. 'And can we get a dog?'

Jesus Christ. 'No. Definitely not. You don't even clean out Morris.' She nodded to the hamster. 'Dogs need lots of looking after.'

'I could do that. I promise,' Matt said.

'No dogs,' Donna said.

'It would keep Dad company when we're at school.'

'Still no.'

'But—'

'No discussion,' Donna said.

'You're mean.'

'That's why they call me Thunder Bell. Now sleep, I love you. Night night.'

'Night.'

The Harrington brothers were somewhere across town. In strange beds, in a stranger's house. Everything unfamiliar. Missing their parents, confused and homesick.

What had they witnessed of recent events, of the baby's sudden arrival and its just as sudden disappearance? You can't keep a baby quiet. How had Stewart and Gaynor explained it to them?

And with their sister, how did it work?

Evie had never gone to school. None of the neighbours knew she existed. Aidan had included her in his drawing but other than that there was no sign she had ever lived at number fourteen Rosa Street. Did she play with the boys? Watch telly and eat meals with them? Were they instructed not to talk about her?

The case, the unanswered questions, rolled around in her head as the night crept by. Puzzling, frustrating, but easier to mull over than the question of why Jim was lying to her. And the answer that reared up every time she lowered her guard was obvious, clichéd and gut-wrenching. He must have been cheating on her.

Chapter 40

Jade tried to sleep on the sofa in the visitors' room at the police station, where they spoke to families and vulnerable witnesses. A box of toys in the corner, tissues on the table.

But she was too pissed off, anger seething in her, like a virus. Spluttering like salt on a fire. Making her hot and wired. Angry with all of them. Shannon scrounging off her, all over her life like a rash. Bert keeling over at exactly the wrong time and giving Shannon an excuse not to just fuck-the-fuck-off. The boss jerking Jade about, sending her to talk to the child-protection unit instead of keeping her on interviews. And none of the team had given her any credit for working out there'd been a fourth child in the house. For finding out about Evie.

Her life wasn't hers any more. It was slipping out of her control. It'd taken her years to get here, to get her head together, a job, her own flat, not relying on anyone or anything. Safe. And now it was all falling away. The ground dissolving under her feet. The bad stuff boiling up. Dead things clambering out, claws clamped around her ankles, ready to pull her under.

Fear, vast and cold, surged up her spine, forcing her to her feet. She couldn't stay here. She switched the light on. The harsh glare hurt her eyes. There were sounds, faint, in the building. The bump of a door, the walls and floors ticking as the heat dropped.

Is it a fit or something? Shall I call an ambulance? Shannon's horrified concern. *Do you want to go to hospital?*

No. It mustn't come to that. It *wouldn't* come to that. Jade wouldn't let it.

A cascade of memories, frozen in Day-glo colours. The locked ward, two-to-one observation, the assistants stationed at the open door to her room watching her round the clock, one at either side of her whenever she moved, wherever she went. Fighting them off, screaming, when they came at her with the needle. The dull, thick feeling as all her strength left her and she could weep but not stand. The listeners in the walls, in every switch and socket. A hand on her back, gripping her neck, disappearing when she turned. Snakes falling from the ceiling, slithering under the bed. Vomiting, trying to purge herself of the evil. Skin raw from scratching. Bugs there too.

The old woman who beat her head on the doors and tore at her clothes, stripping naked, pitiful. The girl with ginger hair who never spoke. The ones who didn't make it.

The meetings, the drugs, trying on the labels: schizophrenia, dissociative personality disorder, PTSD, paranoia.

Jade took the stairs down to the car park, passing a cleaner who grinned at her. *What're you laughing at?*

The night was cold, almost frosty. The sky held a half-moon, bright until ragged clouds covered it. Jade let her cheeks chill. She bent her head down and bared the back of her neck where sweat had dampened the tendrils of hair.

When she began to shiver she opened the car door. She would drive. Drive and put miles between her and the feelings. Drive away from the flashbacks and the terrors. Drive until the sun rose. Then she could get back to work.

Chapter 41

Jade looked as if she'd slept in her clothes, Donna thought. Something was off. As they prepared for the interviews, Jade's attention kept drifting. Twice Donna had to repeat a point before Jade responded.

Donna waited until the others were out of earshot, starting their agreed tasks, to check on her. 'Are you all right, Jade?'

'Yes, I'm fine.'

'You don't seem fine. If you're sickening for something . . .'

'Boss, I'm fine. I swear.'

'I swear' was what suspects often said in interviews, mostly when they were lying.

'You slept here,' Donna said.

Jade didn't try to deny it. She could probably tell it was a statement, not a question.

Donna recalled Jade's comments about turning off the lights at home to look for trouble outside. She pictured her standing in the dark, anxious, hearing noises. Replaying the assault in her head. Her attacker twice her size and full of hatred, desperate for self-preservation.

When Jade had mentioned personal stuff, was this what she'd meant? Was she struggling to cope with the aftermath of that assault? Donna knew these things didn't always surface straight away.

'Are you OK at home?' Donna said.

Jade tensed, her face sharpened. 'What do you mean?'

'After what happened. You were attacked. Sometimes it can be hard to stay somewhere afterwards. It should be where we feel safest but if that's gone . . . Some people move – they feel violated.'

But Jade smiled, seeming almost relieved by Donna's suggestion. 'No. No, it's not. It's fine. I'm good. I was late last night. I got caught up with stuff here. It just seemed easier to stay.' Jade gave a quick smile, dimples in her cheeks. There was no merriment in her eyes, only a guardedness that left Donna feeling less than reassured.

Jade had come through the attack: she had managed to use her assailant's stun gun against him, get him into cuffs and call for help but not before he'd beaten her bloody and bruised.

Donna's horror on first seeing Jade like that had been tempered by Jade's own attitude. She'd been on a high, triumphant at thwarting him, her brown eyes glittering brightly. She was proud of her achievement and Donna had shared that pride, along with an immense relief that her own trust in Jade had been well placed. But could she trust her now?

'I need you to be firing on all cylinders. If you're not, I can keep Calvin on,' Donna said.

'I'm good,' Jade insisted. 'We should go in harder on Stewart Harrington, right?'

Trying to prove herself?

Donna was tempted to refuse, ill-tempered after Jim's lying. But she had to separate the two worlds, not let her domestic troubles affect her judgement at work. 'OK. But I'll lead. We go deeper into the whole Evie story as agreed.'

Chapter 42

Harrington had the grace of God to look ashamed when Donna asked about Evie and the move to Manchester.

'You brought Evie and William with you, and you rented a place in Whalley Range at first. William was three at the time. When did you move to Rosa Street?'

'About six months after that,' he said. '2013.'

'You were in a relationship with Gaynor by then?' Donna said.

'Yes.'

'How did you meet?'

'She owned the Whalley Range house back then. She gave me work on the other properties, handyman, repairs and refurb. We got to know each other. Eventually she invited us to move in with her.'

'The three of you,' Donna said.

'Yes.'

'That's a lot to take on,' Donna said, glad she was leading. It was an angle she didn't think Jade would have the insight to explore fully. 'Two children.'

'Yes,' Harrington agreed.

'How did they get on, Gaynor and the children?' Donna said.

'Fine.' His nose twitched.

'No strain?' Donna said. 'They'd lost their mum, and now they had a new stepmum. Wasn't it hard for them?'

'No,' he said. 'They were fine.' Donna didn't believe him. OK, maybe William would adjust, being younger, but Evie at nine?

'Why didn't you send Evie to school?' Donna said.

'She didn't like it.' He cast his eyes around, unsettled.

'You know it's a legal requirement that children go to school, or are provided with an alternative education?'

'Yes,' Harrington said.

'In fact you'd been visited in Huddersfield because Evie had stopped going to school after her mother died.'

'Yes.'

'So why didn't you make sure to enrol her in Manchester?' Donna said.

'She didn't want to go.'

'What about the GP?' Donna said. 'Evie wasn't registered there either, was she?'

'She never got sick. There was no need,' Harrington said.

'The dentist?' Donna said.

He moved his hand as if to brace his head, then lowered it again.

'Why didn't you let her see the dentist?' Donna said.

'Just never got round to it,' he said. 'I don't bother going.'

'But William and Aidan and Charlie see the dentist, don't they?' Donna said.

He looked weary.

'Mr Harrington?'

'Yes.'

'But not Evie. How did Evie spend her time, when the others were at school?' Donna said.

'Just . . . helping around the house.'

No doubt helping with the little ones, too.

'What about days out, friends? Does Evie have any friends?'

He looked down at the table. 'No.' At least Harrington was co-operating, she thought. His answers were delivered flatly, as if he'd given up trying to dissemble.

'Anyone online? Groups on her phone?'

'She doesn't have a phone.'

'That sounds very lonely,' Donna said. 'What about holidays? The last time you had a holiday, where did you go?'

He was quiet.

'Mr Harrington?'

She heard him suck in a breath. 'We don't get away much.'

'But when you do. The last time?' Donna said.

'In the summer we'd a week in Abersoch.'

Wales. Jim and Donna had taken the kids there on a caravan holiday one year. 'Did Evie come with you?' Donna said.

'She gets travel sick,' he said.

Oh, please. 'She stayed behind?' Donna said.

'Yes.'

Evie, the odd one out, no biological connection to either Stewart or Gaynor.

'When did she last leave the house?' Donna said.

'I can't remember,' Harrington said.

'Who was the baby's father?' Donna said.

'I don't know,' he said.

'If Evie doesn't leave the house, how did she get pregnant?' Donna said.

'I don't know. We'd no clue she was pregnant till it all— Then she wouldn't say.'

'She's fourteen years old. Sex with a minor is rape. Someone raped her, Mr Harrington. Raped your stepdaughter. Apparently in your home,' Donna said.

He blinked quickly. 'I don't know who it was,' he said.

'Evie didn't exist as far as health or education-welfare agencies were aware. None of your neighbours knew about her. You were hiding her away. Was there a reason for that? Were you abusing her?' Donna said.

'No,' he said, horrified, coming to life for the first time in the session. 'No, nothing like that.'

'Was your wife abusing her?'

'No!' Harrington looked aghast. 'Evie is ... She's just, like, a recluse.'

'A recluse from the age of eight? Mr Harrington, if she was a recluse wasn't that because you forced her into seclusion?'

'No.'

'She had no choice,' Donna said. 'She slept in the utility room. It sounds like she was a prisoner. Locked away. Treated differently from the others.' Donna's voice rose.

'It was the—' He broke off, shaking his head, wiping his hands over his face.

'It was what?' Donna said.

'It was the best thing for her.'

'Why? Can you explain why?'

'It just was,' he said weakly. 'She wasn't very bright. She didn't like school. She was better off at home.'

'You noticed Evie was missing just before seven. When had you last seen her before that?'

'Before work, in the morning.'

'And what made you realise Evie had run away?'

'She wasn't in her room.'

'Why had you gone to her room?' Donna said.

He hesitated for a fraction, then said, 'To take her a cup of tea.' His account was diverging from what Gaynor had told them. In Gaynor's version *she* had gone to Evie's room to see if she wanted another feed making up. Jade had noticed too: Donna could tell from the way her breathing altered and she straightened in her chair.

'And where was the baby at that point?'

'In bed.' His eyes shifted.

'In Evie's bed, in the utility room?' Donna said.

'Yes.'

'Sleeping?'

'Yes.'

'Was she breathing?' Donna said.

'Yes.'

'How could you tell? Did you check?'

Harrington swung his head, faltering. Because he couldn't remember? Or because he was lying? 'She moved,' he said. 'Twitched in her sleep.'

'What was the baby called?'

'She didn't have a name,' he said.

'What did you do then?' Donna said.

'I went out in the van looking for Evie,' Harrington said.

'Where did you go?'

'Just around. I drove around.'

'Where?' Donna said.

'I can't remember.'

'You can remember everything else but not this?' Donna said, scepticism deliberate in her tone.

'I probably went up Stockport Road, into Longsight, round the Anson estate.'

'But you don't remember?'

'No.'

'Then you went to get pizza and came back,' Donna said. 'Who ate the pizza?'

'Just Gaynor and me.' Gaynor, who was supposedly lying in a darkened room, tortured by a migraine.

'Not William or Aidan or Charlie?'

'No. Charlie and Aidan were in bed. Anyway, they'd all had something before.'

'Where did you eat?' Donna said.

'In the living room.'

'Where was the baby?' Donna said.

'Still in bed,' he said.

'Was the television on?' Donna said.

'Yes.' Harrington frowned, not understanding why she was interested in that. 'I think so.'

'Could you hear the baby? If she cried? She was in the back of the house, across the hall. You were in the front with the TV on.'

'We'd have heard her. She's got a loud cry. Had,' he amended.

'Wasn't Gaynor in bed?' Donna said.

'What?'

'Gaynor was in her room with a migraine?'

'But—' Harrington stopped, open-mouthed. He was trembling lightly, his whole frame shaking. A response to the lack of alcohol or the stress of the situation? He shook his head. Caught out.

194

'You didn't report Evie missing. Did you talk about that with Gaynor?' Donna said.

'No.'

'No?' Donna sounded surprised. 'You didn't even discuss it? Why was that?'

'I don't know.'

'Perhaps there was no need. Perhaps Evie hadn't run away at all. Perhaps she'd been hurt.'

'No!' Harrington protested.

'You know we found traces of blood in the utility room. The whole place has been washed with bleach, a mattress and bedding removed. Why?'

'No, you don't understand. We were just clearing up.'

'Clearing up why?' Donna said.

'It was a mess, she'd had the baby there. The mattress was ruined.'

'Where did you take the mattress?' Donna said.

'To the tip.'

'When?'

'On Tuesday,' Harrington said.

'You put the baby in the bin Monday evening?' Donna said.

'Yes,' he said, little more than a whisper.

'And what about Evie, where did you put her?' Donna said, an intensity to her tone.

He baulked. 'I told you, she ran away. She was fine,' he insisted.

'She'd just had a baby. She was fourteen years old. No way was she fine.'

Donna waited a few beats, then said, 'Mr Harrington, when the baby's body was recovered, a post-mortem was carried out. The results of that contradict your account of the baby dying in her sleep. The evidence shows she was smothered.'

'No,' he said, rearing back. 'That's wrong. They got it wrong.'

'Think back to the last time you saw the baby moving or breathing or heard her cry. You told us that was just before seven when you were looking for Evie. Between then and you discovering her unresponsive, someone suffocated her.'

195

'No. No.' Harrington shifted in his seat as if by moving position he could change what he'd been told. 'No. That's not true. They've got it wrong.' He was almost pleading. 'It was a cot death. You have to believe me. You see them, don't you, on the news? The experts – even they get it wrong.' He put his fist to his forehead and closed his eyes.

'But in this case,' Donna said, 'that baby was murdered and some-one in your household is responsible.'

'No. You're wrong. You've got it all wrong.' And that was all he would say.

Chapter 43

'Harrington sounded surprised at the forensics, the suffocation,' Calvin said.

'Like he really believed it was a cot death,' Isla said.

They'd been watching the video of the interview and now the boss wanted their take on it. Jade knew what her take was: Harrington was a lying scrote, who had probably colluded in the murder of his stepdaughter and her baby.

'And, according to Stewart Harrington, the baby was alive when he left,' the boss said.

'But we can't trust a word he says,' Jade argued.

'Like the stuff about where he went in the van looking for Evie . . .' Isla shook her head.

'Sudden amnesia,' the boss said.

'Well dodgy,' Jade said. 'And he's saying Evie had gone when he took her tea but his missus reckons she found her gone when she went to see about the baby's feed. It's bobbins. They didn't work out their story in enough detail.'

'The shouting that Clark Whitman heard. That could have been Evie and Stewart. Or Stewart and Gaynor,' Isla said.

'We've still had nothing from ANPR to pin down his movements,' Calvin said.

'Unlucky?' Tessa said. 'Or did he just stay in the area? Not pass any cameras?'

'If he wasn't out looking for her, maybe he was getting rid,' Jade said. 'We should check out their other properties.'

'We now know the migraine was a fiction. So what was the point of that?' the boss said.

'It was the reason Gaynor gave originally for not answering the door to the PCSO,' Jade said. 'So there must be some other reason she didn't. Like they'd just killed Evie and she was cleaning up the mess—'

'Jade—'

'Wiping the blood, using the bleach. He's already gone off and—'

'Jade, slow down,' the boss said.

Isla looked away, flushed a little. Embarrassed.

'We should be out there searching *now*. What are we waiting for?' Jade heard herself sounding shrill, hysterical. Why were they still debating? They needed to get out there and find Evie.

The boss stared at her, a beat too long, then said, 'I'll get warrants sorted out. Meanwhile we go back to Gaynor. Why didn't she want to answer the door to the police at that point? Let's home in on that and the migraine, then the forensics. We give her an idea of how cooperative her husband is being and we challenge her. Demonstrate the gaping holes in her version of events. We know someone in the house smothered Rosa. By my reckoning that gives us three candidates: Stewart, Gaynor and Evie.'

'Or one of the boys,' Jade said.

For a moment it looked like the boss would trash that idea but then she nodded. 'Or one of the boys.' She stretched, rubbed at the back of her neck. 'Do you want to take a break, Jade?'

'What?'

They were all staring at her. The boss directed her gaze to the table. Scraps from Jade's notebook strewn about. Pages torn through with scribbles. Pen marks all over the desk. *How did that happen?*

'No. No, boss.' Jade fought to keep the flare of fear from her voice.

The boss rolled her eyes. Fucking cow. Actually rolled her eyes. Jade's cheeks were hot, her mouth dry. She reined in the impulse to call her out. *If anyone needs a break it's you. You look shagged out. You've not got the staying power any more.*

Jade said, 'I'm good. Ready when you are.'

Chapter 44

'You sent Mr Harrington to get a pizza and then you texted him,' the boss said.

'I've already told you about that,' Gaynor snapped.

Her solicitor looked up sharply, eyes swimming smaller then bigger behind his old-man glasses. An angry client might say something reckless.

'You also told us you had a migraine?' the boss said.

'Yes.'

'That's not true, is it? When your husband returned with a take-away you shared it with him. You weren't upstairs in bed. Would you care to comment?' the boss said.

'Do I have to?' Gaynor said to the lawyer.

'You can offer no comment to any questions put,' he said.

Fuck, no. Don't clam up now.

'No comment.' A snide little smile tugged at the corners of Gaynor's lips. Was that it? Was she going to stop answering their questions?

'Just after you texted Stewart, the police community support officer called at your house. Why didn't you answer the door?' the boss said.

Gaynor shrugged.

'Why didn't you answer the door, Mrs Harrington?'

'Maybe I didn't hear it.'

'Or maybe you couldn't answer, in case that officer saw something was very wrong,' the boss said.

199

'Nothing was wrong.'

'A fourteen-year-old had given birth to a baby on a mattress on the floor in your utility room. A girl to whom you have a duty of care but who had no access to education or medical help. She was isolated and, in effect, imprisoned. You've told us she ran away. Is that likely, given she hadn't left the house, after what, six years of incarceration? She wouldn't know how to function.'

Gaynor shook her head slowly. 'She ran away. I don't know what she was thinking. She was off her head.'

'What makes you say that?'

'She didn't know what to do with the baby. She was freaking out.'

Jade pressed the pen hard onto the paper.

'She was a child. She was traumatised,' the boss said. 'You wouldn't open the door because you were hiding something. Rosa, perhaps.'

'She was asleep, like I told you,' Gaynor said.

'Rosa was suffocated. Someone stopped her breathing.'

Gaynor grimaced. 'No.'

'Yes,' the boss said. 'We have clear forensic evidence from the post-mortem. Someone put their hand over her nose and mouth and held it there until she was dead.'

'There's your answer, then,' Gaynor said, spitting out the words, eyes shining.

'What?'

'That's why Evie ran away. She killed the baby, she knew we'd find out, and she couldn't face it.' She nodded once for emphasis.

'You said Rosa was sleeping,' the boss said.

'I *thought* she was sleeping. She was quiet, she was in bed. Newborns sleep a lot. And then later I *thought* she'd died in her sleep. But what you're saying, if that's true, then Evie did it. It's obvious, isn't it? She must have panicked and left her and we thought it was cot death.' She folded her arms, smug.

Jade thought of them stuffing their mouths with pizza, telly on, the baby alone on the soiled mattress, growing cold. The image made her mind stutter and freeze. Then a wind of rage swept through her.

She lunged forward, hands on the desk. 'What were you going to do about Rosa before you knew she was dead?' Jade said.

'How do you mean?' Gaynor said.

'Evie had run off, according to you. So what were you going to do with the baby?'

'I don't know. We'd not had time to think about any of that,' Gaynor said.

'You couldn't go to social services, not after what you'd done to Evie,' Jade said.

'We didn't *do* anything to Evie, she *ran away*.' Gaynor's face contorted as she emphasised the words.

'Before that,' Jade said. 'When you kept her like a slave.'

'That's ridiculous.'

'Really?'

'She was fed and watered, she had a roof over her head, clothes on her back,' Gaynor said.

'In return for what? She was your skivvy, wasn't she?' Jade said, her cheeks hot. She wanted to deck the woman, shove her off her chair. Throttle her till she told the truth. She'd shown no shred of shame or guilt. 'You bitch. You treated her like a piece of shit.'

The solicitor said, 'That is out of order.'

'Too fucking right,' Jade muttered.

The boss grabbed Jade's arm, yanked at her to sit. Said, 'Mrs Harrington, it is likely we will be applying for an extension to your detention until we make a decision whether to charge or release you. Your children will remain in care. And we have applied for warrants to search your other premises, the rental properties. If Evie's there, we will find her.'

'That's ridiculous,' Gaynor scoffed. 'There are tenants in two of them.'

'I'm sure they'll understand, a vulnerable girl, a rape survivor.'

Gaynor's face pinched, eyes blazed. 'I've told you everything I know. I haven't done anything wrong. It's all Evie. It's all her. She was trouble from the get-go. He should have left her in Huddersfield. She wasn't even his kid. She's slow and sly, hopeless. I took her in and then she spreads her legs for God knows who and hides it from us. Then she kills the baby. She needs locking up.'

Jade snapped her pen. The boss glared at her. *WTF is wrong with you?* Jade shoved back her chair and left. The air was toxic. She'd had enough.

Chapter 45

Jade's head felt frantic, thoughts racing too fast to grasp. She was raw all the time, nerves too close to the surface, exposed. She needed to rest, but the trouble was, when she got like this it was hard to sleep. A vicious circle. She had to break it. Soon. When Shannon was gone, when the case was done. *I'll sleep when I'm dead.*

The boss glared at her in the corridor, shaking her head, like Jade was giving her grief, and taking a breath, about to lay into her, Jade reckoned, when the call came. The warrants were through. There was no time to lose.

It made sense to go first to the house that Stewart Harrington had been working on as it was unoccupied, giving greater opportunity to leave a body undetected.

The place was a shell, no furniture, carpets, curtains. The plaster had been knocked off the walls in large sections, lumps of it swept into piles. Dust coated everything. A new double-glazed window in the kitchen still had plastic, patterned with chevrons, covering the frame. A bare bulb hung from the ceiling.

Outside they surveyed the small garden, full of discarded building materials, the carcasses of kitchen units, the old window, bricks and broken roof tiles. No shed or outhouse. No stained mattress to complete the picture. And no sign of a grave, shallow or otherwise.

'It's clear,' Jade said to the boss.

In the house opposite a young lad was washing a car and his eyes were on them.

'I'll have a word.' Jade signalled over the road. 'Check if they saw the van here Monday evening or Tuesday.'

'Not Monday evening,' the boy's mother said to Jade. 'In the day, yes. But never the evenings.'

The other two properties were side by side not far from Maine Road, once the site of Manchester City's football ground.

In the first they found an old couple and their teenage grandson. The woman was bedbound, living downstairs in the front room, surrounded by medicines and equipment. The place smelt half dead.

Jade thought of Bert in the hospital. He'd be fuming to find himself there when he came round. He would come round, wouldn't he? A shiver of alarm clutched at her. *Course he will. Tough as old boots.* And they'd ring her if not. She was down as next of kin.

'There's no one else,' Bert had said. 'Besides, you'll inherit, Jade. Think of that.'

'Made a will, have you?'

'No. Bugger all to leave. But I've paid into the Co-op for the funeral, so no worries on that score.'

'Put me out with the bins,' something else he used to say. Felt weird now.

The old woman was wittering on about the bedroom tax and how they were thrown on the scrapheap, treated like criminals, and it took the boss a few goes to get her back on track. Then the couple were bickering back and forth about whether it was July or August when they'd last seen Mr Harrington – the sink had needed fixing. Whichever of them was right, it meant it wasn't in the last week. That was all they needed to know.

In the neighbouring house no one was up. Jade belted the door for about half an hour before a sullen-looking young woman, wearing last night's eyeliner and a zebra onesie, opened it. Guilt flooded her face when the boss said they were police.

Drugs, Jade guessed. Coke or weed, probably. Maybe Es.

'We want to ask you a few questions, if we can come in for a moment,' the boss said.

'It's a bit of a mess,' she said, stepping back.

It looked like it had been trashed. Bottles and glasses on the low table, with threads of loose tobacco and torn cigarette papers. More cans and bottles around the feet of the boxy sofas. The smell of alcohol hung fruity in the air. A poster had peeled off the wall, clinging wrong side up by the last blob of Blu Tack.

The girl shoved her hands into the pouch in the front of her onesie. Should be a kangaroo, Jade thought, not a zebra.

'How many of you here?' the boss said.

'Eight or nine. Not exactly sure.'

'Usually?' the boss said.

'Oh, four.'

'Students?'

'Second years.'

'So you've not been in the property very long?'

'We rented it from the start of the summer. It's the only way to get anywhere,' the student said.

'Did you meet the landlords?'

'Gaynor? Yes.'

'What about Mr Harrington? He does the repairs.'

'We saw him at the start. He was bringing furniture from the store. New mattresses.'

'And recently?' the boss said.

'Sorry?'

'Have you seen him in the last week?' the boss said.

'No.'

The backyard was flagged, uneven. Standing water where one of the stones had broken, a ball of gnats rolling above it. A line of wheelie bins and bicycles chained together. A padlock on the back gate. *Nobody buried here.*

Overhead, leaden clouds were stealing the light. Gusts of wind rattled the panel fencing.

As they returned to their cars, Jade stopped short. *The store.*

'Boss, the store. She said Harrington fetched stuff from the store.'

'It could mean a shop,' the boss said.

'Or another place. Where he keeps his tools and that. There weren't any at the house, were there?'

Jade ran back and knocked on the door again. 'You said the landlord fetched new furniture from the store. Do you know where that was?'

'No idea,' the student said. 'But it wasn't long between trips so it can't be very far.'

'Was it a shop?' Jade said.

'I don't know. It could have been.'

Jade caught up with the boss. 'If they have somewhere to store stuff, the rental for that will be in their business expenses, in the records,' she said.

'I'll get Isla to look through, first thing,' the boss said.

'I can do it now.'

'Go home, Jade.'

'What?'

'Home time.'

'But, boss—'

'Look, we're making good progress and I want an early start tomorrow, six a.m. I'm going to talk to the CPS about charging Stewart Harrington.'

'We haven't got enough for murder,' Jade said.

'We can charge him on the other counts and release him under investigation,' the boss said.

'But if we can find Evie first, find out what they did to her —'

'Yes, we keep looking. But now – go home. Go out, have a drink, make a meal, watch a box set, get your eight hours, and I'll see you in the morning.'

Was she edging Jade out? Going back to the station to carry on without her? Just the boss and the others.

'I could help Isla,' Jade said. 'It's no bother.'

'What is going on with you?' The boss rounded on her.

'Nothing.'

206

'Are you sure about that? Because something is affecting your ability to take on board what I'm telling you to do.'

Jade bit her tongue, the pain flooding her mouth.

'I don't want you anywhere near the office until six tomorrow morning. You're no good to me half dead and going off script.'

'What – just because I said she'd kept her like a slave, treated her like shit? It's true! You've never said anything like that?'

'You *swore* at a suspect. You were shouting. That could be construed as hostile and aggressive questioning. I've twenty-five years more experience than you and a far better grasp of when to shut up and hold my tongue. And I am your senior officer.'

Jade trembled with the effort of not letting rip.

'See you in the morning,' the boss said. She walked away.

Jade tasted blood, hot brass. Her eyes stung, her throat ached.

She pointed her key fob to her car down the road.

A kid on a scooter was staring at her, red hoodie and new trainers, neon bright.

He was watching her. Why so interested? And the Asian couple walking up on the other side of the pavement, all lovey-dovey. Were they following her? Who were they working for? She felt a shove at her back and wheeled round. There was no one there.

The trees over the way were shaking, waving, warning her. Branches thrashing. A roaring noise filled her head. Terror gripped her spine, her bowels, closed her throat. Jade raced to her car, trying to outrun the storm.

Her fingers shook as she tried to fasten her seatbelt. *Come on, come on.* She floored the accelerator and peeled away from the kerb. She had to get away before they caught her.

Chapter 46

When she was sure that no one was still following her, she looked for somewhere to stop. Saw a Lidl ahead and pulled in there.

A big display of pumpkins outside the entrance.

She'd made a lantern one time, in one of the homes. The orange pulp was slippery in the middle, smelling weird. Jade had thought about stealing the knife, keeping it for protection. But the worker had been wise to that, clocked her when they were clearing up, signalled to her to give it back.

Her hand had slipped when she was carving the teeth, all the fiddly triangles, so Jade had cut them all off leaving her lantern with two eyes and a big fat hole for the mouth.

'Like Munch, the scream,' the worker said. 'I like it.'

Jade didn't know what the fuck he was on about.

'Go home,' the boss had said. But home wasn't hers any more.

Should she visit the hospital and see how Bert was? Call Shannon and make sure she'd sorted out somewhere else to stay? The thought curdled her stomach. She'd still be there, Jade knew it.

She watched a taxi pull in, picking up an old man who was wearing a beanie and carrying a stick, piles of shopping bags at his feet. A white van pulled into the bay next to Jade.

Where had Stewart Harrington gone on Monday night?

Jade pulled up her copy of Isla's geographical timeline. Ran it through from 18.55 until 19.30: George Peel hearing the argy-bargy, Clark Whitman watching Harrington's van drive away, PCSO Evans speaking to Whitman at the flats, getting no answer at the

Harringtons'. After that nothing. No one about. She threw her tablet down on the seat.

Jade started the engine and drove up to the dual carriageway, with no idea where she'd go next. Keeping on the move felt safer.

She thought about the van again. And what he might have been carrying.

The Harringtons had removed all traces of Evie and Rosa from the house. Or tried to. But they'd missed the long hairs in the vacuum cleaner, the drops of blood that Jade was sure were Evie's. Had they cleaned the van too? Taken it for valeting? To a car wash? *Vasile!* Her heart missed a beat, and blood rushed to her head, making her giddy. Would he be at work still? Or finished for the day?

There was a blare of horns to her right and Jade swerved and slammed on her brakes, stopping inches from the car in front. The driver in the outside lane, the one who had sounded the horn, was screaming at her, swearing. She wasn't a lip-reader but she'd no problem making out what he was shouting: 'Fucking Paki bitch. Fucking Paki.'

Jade snapped open her seatbelt, grabbed her bag and flung open her door. She was at his passenger side in an instant.

He rose to the challenge, jumped out of his car, bellowing, 'Stupid Paki bitch. You asleep at the wheel? Why don't you fuck off back where you came from? We don't want you here, dirty fucking Muslim terrorists.' He was young, clean cut, suit and tie. Teeth bared and spit flying.

Jade could have arrested him for racist abuse, ruined his day, his week, but the water was muddied. It could be argued that she'd been driving without due care and attention. The thoughts flew through her mind and away, even as she raised her arm, steadying the can, and squirted pepper spray in his face. 'Racist prick.'

He screeched and clawed at his face, doubling over.

Jade strode back to her car. She drove away, heart thumping hard. Saw in the rear-view mirror people rush to his aid.

Chapter 47

Donna was halfway home when a call came through from headquarters.

'Sergeant Middleton here. We've been attending an unexplained death, a body in the Bridgewater Canal near Castlefield.'

Evie?

'Yes?' Donna said.

'We've yet to identify her.'

Donna thought of the appeal posters, Evie's photograph. The girl who had no friends, locked in the house, sleeping by the washing-machine.

'No ID but we found your card in her pocket.'

'My card?' *Oh, Christ.* 'Can you give me any description?'

'Middle-aged, white, average build, brown hair.'

'I think it's Colette Pritchard, no fixed abode. She's a witness in the baby Rosa investigation. She found the baby. Just a moment.'

Donna pulled into a car park beside an M&S food store and stopped the car. She looked up, blinking, and cleared her throat.

'Does it look suspicious?' *Could someone have wanted to silence Colette?*

'Nothing to suggest that. Likely a drowning. She had bricks in her pockets, stuffed under her clothes, in a backpack.'

Oh, my God.

'Ma'am, could you make a formal identification?' he said.

'Yes, of course.'

'It'll probably be tomorrow afternoon. If I can pass your number on to the pathologist?'

'Yes, do that. Bye.' A hitch in her voice.

She gazed unseeing out of the window, imagining the woman's despair, the terror that made her end her life. A stream of anger bubbled under the tide of Donna's sadness, anger at what Colette's life had become, anger that Donna had been unable to help her, get her the support to turn things around, rebuild a life that was secure, safe. *A direct debit to Marie Curie and another to the Dogs Trust. A fucking cherry tree.* The life Colette had had before it had all been torn away.

They ate together, the whole family. Practically unheard of when Donna was leading an investigation.

'Mum's back!' Matt whooped, as the pasta was being doled out.

She let the chatter, the bickering, wash over her. The twins debating whether Pogba or Rashford was the better player. Bryony relaying the latest advice on university applications and how her best friend had decided not to bother applying and her mum was going mental about it.

'Mum, Mrs Jones is back,' Kirsten said.

'Oh, brilliant.' Kirsten's piano teacher had been over to New Zealand for her daughter's wedding, a trip that had lasted several weeks. Piano was the one thing that Kirsten loved unequivocally, but without the regular discipline of lessons, her practice had slipped and so had her mood.

'You'd better get practising again,' Donna said.

'Does she have to?' Matt said.

'Hey, she's very good. You don't know talent when you hear it,' Donna said.

Kirsten smiled and Donna relished the moment.

'We need costumes for the Halloween party. Either zombies or mummies,' Rob said. 'Loads of bandages and fake blood.'

Donna noticed a flicker of unease on Matt's face at the zombies.

'Red paint'll do,' Lewis said.

211

'I'm not putting paint on my face,' Rob said.

'Ooh, precious.' Lewis mocked his brother.

'What are you going as?' Matt asked Bryony.

'Not decided,' she said.

'Can we come?' Kirsten said.

'No kids allowed,' Rob said.

'You're kids,' Kirsten argued.

'Braindead.' Rob shook his head at her.

'Will you take us trick or treating, Dad?' Matt said.

'Of course. I'm not dressing up, though,' Jim said.

'I've still got my skeleton suit,' Matt said.

'I want to get a Bat Girl costume,' Kirsten said. 'I've seen them online.'

'Fine,' Jim said.

'How much?' Donna added quickly.

'I don't know,' Kirsten said.

'Well, check. You can spend up to . . .' How much should she say? The thing would probably be worn just once. 'Twenty pounds.'

'Can I too?' Matt said.

'You've got a skeleton suit,' Donna said.

'If it doesn't fit, though?'

'Oh, I suppose so,' Donna said.

It was all so normal, Jim so relaxed. Could she be mistaken about what he was hiding? It was hard to imagine Jim sleeping with anyone else. He loved her. They'd been together for twenty-four years. He'd never been the type to chase after other women. He just wouldn't. Was she naive to think like that?

'There's pudding,' Matt said.

'Pudding!' Donna said. They usually had a biscuit or yoghurt after a meal.

'With ice cream.' Matt waved his arms in the air.

'What's the occasion?' Donna said.

'We wanted ice cream,' Matt said.

'*You* wanted ice cream,' Kirsten said.

'Shut up,' Matt said.

'You shut up,' Kirsten retorted.

'You shut up,' the twins mimicked her.

'Hey, enough!' Jim said.

Bryony's phone rang and she fished it out.

'Mum, tell her!' Kirsten said. They had a no-phones-at-the-table rule.

'It's important,' Bryony said.

'Bryony,' Donna warned.

'Dad's always on his phone,' Bryony said.

'Not at the table,' Jim said.

Bryony pushed back her chair and stood up. 'Well, I'm not at the table now, am I?' She walked off.

'You won't get any pudding,' Matt called after her.

When the meal was finished, Donna left the twins arguing about whose turn it was to load the dishwasher and grabbed a quick shower while the bathroom was free.

Back downstairs she poured herself a glass of sauvignon, deliciously cold, and took it to the living room.

The kids had scattered to their separate spaces, plugged into their social networks. Bryony had gone round to her boyfriend's.

Jim was doing the crossword, one eye on the television, a spy series set in 1980s Germany. Donna had missed far too many episodes to be able to follow.

'You want to watch something else?' Jim said.

'No. I'm fine.'

'Hard day?' Could he tell? Did he really care?

She thought of Colette, bricks in her pockets, mind splintering, oblivion preferable to another day on earth. Of Jade becoming more . . . erratic, chaotic. And the Harringtons, who seemed to think it was acceptable to keep a young girl locked in a utility room, leave her there while the rest of the family went on holiday. Who hadn't had the humanity to report a baby's death.

'Not great,' Donna said.

'But you're winning?' Jim said.

She tried to smile. 'I suppose. Doesn't really feel that way.'

'I got a letter through from the hospital,' he said. 'An appointment next month. So, hopefully, they'll be able to clear me to drive again.'

'Will you be able to get insurance?' Donna said.

'I've still to look into it. No point getting quotes until I've got the medical say-so.'

The suspicion she harboured about him was like an abscess under her skin that needed lancing. Just not now. She really couldn't deal with it now. She needed a few hours' peace.

'Six o'clock start.' She yawned. Took a sip of her wine.

The newspaper headline was about the murder of the journalist Jamal Khashoggi. Saudi Arabia was now claiming he was killed in their consulate in Istanbul after a fight broke out.

Donna turned to the magazine, looking for something less depressing. She glanced at the television, the subtitles, *West Berlin 1986*. 'When did the Wall come down?'

Jim checked his phone. '1989.'

'Remember how exciting it all seemed, peace and freedom, a new age?' Donna said. 'Now it feels like everyone is building walls again.'

'Cheery,' Jim said.

'Sorry.'

'Mum?' Matt's voice rang down the stairs. 'Mum?'

Donna groaned.

'I'll go,' Jim said.

'You sure?'

'Yes. Good exercise.' He dropped his phone onto the coffee-table at her side. 'More wine?'

'I'll finish this first.' One more glass, she thought. That'll be enough.

Matt was still calling as she heard Jim climb the stairs.

Jim's phone rang, the screen flashing a name. *Pen.*

Pen? They didn't know anyone called Pen. Donna felt dizzy, something inside shifting, darkening, turning rotten.

The caller gave up.

Pen?

214

Jim waking in the night, calling out. *Pain*, she'd thought he'd said, *pain*. She'd translated it wrong. Not *pain* but *Pen*.

A text-message alert sounded. Without compunction, Donna pressed the symbol for his messages. It was short. No need to open the envelope to read it. *Monday is good. Can't wait!* And three red hearts. Emojis. Like three blows to her abdomen. Crippling her, snatching her breath. The truth laser sharp in her mind.

The messages stretched back, several a day for the previous weeks, back through the summer and earlier. Into last year. Words leaped out, burning her like hot coals. *Sexy beast. Harder next time. Friday lunch. Drive me crazy, babe. Got the kids.* Scattered with heart emojis and kisses, grinning devils and wine glasses.

Like fucking teenagers.

A look at his contacts and there was Pen. Her image in the circle, short red hair, freckles. Donna's skin tightened, felt as if it was freezing and fracturing. Pen – the woman who had been at the inquest. The lie about the petrol station. He hadn't been going to fill up the car. He'd been— Ah, Jesus. She was too angry to admit any sorrow. Enraged. Her teeth set together, skin on fire, cold rage in her belly vibrating through every sinew.

Donna walked into the kitchen and filled her glass to the brim, drank half of it. She returned to the lounge where the East German planning committee in their green and brown office, cigarettes in hand, the picture of Lenin on the wall, were frozen mid-sentence.

Jim came in. 'Spider. Right up in the corner of his room.' He sighed, about to sit down till he saw Donna's face, read her body language.

'Pen,' she said. 'Who the fuck is Pen?' She held up his phone. 'You fucking bastard.' She hurled the handset as hard as she could at the wall opposite. Felt a tiny glimmer of satisfaction at the crack it made on impact.

Chapter 48

The car wash was closed so Jade drove on and parked near Vasile's house. The road in shadow, a streetlamp broken. The place was deserted – it could have been the middle of the night. A dog was yapping nearby and, further away, Jade could hear the drone of machinery. A blast of wind threw rain at her face as she hurried to the door. Dim light leached through the faded parts of the curtains.

The man with the rotting feet answered the door. His face fell as he recognised her.

'Vasile?' Jade said.

He shook his head.

And again when she repeated herself.

'Where?' Jade said, holding open her hands, then mimicked searching, one hand over her eyes, head side to side.

The man gave a shrug.

Jade pulled out her warrant card. Gave him the eye. 'Where?'

'Football,' the man said.

'What?'

'Football.' He lifted a foot, moving gingerly.

'Where?' Jade said. Was there a match on? How could someone like Vasile afford a ticket? 'Man United? Man City?'

Another shake of the head.

'Where is Vasile? Where football?' Jade said.

He jabbed a finger towards the main road.

'That way?' Jade said.

'Paag,' he said.

'Park?'

'Park.'

Jade drove back up to the main road. There were people at the bus stop, and walking on the pavements. Saturday night. Some were dolled up and heading into town. The traffic was steady. A siren wailed, growing louder, the wash of blue light approaching quickly.

Her heart jumped into her throat. They were coming for her! The racist driver had reported her. She pulled in. The windscreen wipers squealed on the glass, the world beyond warped in the rivulets of water. The squad car raced by.

She closed her eyes, took several breaths before moving off.

She left her car on the double-yellows near the park entrance. If she was busted she could explain it was work. An emergency.

The screech and boom of a firework tore through the night, then another, followed by a volley of mortar thuds. Jade couldn't see any lights in the sky, no cascade of stars or shimmering blossoms. What sort of dickhead let off fireworks on a night like this?

The five-a-side courts were visible from the gates, illuminated by a bank of solar lights. She spotted Vasile in the group on the court. He scored, the ball hitting the top corner of the net. He pulled his T-shirt over his face, then jumped, fist in the air. One of the others leaped on him, gave him a bear hug, then patted his face. There was laughter, joking in the language she couldn't fathom.

The rain was heavy and Vasile threw back his head, opened his arms, mouth wide, catching drops.

They started playing again.

Jade ran forward, up to the wire fencing.

'Vasile,' she shouted, shaking the fence.

He turned and the smile died on his face.

She waved him over. His friends melted away.

He picked up his cap and hoodie from the side of the court and came through the wire gate but instead of walking towards her he spun round and bolted in the other direction, running deeper into the park.

'Stop!' Jade took off after him, arms and legs going like pistons.

He was fast.

There was little light and the heavy downpour blurred everything but she could just make him out and hear the slap of his feet on the footpath.

She kept running. Her chest burned, the muscles in her thighs ached. She snatched a breath and yelled again, 'Stop! Wait, Vasile.'

He turned right up ahead where the path curved to skirt the far perimeter.

Jade willed herself to go faster. She was sweating from head to toe, panting, her skin on fire. As she rounded the corner there was a volley of barking and snarling and a voice shouting, 'Cooper! Cooper! Leave! Down!' Someone else screaming.

Jade could see a man with a dog, and Vasile on the ground.

A stitch pierced her side, like a stiletto, making her grunt aloud. Her mouth was watering, like she was going to throw up.

She reached the group, the dog, a pit-bull mix, still growling, its owner holding its collar and struggling to attach a lead.

'He thought you were a threat, running up behind us in the dark,' the man said. 'He didn't bite.' He turned to Jade. 'He doesn't bite.' He looked shaken, out of breath himself.

Jade was still gasping. Her legs felt weak, head woozy. White stars danced at the edge of her vision. 'No harm done, then,' she managed to say.

'You're OK?' the man said to Vasile, who was sitting up.

'He's fine,' Jade said.

Vasile looked at her, loathing on his face. He stood up and tottered. Jade saw that he'd hurt his foot and struggled to put weight on it. Going nowhere fast now.

The dog lunged at him, snarling again.

'Cooper!' The man yanked the lead and jerked the dog back.

'I'd take him away, if I was you,' Jade said.

'Yes. He just thought you were a threat, that's all.' He walked off with the dog.

Jade waited a few seconds as her heartbeat slowed. Her face was glowing with heat. When she glanced at him, Vasile looked bitter, seething.

218

'I'm not going to arrest you, you daft prick,' Jade said. 'Come.' She waved a hand at him.

He limped beside her back through the park in the rain to the car. She motioned to him to get in.

She shook the rain off her jacket as best she could and climbed into the driver's seat. She leaned her head back for a moment, thinking. Had he seen Stewart Harrington at the car wash? How could she put that so he'd understand?

She rang DD with their prearranged signal. But he didn't call her back.

Vasile was nervy, his fists bumping together. He pointed outside. 'I go?'

'No.' Jade got her tablet out. 'You work – car wash.'

He gave a guarded nod.

'OK. This van . . .' Jade opened the browser and searched for images of white Transits. Selected one. Showed him. 'This van – car wash?'

He shrugged. Course he shrugged. Half of Manchester's tradespeople used white vans.

She didn't have a photo of Stewart Harrington to show him. Could she describe him?

She launched Google translate. There was no option for Romani.

'Shit!' She slammed the tablet onto the dashboard. Vasile flinched. *The dashboard. Spider-Man!*

'Spider-Man?' she said. 'Yes, Spider-Man?' She picked up the tablet and tapped the picture of the van. Then she knocked on the dashboard. She held her hands horizontal, one above the other, nine inches apart. 'Dolly? Toy? Spider-Man.' She did a little dance, waggling her head and arms. Banged the dashboard again. 'Spider-Man.'

Vasile looked at her like she was off her fucking rocker.

'In the van? Spider-Man?' she faltered.

He looked at her, embarrassed, pitying, rain still dripping from the peak of his cap.

It was pointless. She let her hands fall.

Time to go.

Then a ripple of something. Mouth opening, his eyes slid off to the side and back to her. Understanding. Eyes wide. Nodding. 'Spider-Man,' he said. 'Yes. Spider-Man.' He touched the dashboard.

Jade couldn't contain herself. She punched the air, like he had with his goal.

'Car wash? Spider-Man at car wash?'

He gave a nod.

'When?'

He looked blank.

Jade pulled up a calendar for the month, showed him. 'When?'

He tapped his index finger, stained yellow with nicotine, on Tuesday the sixteenth, then moved it to Wednesday the seventeenth. Repeated the motion. *Ip, dip, dip.*

So, either Tuesday or Wednesday Harrington had taken the van to be cleaned.

Jade thought of the banner signs that ringed the business: *Quick Clean, Mini Valet, Premier Power*. She reeled them off.

'Premier,' Vasile said. Which would clean everything, inside and out.

'Is he a regular?'

Vasile shook his head slowly, lip curled. He didn't understand.

Jade whirled her hands, a cycle. 'Car wash – many times?'

Vasile scowled.

She tried the calendar again, clicking back through the months. 'Spider-Man – car wash?'

Jade pointed to her eye, then to the van, rotated her hands round each other again, counted on her fingers. She felt like a twat. 'Car wash, many? Many?' Pointed to Vasile, her eye and then the van. *You see Spider-Man van?*

He gave a shake of the head. 'Car wash, no.' He held up a finger. One. 'Work,' he said. And pointed to his eye and the tablet.

You work *at* the car wash. 'What?'

Jade called DD again. Nothing.

'Work,' Vasile said. 'Spider-Man work.'

Jade shook her head.

220

Vasile pointed over his shoulder, towards the back windscreen, down the main road.

Jade hadn't got a clue what he was on about. 'Show me.' She waved him out of the car, opened her door.

Jade walked with Vasile, dodging umbrellas, sidestepping groups who already seemed hammered and the occasional late shopper, laden with bags, shuffling along the centre of the pavement. She tried to ignore the way people were looking at her. The whispers that licked at her from the dark. The roiling in her guts. The sensation of someone just behind her. *We're coming for you.*

They passed the mosque, shutters down, security lights on.

Mitch Cookson was getting off the bus. Jade felt a clutch of alarm. Was he following her? But he turned the other way, didn't seem to notice her. Probably too knackered to see straight.

When they reached the entrance to the industrial estate Vasile stopped.

'Here?' Jade said. 'Spider-Man work here?'

Vasile gave a nod.

'You see?' Jade pointed to Vasile, to her eyes.

Now it was his time to wheel his hands. Lots of times.

Vasile would pass here twice a day at least going to and from the car wash and the shops. And to call in at Chuckie Chicken for his pick-ups. Now he was telling Jade that he'd often seen Harrington's van here. Spider-Man coming and going.

She'd found the store.

Chapter 49

The gates were wide open. A sign proclaimed *24-hour access. No parking. Vehicles obstructing access will be clamped. £150 release fee.*

Evie was here, somewhere here. Harrington hadn't been out looking for her. He'd come here to get rid of her.

Jade sent Vasile on his way. She stared through the gateway at the array of buildings, blurred by the rain. A mish-mash of older workshops, with slate roofs and fancy brickwork, and modern units, mainly corrugated steel and breezeblock. A couple of Portakabins in the mix. Someone was still at work on the estate: Jade could hear a guttural roar and a clunking like a tumble-dryer full of stones.

She walked round the entire estate. It covered more ground than she'd imagined, than she remembered from the area map. The central access road branched off into five subdivisions. The one at the bottom was a maze of shipping containers. The sections nearest the entrance appeared to be a mix of small manufacturing and storage facilities, some no more than single Portakabins, the size of a portable toilet block at a festival. Among the larger ones was a leather-goods factory, where the rumbling sound was coming from, cars parked outside, a pair of people under umbrellas, the glow of cigarette ends. Most of the units were shuttered, alarms blinking. The central areas included a scrap-metal yard, full of crushed car and van chassis stacked in towers. Signs warned of guard dogs, and as Jade passed, a pair of large dogs hurled themselves at the chainlink, barking furiously. The signs weren't just for show, like on so many premises. Jade reckoned she'd made their night giving them something to bark about.

There were no trees or landscaping, nothing but corrugated steel and brick, tarmac and concrete. Here and there the tarmac had been breached leaving craters and scattered grit underfoot, the holes pooled with rain water. Mixed with the smell of the rain, something plasticky, chemical, caught in the back of Jade's throat, making her cough.

Somewhere here was the Harringtons' store. A place for spare furniture and small appliances, building materials and tools.

Jade remembered the smell of bleach. They'd swabbed the floor to cover the crime. Had they killed her because she'd killed the baby? Or had she killed herself after smothering Rosa? Or had the Harringtons killed both mother and child?

Would the security firm have a record of who rented which premises? She walked to the entrance and rang the number on the sign about access, trying to shield her phone from the rain. *The number you have dialled has not been recognised. Please hang up and try again.*

She dialled the landline number, listed beneath the sign for Gore Industrial Estate. It went to voicemail. She didn't want to leave a message.

Jade blinked away the rain and sought shelter under the porch of a discount tiling outlet.

Isla took for ever to answer, then sounded cautious when she did. 'Jade? What is it?'

Jade wouldn't usually call someone if they were off-duty. Only the boss. But the boss had sent her home so that wasn't exactly an option.

'The Harringtons' business records. Can you look for information on a storage unit? Not sure how it'll be listed but I'm guessing they rent it so there may be regular monthly payments. The address would be Gore Industrial Estate, on Stockport Road.'

'Now?' Isla said.

No, a week on fucking Tuesday.

223

'Yes, now,' Jade said. 'Boss wants it soon as. It could be where Evie was taken.'

'Yeah, sure.' Any reluctance gone. 'I'll get back to you.'

'Cheers,' Jade said.

She ran to fetch her car from the park, alive with energy, mind fizzing. *I've found her. I've found her.*

Rapping on the car window.

The boss. *Oh, fuck.* Not happy.

Jade got out.

'Living in your car now, are you?' The boss was livid, mouth pinched, eyes stony. Didn't give Jade a chance to answer. 'Only I remember telling you expressly to go home, in words of one syllable, just so we're clear. Then I get Isla on the phone: do we want her to email copies of the invoice as well? I was on my way to bed and you should have been too. Jesus, Jade, it's like you're set on self-destruct or something.' Her voice was strained with anger.

'She's here. Evie. I think he dumped her here. Did Isla find a unit number?'

The boss shook her head, hands on hips, mouth open fish-style, then snapped, 'Why? Why here?'

'Handy, if the store's one of these.' She gestured round the buildings.

Headlights lit the boss, giving her a Halloween vibe, hair stuck to her head, face chalk white, make-up smudged. Had she been crying? Jade's stomach fell. Must be the rain. A lorry trundled past them and turned into the division further down.

'It's why we couldn't pick him up anywhere on camera. He'd come here, a stone's throw,' Jade said.

'And what made you think of this place?' the boss said, maybe a sliver less ice in her voice.

Could she tell her about Vasile? Jade ran the numbers. If Evie's body was in a unit here then they had a double murder, or infanticide and murder. Jade's dealings with Vasile: she didn't want anyone sniffing into that, paying off DD with the contraband, interviews

224

with a witness off the record. None of that had been carried out according to PACE rules. And if anyone found out it could detonate their case.

'A hunch,' Jade said. 'When the student talked about a store. I looked at the map.'

Jade's phone pinged and the boss's echoed it. The info they needed. Unit 43.

'It's this way, near the middle,' Jade said.

The boss just looked at her.

Jade clenched her teeth together. *What you waiting for? Fucking Christmas?*

Finally the boss closed her eyes, allowing Jade to move.

The unit was a metal Portakabin, the size of a double garage. No windows and a roller shutter for the door, which was locked at the bottom with a heavy-duty padlock.

Jade kicked hard. The sheet metal clanged. She kicked again but there was no way that would breach the shutter. 'We need a battering ram,' she said.

'Or a key,' the boss said crisply. She proceeded to call the station and ask the custody sergeant to recover Stewart Harrington's keys from the evidence locker and courier them to her with a patrol. 'Maintain strict chain of custody,' the boss said. 'I don't want any bastard undermining our case because his keys went walkabout and weren't accounted for in the log.'

'Shall we call the CSIs?' Jade said.

'Let's see if we've actually got a potential crime scene first,' the boss said. 'They won't be thanking us if we call them out and then all we find are spare divans and a stack of toasters.'

Jade felt a rush of dizziness and put a hand out to the shutter to steady herself.

The boss swooped down on that. 'What's wrong?'

'Nothing. I'll lock the car.' Forcing herself to stay upright, Jade walked away, splashing through the puddles, aware of the boss's eyes drilling into her back.

Just tired, she told herself. She shivered, shook her hands trying to throw off some of the tension. She *was* OK, just tired. Was she due her meds? *Avoid stress. Take your meds.* When had she last taken them? This morning, waking at the station, before she'd gone driving? Or when she'd got back? Her memory was shifting, smoke disappearing.

She was thirsty. Thought briefly about going to buy something to drink, water, cola, Red Bull, something to give her some energy, but she didn't want to miss anything. She remembered Vasile, head back, mouth open, drinking rain. But it had slackened off now.

What if Harrington had moved Evie again? He claimed he'd taken the mattress to the tip on Tuesday. What if he'd taken Evie's body with him? In a curtain, or a bag. Or bags. *Blood and bleach.*

They'd be able to find traces, though. If a body *had* been kept here. If a body *had* been in his van. And it was possible to prosecute murder without finding the victim. It was a whole lot harder, relying on forensics and circumstantial evidence, but not hopeless.

Chapter 50

Everything felt unreal to Donna. This coming hot on the heels of the bombshell of Jim's affair. Was she sad about that? She must be, surely, but the main sensation was of shock and disbelief. An almost physical trauma, like a car crash, like tripping and falling. Hitting concrete. And then the emotional backwash of fear and anxiety. Confusion. She found herself repeating the words in her head, *He's having an affair, seeing someone else, sleeping with another woman, cheating on me.* As if ringing through the phrases, the different ways of saying it, might help her comprehend.

Everything had changed. But for now, with no one else knowing, everything remained the same. Her jaw ached, her teeth, her throat. Swallowing it all. Keeping it clamped in tight.

Jade couldn't keep still, pacing back and forth in front of the building, shaking her hands in a strange gesture that Donna hadn't seen her use before. The sort of movement a child makes when they can't contain their excitement. Or their fear.

Jade saw Donna watching and stuffed her hands into her pockets.

'You could wait in your car,' Donna said. 'Keep dry.'

'It's nearly stopped,' Jade said. 'I'm soaked anyway.' She turned and walked away, then back. Sentry duty outside the storage unit.

'Colette Pritchard,' Donna said, after a few moments. 'She's been found dead.'

Jade stopped walking. 'When?'

'This morning. Suicide. Bricks in her pockets. Canal at Castlefield,' Donna said.

'At least we've got a written statement.'

'Christ, Jade! That's your first reaction?' Donna said, thinking of the distraught woman who had carried the baby to the police station, who had wept for her.

'What am I supposed to say?' Jade retorted. 'This is the job. Yeah, maybe it's sad but maybe she's better off. Just because you've been crying it doesn't mean—'

Donna held up one finger. 'Shut it now. You are way out of order, Jade. This behaviour, this has to—'

'Fuck.' Jade flung up her arms, turned away, trying to shut Donna out, close her down.

'Yes, we're here for the job, for work,' Donna said. 'But any half-way decent officer, any professional, understands that we are dealing with *people*. You know the mission statement, our core values: integrity, compassion, justice—'

Jade swung back to face her. Froze. Rising on her toes. 'They're here,' she said. 'They're here with the keys.'

Before Donna could say anything, Jade was moving to meet the patrol cars.

Donna went after her, held out her hand for the keys. She asked the officers to bring their torches. And reminded Jade to put her gloves on. She shouldn't need reminding.

There were a lot of keys on the bunch but only one stamped with the same name as the padlock.

Donna crouched, grunting with the effort, unlocked the padlock and removed it. Jade went forward and helped her push up the door.

Chapter 51

Pitch black inside. The smell, a high reek like dogshit or rotten offal, the sort of smell that made you want to run, sent a blast of fear into Jade's spine. If she hadn't been convinced that Evie was here before, as soon as she breathed in that death stench she knew.

'Any lights?' the boss said.

The patrol officers swung their torches around and Jade saw the switch on the wall. 'Here.' She hit it and brought on the overhead lights.

Jade's eyes flew round the space, mattresses stacked to the left, three of them, and beyond, some cupboards, kitchen units. Toolboxes. Lengths of wood, paint tins and boxes of tiles. She walked through the aisle in the centre breathing through her mouth. Bags of plaster, ladders.

Two sofas stood on their ends.

Jade went forward.

Behind the sofas, among stacked cardboard boxes, she saw her. She was lying on a thin mattress, a blue and white fleece blanket, patterned like snowflakes, covering her feet. Her legs bent weirdly, bowed, like a jockey. Pyjamas soaked with blood around her crotch and her thighs. Long brown hair.

'Oh, Christ,' Jade heard the boss whisper.

Jade stretched to check her pulse, knowing they were too late, tensing her fingers against the chilled density of dead flesh.

Jade touched Evie's neck.

Evie opened her eyes.

Jade reared up. Her heart wild in her chest. 'Ambulance! Now!'

One of the uniformed officers got on his phone.

Jade looked around at the bucket overflowing with human waste, the empty water bottle, a two-litre size, the sharing bag of crisps.

The boss was kneeling down, holding Evie's hand, her voice warm, gentle. 'Evie, you're OK. I'm Donna, I'm a police officer. We've got you now. You're going to be OK. We're going to look after you. There's an ambulance coming. We'll take you to hospital.' She held her hand and stroked her hair. 'You're safe now. We'll keep you safe.'

Someone lifting Jade up, undoing the laces tied at her wrists. Her mother shouting, 'They're just to stop her climbing out.'

A hand stroking her head. 'Come on, Jade. It's all right. We'll get you something to eat. And a nice bath.'

'You can't fucking take her! You can't!'

Glimpses, strobe lit. 'Give you something to cry for, you little fucker.' A slap on her cheek knocking her to the floor, jarring through her. Cheekbone throbbing, her ear sounding all funny. Jade, climbing to her feet. Spitting. 'You dirty little mare.' Another crack. Pain howling through her. 'Wish you'd never been born.'

Jade turned and walked outside, tried to steady her breathing, all jerky and tight.

The dogs guarding the scrapyard were going ape-shit, barks ricocheting around the estate.

People from the leather-bag place had come out to see what all the fuss was about.

Jade called over one of the patrol officers: 'We need a cordon, you got any tape?'

'Yes.'

'OK. No one but the paramedics comes within twenty feet of the building. Secure the area until they come.'

'Yes.'

'Is it her?' the guy said. 'Is that Rosa's mother?'

'That's her,' Jade said.

'Only a kid herself, isn't she?'

'Fourteen,' Jade said.

'Poor little thing, eh?'

Jade wasn't sure if he meant Evie or Rosa.

Jade called base to notify them that Evie had been found, alive. She headed towards the onlookers to caution them against taking photographs and tell them that if anyone had seen activity at this unit in the last week they should give a statement to one of the officers. And to ask if anyone knew who could shut up those fucking dogs.

Chapter 52

Donna made it home just before three in the morning, the house in darkness, though Matt's nightlight would be on in his room. She ate a slice of bread and honey, drank a glass of milk, then went upstairs to wash her face and brush her teeth.

She didn't put the light on in their bedroom, was practised at getting undressed and finding her way to bed in the blackness, though why she should be considerate to Jim at this point was beyond her.

She couldn't fathom what it meant, his betrayal. For her, for the marriage, for the kids. It was still a big, ugly shock and there hadn't been any time to talk about it, even if she'd known where to start, because Isla had rung with the message about the storage unit.

When she thought of the children, telling the children, her guts contracted. He'd always been a good father, a great dad. He delighted in his kids, their kids. Celebrated every achievement, consoled them. Loved them. He'd always pulled his weight, changed nappies and made meals. He'd put the kids to bed many more times than Donna had, with her long hours of work. They'd all be so hurt. Betrayed.

She imagined Bryony outraged at Jim's conduct with all the righteous indignation and moral certainty of a teenager. And the twins dismayed and confused that their male role model had been unmasked as just another dick who couldn't keep it in his pants. Kirsten, who adored Jim, would no doubt find a way to blame Donna. While little Matt would be inconsolable, his scary world even more frightening and unpredictable than it had been.

Of course, the received wisdom was that the errant party was only cheating on their partner, that they still loved the kids unconditionally even if the love between the adults had faded. But how could they be anything but hurt by Jim's actions?

Against the odds Donna fell asleep quickly, a blank, deep sleep, and woke to the alarm at seven. Her first thoughts were of the workday ahead, glad she'd postponed their early start by a couple of hours, then fast after that, like a bomb exploding, she remembered anew that the man beside her was fucking someone else.

'Dad's always on his phone,' Bryony had said. Now it made sense. And the phone call, allegedly to Bradley, when Donna had come in on Friday evening. 'Talk to you later,' he'd said. It'd been Pen, Donna was sure of it. The lie had slid so easily off his tongue. Jim trying to stop Donna going to the inquest, *Look, you just drop me off, I'll be fine.* Fine because *she* would be there. *Christ!*

It was the weekend: the kids would all sleep late and Jim too. She left for work without seeing any of them.

Maybe they don't need me, she thought. A vision of her leaving, of Pen moving in. Of Donna on the outside. Alone.

Oh, stop it! she told herself, hating the self-pity.

She reached the mortuary at nine o'clock ready for the viewing. She'd been there many times before accompanying relatives, supporting them through the terrible business of formally identifying their loved one. Bewildered, grief-stricken, half mad, resolute, shattered, raging, numb, stoic: a myriad reactions to sudden, violent bereavement.

And each time it reinforced her determination to do all she could for them – which was simply to discover the truth. Who did this? How? Sometimes, though not always, why? To gather the proof that might bring justice.

Nothing so intense today.

She looked at Colette through the window. Colette on the trolley, her body covered with a sheet. Messy brown hair. Looking older in death than her thirty-seven years.

'Yes, that's Colette Pritchard,' Donna said, in answer to the mortuary assistant's question.

I thought it was a cat. I just wanted you to know. Why hadn't Donna heard the ring of finality in that statement.

'We're not aware of any next of kin,' Donna said. 'But I'll be attending the service when it's arranged.'

You were right, Colette, Donna thought. You probably did hear a baby crying on Saturday. But you couldn't have saved her. And I couldn't save you. I'm so sorry.

'Do you need a few minutes, ma'am?' the assistant asked.

'No,' Donna said. 'That's fine. I'll be on my way.'

Chapter 53

The doctor met Donna and Jade in an anteroom on the ward at Manchester Children's Hospital before they went in to speak to Evie.

'She's traumatised and exhausted so, please, no more than fifteen minutes. We're treating her for a serious infection, any longer without medical care and we'd have been dealing with full-blown sepsis. She was badly dehydrated and anaemic. She also has chronic problems, acute vitamin D deficiency that has caused rickets.'

Donna remembered the bowing of Evie's legs. 'She wasn't allowed out. No sunlight.'

'I've asked Stella Padiham, the child-protection social worker, to attend,' the doctor said. 'Stella spoke briefly with Evie earlier and will manage her eventual discharge. Into the care of the local authority, in all likelihood.'

'Yes,' Donna said. If Evie was charged with infanticide or murder, she'd probably be detained in a secure children's home.

'Could we talk to Stella first, fill her in on the background?' Donna said.

'Of course. She should be here soon. I'll tell her where to find you.'

Stella arrived ten minutes later, carrying a bag full of files. She wore a tartan skirt, a white blouse and chunky Perspex earrings. Donna guessed she was in her late twenties.

Donna gave her a résumé of what they knew, and what they were still trying to establish, before the three of them went into Evie's room.

'Just to warn you, she's pretty withdrawn,' Stella said. 'She was probably told never to talk to anyone. I'll explain who you are. We need chairs from the corridor.'

Evie looked tiny, more like a ten-year-old, though the expression in her eyes was ancient. Her long hair was brittle and matted, her lips chapped, and angry pimples peppered her nose and cheeks.

She was still on a drip, the cannula taped to the back of her hand.

'Hello, Evie,' Stella said, setting her chair down. 'It's Stella again. You were pretty sleepy before. I'm your social worker, and these ladies here are Donna and Jade. They're police officers. They found you last night.'

Evie shifted a little, drawing back.

'We're here because we need your help,' Donna said. 'Can you tell us what happened to you, Evie?'

She was picking at her nails, eyes cast down.

'Evie?'

'I don't know.' Her voice wavered.

'We found you in a unit on the industrial estate. You were very poorly. Someone had left you there. Can you tell me who?'

She shook her head.

'Do you know who left you there?' Donna said.

She didn't speak.

'I want to help you, Evie. But I need you to help me, too,' Donna said.

'I don't want to go to prison,' Evie said. Her teeth were grey, translucent, the colour of rotten potatoes, her gums edged with blood.

'No one's talking about prison,' Donna said.

'Where's Annabel?' she said quietly.

Donna looked at Jade, who flashed her a glance in return.

'Is that your baby?' Donna said.

A nod.

'Tell me about Annabel,' Donna said.

'She kept crying,' Evie said.

Oh, God.

'Yes,' Donna said.

'Sometimes she wouldn't stop. Not for ages. I tried to make her stop.'

Donna felt a chill down her arms. She imagined the baby's cries, piercing, unrelenting. Evie half crazed with the trauma of giving birth alone, with the lack of sleep, at the mercy of her hormones, her youth. Becoming increasingly distraught. Needing the noise to stop. Just a second's peace. Her hand over the baby's nose and mouth, a pinch, just a brief pinch. Silence. The blessed silence. The terrible silence.

'How did you do that?' Donna said.

'With the bottle, feeding her. Cuddling her.'

'Yes.'

'But I couldn't do it properly. I wanted to but I couldn't. And they were going to take her away.'

'Who were going to take her?' Donna said.

'Daddy— Stewart and Gaynor.' She called him Daddy.

'Take her away?' Donna said.

'To a good home. Because I couldn't look after her properly. She was always crying. And it was illegal anyway, me having a baby, so if anyone ever found out they'd put me in prison. They were talking about how much money they'd get so it must be a rich family. Did they already take her?' She looked up, quaking.

Donna took a breath. The room felt still, hesitant. The tension electric in the air.

'When did you last see Annabel?' Donna asked.

'On Monday. I tried to run away with her, so we could stay together, but she started crying and they heard her.'

'What happened then?'

'Gaynor grabbed her off me and Stewart put me in the van. Is she still at home?' Hope trembled in her eyes and Donna's heart split. This child who had been so terribly mistreated yet had found the courage to try to protect her own.

'You tried to escape,' Donna said. 'That was very brave. You tried to save Annabel.' Ah, Jesus, how could she tell her? And how could she not?

237

'Has she gone?' Evie said, nose reddening, tears spilling, dripping off her chin.

'Evie, I'm so sorry,' Donna said, 'but Annabel died.'

'No.' Anguish frozen on her face.

'We're trying to find out exactly what happened but she's—' There was a lump in Donna's throat, she cleared it with a cough. 'But she's dead and I'm so, so sorry.'

Evie keened a high wail, rocking. Moaned, 'No, no, no.'

Donna sought her hand. And Stella moved to go and hug the child.

Donna looked up at the ceiling, suppressing tears and counting the squares in the grid there as a way of clinging to her composure.

Chapter 54

They grabbed a drink in the café at the hospital. The boss looked dead on her feet, silent in the queue at the counter, shoulders rounded like Mina's when she was nodding off. Jade knew she'd had to make the formal identification of Colette's body this morning after being up half the night, like herself. She hadn't even got any make-up on. She didn't wear much, as far as Jade could tell, but without any at all she looked sort of exposed.

But as soon as they'd been served and were seated the boss snapped back into action.

'OK, we need more from her. There are still loads of gaps.' She ticked things off on her fingers as she spoke. 'The exact situation of her life in that house, who the baby's father is, the circumstances under which he raped her, what Stewart and Gaynor know about that, precisely what was said about getting payment for Annabel and by whom. We're probably looking at staggering interviews over several days. But we have enough now to challenge the Harringtons. When Evie was taken from the house, Annabel was alive. A couple of hours later she was dead. I believe Evie and I believe any jury would too.'

'Harrington has said all along it's a cot death,' Jade pointed out. 'And his wife the same. *Until* you told her about the post-mortem, the bruising. Then she accuses Evie.'

'Pointing the finger, deflecting the blame.' The boss blew on her drink.

'If Gaynor did it and left the baby in the bed, that means she set him up to find her. She *set him up*,' Jade insisted.

'So . . . what?' the boss said. 'He goes out and locks Evie in the storage unit. And she smothers the baby.'

'Then sits and eats pizza with him and sends him to check on the baby later. Cold,' Jade said.

The boss drank some coffee, eyes closed.

Jade watched an ancient man pushing a woman in a wheelchair up to the counter. He said something to the staff and they all burst out laughing.

'But why do that?' Jade said. 'If they're looking to make some money selling the baby, that's several grand or whatever. Doesn't make sense.'

'No,' the boss said. 'We press him. Lay it out and see if he joins the dots. With Evie back in the picture, any hope they have of blaming it all on her and getting away with minor charges is long gone. No riding off into the sunset together.'

'You think he'll turn?' Jade said.

'Hard to call. They've been living together for five years. When he moved Evie and William in with Gaynor, which of them decided Evie would be better off staying at home and working for her keep? A nine-year-old. Clearing up after the rest of them. Seen and not heard.'

'My money's on Gaynor,' Jade said. 'You can see it every time she talks about her. She hates her. He seems more . . . guilty.'

'They're both guilty. In it together,' the boss said.

'Ashamed, then,' Jade said.

The boss put her cup down. 'Jade, last night. We still need to deal with that.'

Oh, for fuck's sake. 'I found Evie,' Jade said.

'And you ignored my express instructions,' the boss said.

'But if I hadn't—' Jade said.

The boss held up her hand. 'I'm not discussing it now. But it will be discussed. Because it raises very clear concerns for me, Jade. And they're not new. So there *will be* a debriefing and I will be reviewing your performance. Now, you've said you've got some personal stuff going on, and I've respected that, but if you're bringing that to work with you, if it's interfering with your performance, with your—'

'How? How is it? I'm not doing anything different. I worked out there was a fourth child. That was a breakthrough. Solid work. And last night I found her. I found her!' Jade's frustration boiled over. 'That probably saved her life – you heard what the doctor said: full-blown sepsis. You talk about mission statements. Well, what about the preservation of life? That doesn't count? What is your problem? You're fucked off because I got ahead of the game? Cos I took a chance? Stuck my neck out and got results. And now you're shitting on me. It's all right for you with your perfect Disney life—'

The boss lunged forward, face furious. 'I've just found out my husband is having an affair. There's nothing remotely fucking perfect about that. My daughter's struggling to cope at high school and we're running out of money. That do you?' She slammed her palms against the edge of the table, the shove slopping her coffee over the edge of the cup.

Fuck!

'Twenty-four years, Jade. Twenty-four years and five kids.'

Jade didn't know what to do, what to say. Everyone was looking at them, pretending not to.

The boss grabbed a serviette, started mopping up.

'I'll get a cloth,' Jade said.

She came back with some kitchen roll and cleared the last of it up, feeling like a right tit.

'Don't hover,' the boss said. 'Sit down.'

Jade did.

The boss, hand on her forehead, was staring at the table.

'That must be . . . You just found out?' Jade said.

'Yes. Messages on his phone.'

'I'm sorry,' Jade said. 'What are you gonna do?'

'I've no idea. It's still unreal. And don't tell anybody.' The boss looked wounded. Eyes like a dog's when it knows it's about to be belted. 'I shouldn't have told you. I didn't mean to. I need to get my head round it.'

'OK. I won't say a word. Swear down.'

The boss blew out a breath, pressed her lips together. 'She was at the inquest – the woman.'

241

'Really?' Jade felt like she was trapped, waters rising, ankle tethered.

'I'm sorry,' the boss said. 'I didn't mean to dump it on you.'

'It's fine,' Jade said, desperate to draw a line under the conversation. But at least the boss wasn't having a go at her any more. 'Shit happens.'

The boss laughed in surprise. She shook her head. 'Oh, Jade,' she said. 'It certainly does. Shit happens.' She rubbed at her face, like she was waking herself up. Groaned. 'So, if my game's a bit off, that's why.' She pushed herself to her feet. 'But you'd tell me about it, wouldn't you?'

You joking?

'Just like I'm calling you out when I need to.'

A dog with a fucking bone.

'You need to follow instructions,' the boss went on.

Yeah, right. And if I had, Evie would be dead.

She bit the inside of her cheek and watched the wheelchair woman stuffing cake down herself and the old fellow stirring his tea.

The boss walked away.

Jade followed, blood seething, the taste of copper on her tongue. Her vision too bright, too sharp, and a black hole in the pit of her stomach.

Chapter 55

The journey back took for ever. The Mancunian Way was closed and two accidents were blocking alternative routes. Outside it was foggy, everything wreathed in grey. A yellow tram trundled past, almost empty. They were always either like that or rammed to the gills. The tram gave a mournful hoot, perfectly matched to the weather.

Jade tried to imagine what it must be like for the boss to find out her husband was shagging around. Not easy, that was for sure, the way she'd lost it in the canteen.

You couldn't trust people: Jade had learned that early on. Most people, they look after number one. So, you didn't let anyone get too close and then they couldn't take you down.

Twenty-four years. They must have known each other for the whole of Jade's life. And it'd all be tangled up together, wouldn't it? Home, possessions, the kids. Not like the boss could just walk away. Maybe she should chuck him out and change the locks.

Jade thought of Shannon, with a cold, sick sensation. How hard it was to get shut of her. So imagine that, after twenty-four years and with someone you actually loved. Who you saw day and night, month after month. Who you thought you knew inside out.

Jade had never lived in a home where there was a happy marriage, or any settled relationships. By all accounts both Bert and Mina had been with their respective partners a long time but their other halves had been dead way before Jade had moved into the flats.

She suddenly remembered there *was* one set of foster parents. They'd been all loved up. Like a family from the adverts. Except they smoked. There were always teacakes and toast, and you could pick whatever you wanted on top. But then one of their own kids had got really sick and they'd stopped fostering. That was before— The shadow fell and a ripple of dread crashed through Jade's stomach. She wrenched her mind away from all that. Coughed and stretched in her seat.

Jade cast a glance at the boss as they pulled up at the station car park. She was still looking wrecked. Like the wrong side of a hang-over. If you didn't know what was going on, you'd think she was on the booze.

The boss'd be OK, wouldn't she? Because maybe sometimes she was hard going but anyone else would be ten times worse. And, among the lectures and the smacked wrists and sticking her nose where it wasn't wanted, she was a great team leader and liked nothing better than to see her junior officers come good. She'd stuck by Jade when Jade had really needed support. After a little persuasion. So, yeah, OK, Jade respected her. Rated her. The way she took all that shit from the chief constable and just kept going, the way she drew the team together, the sheer work she put in.

'Boss,' Jade said, 'I could do the Harrington interview. Put Calvin with me. And you can get a break.'

'I don't know.' Not even taking time to think about it.

'You can prep it with us,' Jade said.

'Oh, that's good of you,' the boss said.

'Well, to be honest, you look like you need it,' Jade said. 'A break, like. We've got this. It would take the pressure off.'

The boss looked as if she was trying to figure something out, mouth working as though she was going to speak, then hesitating. Finally she said, 'Look, what's going on for me, I don't have any problem carrying out my duties.' Like Jade was dissing her.

'Yeah, I know that. That's not what I'm saying,' Jade countered. 'But you look wasted. I was just trying to help.'

The boss glanced away, out of the side window. Nothing to see out there but cars, brick walls and a row of pigeons along the roof.

'OK, then,' the boss said. 'You and Calvin.' She opened the car door. 'And, Jade, I do appreciate it.'

Jade felt a rush of embarrassment. 'No problem,' she said, wanting to vanish. 'I'll find Calvin.'

Chapter 56

'Mr Harrington,' Jade said. 'Last night we visited a unit on the Gore Industrial Estate near your home. Unit forty-three.'

He blew out his cheeks, rubbed his forehead.

'You rent that unit for the business. Is that correct?'

He pressed his hands on the top of his head, bowed forward. Then let them fall. Defences lowered. 'Is she all right?' he said, eyes averted.

'Evie's in hospital,' Jade said.

'Is she going to be OK?'

'She's not in any immediate danger but she needed urgent medical attention. You locked her in there and concealed the fact. You lied to us, knowing she'd have nothing left to eat or drink. You were prepared to sacrifice her,' Jade said.

'I never meant . . . It just got out of hand.' His jaw worked, he blinked rapidly.

'You could have said the word at any time. You didn't. Evie's told us what happened on Monday. It's very different from what you've been telling us. We'll be questioning you about this matter, the abduction, the physical abuse and neglect.'

There was an echo in Jade's head: the words seemed to bounce off the walls, whispers trailing in their wake. She clenched her fists, willed herself to concentrate.

'But in this interview we want to talk to you about what happened between seven o'clock and nine forty-five when you found the baby unresponsive.'

He looked down. 'I can't do this.'

Can't! Jade swallowed the anger that coursed through her. 'At seven o'clock Evie took the baby and left the house. Is that right?'

He just shook his head.

'Mr Harrington?'

Silence.

'Do I need to repeat the question?'

'No. That's right.' Jade could barely hear him.

'Where were you then?'

'Putting the boys to bed,' he said.

'Aidan and Charlie?' Jade said.

'Yes,' Harrington said.

'Where was William?' Jade said.

'In his room, playing games.'

'What alerted you to Evie leaving?' Jade said.

'Gaynor called me,' he said.

'What did you do?' Jade said.

'I went outside. They were outside.'

'And then?' Jade said.

He rubbed at his knuckles.

'Mr Harrington?'

'I got Evie and put her in the van,' he said.

'And where was the baby?'

'Gaynor had her. She took her inside,' Harrington said.

'Think carefully before you answer this next question,' Jade said. 'Was the baby alive at that point?'

'Yes!' He came to life. 'She was crying. She was fine.'

Give you something to cry for. A chill on the back of her neck. Someone touching her there, an icy grip. She straightened up, rubbed at her neck, dragged herself back to the sequence of the interview.

'When did you next see the baby?' she said.

'At quarter to ten.'

'You went to check on her?' Jade said.

'Yes.'

'And you said you thought she'd died in her sleep?'

247

'She had.'

Jade let that go. 'Between you returning with pizza and checking on the baby at quarter to ten, did Gaynor say anything about the baby?'

'Just that—' He coughed. 'Just that she'd fed her and she was asleep.'

'When did she tell you that?' Jade said.

'When I got in with the takeaway.'

'And when you found the baby wasn't breathing, did you notice if she was cold to the touch?'

'No.' His eyes were swinging around the space, unable to settle.

'She wasn't cold, or you didn't notice?' Jade said.

'I don't know,' he said.

But he did. Jade could tell. And the wheels were whirring away behind that raddled face. *Click, click, click.*

'For the record, Mr Harrington, can you tell me anything about the injuries to the baby? The evidence shows that she was smothered, that someone held a hand over her nose and mouth until she suffocated.'

'No!'

'You know nothing about that?'

He shook his head, his lips compressed. The map of broken veins on his face burned darker, cheeks trembling. Hand rubbing his knuckles hard, over and over. As if he'd rub away the truth.

Chapter 57

Jade saw she'd a missed call on her phone. Unknown number.

It was the discharge lounge at the hospital. 'Just confirming Mr Jowett will be with you sometime this afternoon if you could be there to meet the transport.'

Bert?

'What?' Jade said.

'You're down as next of kin. This is just a courtesy call to let you know he's on his way.'

'I'm at work,' Jade said.

'We understood you would be available.'

'Well, you understood wrong,' Jade said.

'When the discharge unit spoke to you earlier—'

'No one spoke to me,' Jade said. 'When did he leave?'

'About eleven thirty. There are several patients to drop off so it could be anytime.'

Christ! Jade hung up.

She'd nip home, see if he was there. And, if not, Mina would have to help out. No way was Jade going to sit at home waiting for him to land.

When she reached their floor she could hear voices from Bert's flat. She knocked and Shannon answered the door.

'Oh, hi, Jade,' she said. 'What are you doing here?'

'I live here,' Jade said, pushing past her.

Bert was in his chair. He had a bandage around his head. He was eating a sandwich, and put it down on his plate. 'Jade.' He smiled.

'How are you?' she said.

'I'm fine. I told them I was fine. They never listen.'

'You had stitches,' Shannon chipped in. 'And they had to check you for concussion.' She was wearing an old navy sweatshirt and trackie bottoms of Jade's, the fabric straining across her breasts and thighs.

'They rang me, the discharge lounge,' Jade said. 'Last minute.'

'They said yesterday they'd let you know,' Bert said, frowning.

'They thought I was Jade, when I visited,' Shannon said. 'I didn't click at first when they were saying about the times.'

'You pretended to be me?' Jade said.

'No, not really. They just got their wires crossed,' Shannon said.

'And you didn't put them straight?'

'I was only trying to help,' Shannon said. 'You're so busy at work, aren't you, *keeping us all safe*? I thought it would help.'

Jade's palms itched. She flexed her fingers. 'Bert?' Was he all right with this?

'Is there any more tea?' he said to Shannon.

Shannon huffed, looked from Jade to Bert, then grabbed his cup and flounced into the kitchen.

'You OK?' Jade mouthed. She sat opposite him.

'She means well,' he whispered.

'But?' Jade said.

'I like my own company, Jade. You know that.'

'Me too. I'll talk to her.'

'She'll soon get bored,' Bert said.

'Don't bank on it.'

Jade didn't want to drag Bert any further into her dealings with Shannon. But here Shannon was cosying up to him, expecting what? To be on his sofa next? The cuckoo muscling into someone else's nest.

Shannon brought Bert his tea. She hadn't offered any to Jade.

'A word?' Jade said to Shannon.

Shannon joined her in the corridor.

'It's an offence, you know,' Jade said, 'impersonating a police officer.'

'I wasn't impersonating a police officer. I was impersonating a good neighbour.' She screwed up her face. 'Fuck's sake, Jade, get over yourself. What you going to do, nick me?'

'Do I have to change the locks?' Jade said. 'You pitch up, a complete stranger and it's "just for a night". That was four days ago. You chat shit about how your mates are busy and how Dick-brain'll take you back—'

'You'd put me on the streets?' Shannon jutted her chin up.

'I don't owe you anything. I can't be doing with you. Not now.' *Not ever probably.* 'Key.' Jade held out her hand. 'Shut my door when you've got your stuff.'

Shannon pulled the key from the trackie pocket, slammed it onto Jade's palm. 'You're just like her, aren't you? You don't care. You don't care about anyone. All you know is hate. You're dead inside.' Shannon came closer. Spit flew as she hissed, 'You've a cold, black heart and a fucked-up head. Who'd want you for a fucking sister anyway? You're a selfish, twisted bitch, just the same as she is.'

'Fuck off!' Jade shouted. 'I'm nothing like that. I'm not. She's—'

'You don't know what love is. Have you ever been with anyone? Ever been in love? No, course not. Frigid bitch. Who the fuck'd have you, anyway? Mad cow like you.'

Jade was choking, saliva thick in her throat.

'You think you're better than me?' Shannon waggled her head, plump cheeks shiny, eyes like beads. 'Just cos you're police. But you don't give a toss, do you?'

'Jade?' Mina in the corridor, leaning on her stick. 'I heard shouting.' Her eyes darted between them.

'Hi, Mina.' Shannon was syrup, oozing, sticky. 'Bert's back from hospital. I've just made tea, if you'd like some?'

'No,' Mina said. 'I've had a cup.' She gave Jade a glance, curious still. Jade didn't know how to return it. She was going to be sick.

'Later,' she managed. She rushed to the stairs, lips pressed together, clattered down the flights, head spinning. She burst out of the entrance door and ran to the side of the building, then doubled over, hands on her knees, and vomited acrid bile until she was empty.

Chapter 58

'He gets it,' Donna had said to Jade, after the Stewart Harrington interview. He understood that Gaynor must have been responsible for Annabel's death.

'But he's still protecting her,' Jade said.

'For better or worse,' Donna said. And she saw Jim's face, the guilt, then the defiance as he'd said, 'She's someone I'm seeing.' Eyes hard on her, face set. And he'd left it like that. No justifications or explanations or apology. Just that – a fucking gauntlet.

She couldn't imagine them splitting up, the impact on the kids, the implosion of all their lives. But how could they share a bed, a home, after this? People stay together for the sake of the kids. How? she wondered. How on earth do they function? Just the thought of him flooded her with rage. She wanted to hurt him, to belittle him, slap and punch and humiliate him. Would she feel the same if he'd shown a shred of remorse, exhibited any grief for the destruction of their marriage? If he'd tried to justify it, blame her absences, her long hours, for him straying. Straying? Jesus! He wasn't a fucking sheep. He hadn't said sorry once. He *wasn't* sorry. Whoever she was, this Pen, she was worth breaking everything else for. She was his world now, the person he dreamed of, the person his thoughts lit on when he woke. The one who made his heart rise and his blood sing and his prick hard. *Jesus.*

Had it all been a mirage? A fake marriage, a fake relationship? Months, he'd been lying to her. She wanted to scream, a tidal wave of rage. She felt sweat sticky across the back of her neck; her mouth went dry, a sense of dislocation, the ground no longer firm under her feet.

She excused herself and escaped to the toilets. Washing her hands she stared into the mirror and took in the face looking back. Tired and wrinkled.

Questions, invasive, prurient, painful, wormed their way into her mind. Where did they have sex? What did they do? Who took the lead? Did Jim make the same sounds with her? Were there games and sex toys? Different positions? Was it just sex or more than that? How old was Pen? How had they met? What had Jim told her about Donna? What else did they share? A sense of humour? A love of the same music or films? The same things that Jim and Donna shared?

And, like a death knell, mournful and plaintive, *How could he? How could he do that? How could he do that to me?*

She drew a deep breath, then another. Dried her hands. She smiled at her reflection, bright and false. She had to hold it together. Maybe her marriage was rotten, dead or dying, but she still had work. An investigation to lead, a team to manage. 'OK,' she said aloud, and gave a nod. 'OK, then, let's do this.'

Now Donna looked steadily at Gaynor and said, 'On the evening of Monday, the fifteenth of October, Evie Potter attempted to leave your home, where she'd been held captive for six years. Evie was running away with her baby, Annabel.'

Gaynor reacted to the name, a flicker of surprise in her eyes.

'She alleges that you and your husband were making plans to traffic her baby for monetary gain.'

Gaynor gave a snort, folded her arms.

'You stopped her,' Donna said. 'Your husband put Evie in his van and drove to a nearby storage unit where he left her locked in. You had taken Annabel back into the house. Less than three hours later your husband found Annabel dead. She had been murdered. We intend charging you with that murder. Have you anything to say?'

Gaynor was stock still. Silent. Then she began to tremble, her mouth worked, her arms fell open, her face collapsed. Tears brimmed in her eyes. Furrows made sharp lines between them.

'I'm so sorry.' She cupped her hands over her nose and mouth, then took a shaky breath. 'I'm so sorry. I didn't want to say. I didn't want to tell you. He didn't realise. That's why I lied.' Gaynor's eyes glittered. 'He just wanted to stop her crying.'

'Who are you talking about?' Donna said, a shiver running up her back.

'Charlie. He's only a baby himself. I'd gone to make her a bottle. I wasn't long, I swear. And when I came back she'd stopped crying. He was just playing. He didn't know he'd done anything wrong. He's only a baby.'

'You're telling me Charlie smothered Annabel?' Donna said.

'Yes, but he didn't mean to. He didn't understand.'

'Where was this?'

'In the living room,' Gaynor said.

'Wasn't Charlie already in bed?' Jade said.

'He wasn't asleep.' She sniffed, gave a shaky breath. 'He came down when he heard her crying.'

'You didn't tell your husband?' Donna said.

'I thought he'd be angry,' Gaynor said.

'Because you'd been going to make money by selling the baby?' Donna said.

'That's not true,' she said. 'I don't know who told you that but it's not true. We had talked about adoption. Evie couldn't keep the baby – she could barely look after herself.'

'But she helped around the house? Cooking, cleaning, washing, ironing?' Donna said.

A pause. 'Yes.'

'Why didn't you report Annabel's death?' Donna said.

'What good would it have done? And he's just a little boy. It was an accident.'

'And you would also have had to explain about Evie, her sustained ill-treatment,' Donna said.

'She wasn't ill-treated,' Gaynor said. 'She had a roof over her head, food, clothes.'

'No education,' said Donna.

'She's slow. And phobic, school phobic. That's why she never went out. She's happier at home. We were doing our best. We were.'

'She was never given the care and attention that her brothers enjoyed,' Donna said.

'They're not—' Gaynor cut herself off. 'She needed different things. Look, Stewart ended up with her. He could have put her in care but he felt obliged. She's not an easy child but we gave her a home.'

A bed on the floor by the washing-machine. A life locked away.

Donna waited a moment before saying, 'What did you plan to do about Evie?'

'Nothing. Just wait for her to calm down and . . . fetch her back.'

'She was left unattended without heat or light, with scarcely any food or drink, without any medical attention, days after giving birth. Perhaps you left her there to die,' Donna said.

'No. Look, it was only because you kept turning up. We couldn't risk it.'

'So you endangered her life to protect yourselves?'

'No,' Gaynor said. 'I couldn't tell you because of Charlie, because of the boys. What would have happened to them?'

What has happened to them?

Gaynor looked down at her lap, her words echoing in the silence. She took off her glasses and wiped at the corners of her eyes.

'We'll take a short break,' Donna said briskly. 'Half an hour.'

'No way,' Calvin said, when Jade and Donna returned to the incident room.

He'd retrieved the post-mortem photographs of Annabel's face, put them up on the big screen. 'Look at the size of the bruising. My sister's kid is that age – his fingers are tiny.'

'She's throwing him under the bus – Charlie,' Jade said. 'Knows he can't be held culpable. She gets off with minor charges. Normal service resumes.'

'She'd still get several years,' Isla said. 'Surely.'

'And no one's going to let those kids go back to her. Not after the way she treated Evie,' Tessa said.

Jade gave a shake of her head. 'Depends if her kids are judged to be at risk.'

'Come on! With someone who was happy to see a baby dumped in a bin and a teenage mother locked in a Portakabin,' Isla said.

'But who never put a foot wrong with the boys?' Donna said. 'It's not beyond the realms of possibility at some stage. But it'll be years away if we have anything to do with it.'

'With Gaynor convicted of murder,' Calvin said.

'Exactly. I'm going to talk to the CPS, find out what they say, make sure we're on firm ground. But first . . .' She checked the time: Sunday afternoon, three o'clock. Django would probably be busy at home but, given how critical this point was, she trusted he'd be OK with her interrupting his family time.

When he answered, all she could hear was distorted music and children screaming.

'A moment, please,' Django said.

He found somewhere quieter.

'Sorry to interrupt your fun,' Donna said.

'This is OK,' he said. 'This is not my idea of fun. This is roller disco.'

'Understood.' Donna laughed. 'It's about baby Rosa, now called Annabel.'

'I heard you found the mother,' he said.

'Yes. One of our suspects is blaming a child, a three-year-old, of smothering her, of leaving those bruises.'

'This is most improbable,' he said. 'We can see from the size of the contusions that these are consistent with an adult. If this child is large to an extreme . . .'

'No, he's not,' Donna said. 'That's what we thought. Thanks, Django.'

'Anything else?' he said.

'It's more of a CPS question, but would the defence be able to argue otherwise, to say it could have been the child?'

'If they wish to. But then you would have to consider the child's account also.'

'Yes.' Donna didn't think three-year-old Charlie would have been primed to confess to hurting Annabel. Gaynor blaming him smacked of a last resort. A cynical, self-serving ploy.

Donna nodded to the team. 'She's busted.'

Jade was twitchy again. If she wasn't scratching at her arms she was drumming her fingers on the nearest surface or chewing her lip. Now she started wandering between the desks.

'Jade?' Donna said.

'Monday – they've put Evie in the store. They'll want to get rid of the baby soon as, won't they? Make the sale, then bring Evie back. Draw a line under the whole thing. And they'll be a few grand richer. So why? Why kill the golden goose?'

'We'll ask her,' Donna said. 'Then we'll charge her.'

Chapter 59

Jade couldn't focus properly on what the boss was saying to Gaynor. She was still stuck with why. Why smother the baby? Like an earworm, on and on.

Selling the baby would have killed two birds with one stone: got rid of the problem of a waking nightmare and beefed up the family fortunes. Why would Gaynor Harrington sabotage that? Did she hate Evie so much that the hatred spread to include the baby? The baby enraged her to the point of murder?

All you know is hate.

Jade tried to get past the mess in her head.

The boss said, 'You were prepared to accuse your own three-year-old of the crime, rather than admit you were responsible. You have a chance now to change your account. Is there anything you wish to tell us?'

Patches of red bloomed on Gaynor's cheeks. 'No,' she said.

'You claim to care for your children.'

'Of course I do.'

Stop your fucking whining. Slap. Jade's head smacking into the wall.

Jade thought of Evie sneaking into the hall, the babe in her arms, trying to creep out. Annabel screaming. The sound bringing Gaynor after them.

She was always crying.

Gaynor snatching the baby. Evie shouting. Stewart yelling too. Pushing Evie into the van. George Peel looking out, nothing to see.

258

Clark Whitman watching the van drive away. Seven o'clock. Gaynor with the baby. *She wouldn't stop crying.* The lies about the migraine. PCSO Evans knocking on doors.

'The police!' Jade shouted. She leaped up.

The boss whipped round, alarm in her eyes.

'The police were at the door,' Jade said. 'Minutes after Stewart had driven away. Minutes after you'd run inside with the baby. A baby that shouldn't exist. And a girl that didn't exist. Your slave.'

'Jade.' The boss touched her arm. Jade jerked it away. 'Get off me.' Back to Gaynor. 'You thought they'd come for you. You thought you'd been seen, been reported. That someone had witnessed the struggle and seen Evie being snatched and bundled into the van. Or they heard the baby too. The baby who wouldn't stop crying. And there's an officer in uniform knocking on your door. You had to keep her quiet. Stop her making any sound. You panicked. And you killed her. Then you left her in the bed to go cold, left her for your husband to find.'

Gaynor stared up at Jade for long enough. Silence apart from their breathing, the rustle of fabric, the boom of Jade's pulse in her head. The solicitor sniffing, once.

'That's right, isn't it?' Jade said.

Gaynor licked her upper lip with the tip of her tongue, pink, moist. She moved back in her seat. 'No comment.'

'Interview concluded,' the boss said. 'Gaynor Harrington, I am charging you with the following offences . . .'

'I thought she'd lost the plot,' the boss was saying, laughing, point- ing at Jade. Re-enacting it for Calvin and Isla. '"Police!" she shouts. I nearly had a heart attack.'

'You nailed it,' Calvin said, grin like a toothpaste ad.

'Good catch,' Isla agreed.

'We lose intent,' Jade said. 'She didn't intend to kill the baby, just shut it up.'

'She might plead to manslaughter,' Isla said.

'No,' the boss said. 'She'll not go quietly. She'll take it to the wire. Keep blaming Charlie. Hard as granite, that one.'

The charges had been laid against Stewart Harrington as well and they would both appear in the magistrates' court to face committal to Crown Court first thing in the morning.

There was a shed load of paperwork to start on, preparing all the evidence, building the case file, but the boss said it could wait until the next day. 'We all need a few hours' R and R,' she said. 'So go home. Chill out. Get pissed. Whatever. See you all tomorrow. Good work. Thank you. All of you.'

Chapter 60

Jade parked and sat in the car, looking up at the flats. At her window. The glow of light. Her guts were knotted, cramping, and she was sweating.

Shannon had been deaf to her threats, to her deadlines. There was no point in just repeating them.

Avoid stress.

She'd tell her to leave then and there. And even if Shannon was at Bert's or Mina's she'd make it plain: You can't sleep here tonight. That's it. Pack your stuff and go.

Surely even Shannon would understand that the game was up.

You'd put me on the streets?

Ringing round to find Colette a bed. Colette getting raped. And Evie. Jade couldn't breathe. *You're dead inside.* Was she dead? She pressed her palm over her heart. *Cold, black heart.* Felt the fast thud of it. Too fast. The heat of her body. Not dead. Playing dead. Because everything inside, the anger, the pain, the sorrow, was too powerful. It would eat her alive, destroy her. The boundaries, they kept stuff out and they kept stuff in. A way to survive.

Her throat ached.

She wanted it to stop. All of it. To not feel anything. Like Colette, bricks in her pockets. The water taking her under. Taking everything away.

Jade had to protect herself. Shannon was a grenade, pin pulled, ticking and ready to blow her apart.

She climbed the stairs slowly; vertigo threatened to send her slamming down, bones snapping on concrete.

She heard the scrape of footsteps, faint behind her. Wheeled round but there was no one.

She gave the usual knock on Mina's door, then went and unlocked her own.

The air was still, the flat quiet. Her eyes flew around, ears pricked, nose scenting for Shannon's smell.

Nothing.

Jade checked her bedroom, kitchen, bathroom, even though her sixth sense told her she was alone. There was a ticking sound, a clicking. She didn't like it. She couldn't tell where it was coming from. Tapping. Like a message.

Was Shannon at Bert's?

'Come in,' he called, when she knocked.

She waited for him to reach the door.

'Has she gone?' Jade said, when he opened it.

He nodded. 'Not long after you left.'

Good.

'Are you all right? You sickening for something?' Bert said.

'Will everybody just get off telling me I'm sick? I'm fine, fucking brilliant. She was . . . she's been . . . Anyway, you OK in there?'

'Yes.' Then his eyes did a sort of swerve. *Oh, what now?*

'Bert? What?'

'I'll sit down a minute.'

Jade went in after him, the atmosphere edgy.

'Well?' Jade said, once he'd lowered himself into his chair.

His twiggy fingers were shaking, his head too. Jade felt the same inside, everything quivering. And something lodged in her throat that she couldn't shift.

'I had some cash,' he said.

Oh, Christ. 'Tell me, not under your mattress.'

'No.' Sheepish. 'Sock drawer.'

'Bert!' Every burglar's first port of call. 'How much?'

'A thousand,' he said.

'A thousand!' *Jesus wept.* A thousand pounds. Jade imagined Shannon, wad of twenties in her fat fist, hitting the shops or clubs or however she got her buzz.

Bert was tapping his fist on the arm of his chair, eyes lowered. Pumping up to saying, 'That's not the worst of it. My watch. I brought it home in a bag from the hospital.' He always wore it, gold watch, big old face, a thick leather strap. Too chunky for his skinny wrist.

'It was my grandfather's, my father's after that.' He cleared his throat. 'Only thing of his I've got. Sentimental value, really. They could melt it down for the gold.'

'I'll fucking kill her,' Jade said.

'I'd rather you didn't.'

Jade went dizzy. The room swung. She perched on the arm of the other chair. 'Look, I'll figure something out. Have you got a photo of the watch? For insurance?'

'I'm not insured. I never thought . . .'

He wouldn't need a crime number, then, if he wasn't going to make a claim. Jade could report it, but what good would it do? The chances of recovering the money were next to none. They hadn't enough officers to look into petty crimes anymore. She'd no idea where they might find Shannon either. Would she go back to Ryan, flashing the cash, and bribe him into giving her another chance? Even then, Jade didn't know where he lived. Or his surname.

But if she didn't report it, how could she get an alert sent to the jewellers and pawnbrokers?

Jade would look like a complete tool, letting Shannon rob from her neighbours, steal her identity.

She wanted to break every bone in Shannon's body and rip out her hornet nails one by one.

She struggled to decide, her thoughts ripped apart by darts of fear. The feeling someone was behind her, waiting to push. She shook her head, rubbed her face. 'I'll ring it in. You do me a description and they can circulate it to jewellers, pawn shops, gold merchants.' She got to her feet. 'What a shitshow.'

'Troubled young lady, I'd say.'

'She's a thieving little bitch, that's what she is,' Jade said.

'It's worse, somehow,' Bert said, 'when it's someone you trust, and they're acting all friendly.'

'I never trusted her an inch,' Jade said.

'You'd better check *your* sock drawer,' Bert said.

'Funny,' Jade said.

Still, when she went back she made a quick inventory. Telly fine, too big anyway. Shannon would want stuff she could stick in her pockets or her bag. Jade had no jewellery to speak of, a chain, a few studs, no precious metals.

But where was the iPad? The one she had for personal use. No work on it. She wasn't sure which room she'd left it in but it was a matter of seconds to confirm it had disappeared.

So had her passport and driving licence, both missing from the kitchen drawer. Choice items for identity fraud.

Fuck!

Never mind impersonating a police officer, impersonating a human being more like. Was Shannon even Shannon? Her blood chilled. Was that part of the con? But no one else could have said those things, known those things. Could they?

Jade called round to Mina. 'Did you see Shannon today? After I went back to work?'

'Yes, she came to say goodbye. We had tea and cake. That Marks & Spencer lemon sponge. There's a piece left, if you like.' Mina settled in her chair.

'Mina, is anything missing?'

'Missing?'

'Any valuables?' Jade said.

'Why?'

'Just look, will you?'

Mina scanned the room. It all looked as usual. The knick-knacks on the mantelpiece, the statue of the Virgin Mary.

'Nothing.'

'Money under your mattress?' Jade said.

'I'm not stupid,' Mina said. 'I keep it in my purse.' She pointed to the handbag by her feet, next to the basket of knitting wool. 'I know you quarrel, you and your sister—'

Not my sister.

'But to think she's taken something. Why would you act like that?' Mina said crossly.

'Your purse is there, is it?' Jade said.

'Yes, it's there.' Mina shook her head, irritated. She bent over from the waist, lifted her bag, looked inside, then at Jade.

And swore in Polish.

Jade heated risotto in the microwave but spat out the first mouthful. Grains of rice like maggots, soft and plump and white. She'd seen that with some dead bodies, movement under the skin. The first time it had happened, Jade had thought the rotting corpse must still be alive. She'd touched it and the skin split, revealing the grubs seething inside.

She shivered and pushed the food away.

When she'd reported the theft on the non-emergency line, they'd said they'd try to send someone round next week or the week after. Her missing passport and driver's licence she could report online. Mina was going to call her own bank and cancel her cards.

Fuck! Shannon had access to their keys! She could have made copies. Jade rang for a locksmith to come and change the locks for all three flats.

She could smell the risotto, a sickly garlic and cheese combo. She took it into the kitchen, scraped it into the compost caddy and put the carton into the bin. But back at the table she could still smell it.

Shit! She grabbed her keys and both bins and went downstairs.

Outside the moon washed everything in neon white. Jade's feet were cold. She'd forgotten her shoes.

It hit her climbing back up. The falling sensation, frothing blood in the back of her skull. Terror scorching through her. She grabbed the handrail and sat on the stairs, buried her head in her arms. The chorus grew louder: *Wish you'd never been born, stop your fucking whining, I'm going to kill you, psycho bitch, dead inside.* She felt breath cold on her neck. Slapped at it. *Something you deserve, slut.*

265

The buzzer sounded downstairs, forcing her to move. The lock-smith arriving.

'I didn't realise you were locked out,' he said, looking at Jade's socks.

She didn't bother trying to explain.

It was late by the time he'd finished, leaving a bill for £360.

Jade thought a shower might help stop the itching, the way her skin crawled. The thunder of water would drown out the chatter of filthy voices that plagued her. But they screeched, venomous, rapid and overlapping. *Dirtylittlemare ... dirtylittleslut ... getwhat-youdeserve ... justlikeherdeserve ... psychoslut ... deadinsidebitch ... somethingtocryforwhining ... goingtokillyou.*

She left the overhead light on when she got into bed, trying to fool herself into thinking she was safe. But she had no hope of sleep.

There were maggots under her skin, eels slithering in her belly.

She heard the television come on, threw back the duvet and went to see. The screen was black. Jade switched the set on, then off again.

No! You shouldn't have done that!

They were watching her, monitoring her. Testing her. They were inside the flat. And they'd probably bugged the rest of the rooms. That ticking sound. Maybe Shannon had done it. Working for them.

She had to find the devices, get them far away.

She began in the kitchen. Emptying each cupboard in turn. Then the drawers. The fridge. The freezer. They were laughing at her. Cackling. *DirtylittlePaki. Daftbitch. Frigidpsycho. We can see you.*

She found nothing. Not yet. She'd try the living room next. They must be in the living room. She stumbled over tins and soggy packets in her race to start.

Chapter 61

Evie was withdrawn, Stella, the social worker, warned them. Stunned by grief, no doubt. But Donna needed to coax some more from her. And judge whether to tell her yet that Gaynor and Stewart had been charged, that the police believed Gaynor had killed Annabel.

Donna asked Stella what she'd advise.

'I'd be guided by her,' Stella said. 'If she asks, if she raises it, then tell her the truth. Otherwise wait.'

Evie was sitting in the chair beside the hospital bed, leaning back, eyes closed.

Stella called her by name, woke her.

The women arranged their chairs, apart from Jade, who said she'd stand. Stayed by the door, looking like a quirky bouncer, with her leather jacket and spiky hair. Wasn't she boiling, dressed in that? Like all the hospitals Donna had been in, the room was too hot, airless.

'How're you, Evie?' Donna said.

'All right.'

'Evie, there are some questions we want to ask you but if there's anything comes up that you aren't ready to talk about, just say. OK?'

She was so still, her arms folded round her belly, head lowered, wearing a hospital nightdress. Donna noticed bruises along her forearms, most faded to yellow, a few dark purple ones, which would be more recent. From the struggle when Harrington dragged her into the van? And there were several shiny scars on her right arm, places where the skin puckered.

267

'Can you tell me about home, life at home, before you had Annabel?'

'What about it?'

'What did you do every day?' Donna said.

'My jobs.'

'What jobs did you do?'

'Breakfast and washing-up and doing the clothes and the ironing. Making tea and washing-up. Cleaning the bathroom on Monday and Friday. And looking after the boys.' All said in a monotone, reciting a list familiar from repetition. But then she became animated, sat up straight and said to Donna, 'Are they OK? Are the boys OK?'

'They're fine,' Donna said.

'Are they at home?'

'No. They've gone to stay with a foster family.'

'Can I see them?' Evie said, eagerness in her keen brown eyes.

Donna looked to Stella for an answer.

'We'll try to arrange that,' Stella said.

'The boys, they went to school, didn't they?' Donna said. 'But you stayed at home. Do you know why that was?'

Jade had her arms crossed now, jaw tight. Donna couldn't work out what was going on with her. Was she even listening to what Evie was saying?

'Cos I had my jobs to do. Earn my keep,' she added. No trace of bitterness.

'And you didn't go out anywhere else, shopping or to the park?'

'No. Gaynor said it wasn't safe. The police would—' She gripped her elbows.

'It's OK,' Donna said. 'You're safe here. What did Gaynor say?'

'The police would lock me up.'

'Why?'

'For being bad,' Evie said.

'When were you bad?' Donna said.

'I don't know. Lots of times.'

'Can you tell me what sort of things she told you were bad?' Donna said.

268

'Shouting?' Evie said uncertainly.

'I see. What else?'

'Not clearing up properly. Or forgetting things.'

'What happened at home when you were bad?'

'Gaynor was cross,' Evie said. A frown puckered her brow.

'What did she do when she got cross?'

'Told me off.'

'Did Gaynor ever hurt you?' Donna said.

'Not really.' A shrug of her shoulder.

'Did she smack you?'

'Sometimes. If I was too slow.'

'How did you get those bruises on your arms?' Donna said.

Evie looked at the marks. 'Cos I was daydreaming. Too slow.'

'What would happen if you were too slow?'

'Gaynor pinched me, to wake me up,' Evie said.

'Did Stewart ever hurt you?'

'No. He just shouted.'

'And this here? Is this a burn, Evie?' Donna pointed to the silvery skin without touching the girl's arm.

'From the oven. And that's the iron. I'm clumsy. You have to be careful.'

'You were making the dinner?' Donna said.

'Yes.'

'You must be a good cook.'

A ripple of pleasure, swift as blinking, crossed her face. A blush of pink. Then her eyes filled with tears and her mouth trembled.

'What you told me about Annabel, is it really true?'

'Yes, I'm so sorry,' Donna said.

'It's not fair.' Her eyes filled with tears and she began to cry.

At the door, Jade turned to peer through the small window onto the corridor.

'It's not fair,' Donna agreed. 'It's so sad. For you and for Annabel.'

Evie didn't ask any more. Donna waited for her to quieten before she said, 'Evie, please, can you tell me who was Annabel's father?'

'I'm not allowed to say. I don't know his name.'

'Did he come to the house?' Donna said.

'Yes.'

'When?'

She sniffed. 'When Gaynor was away and Dad— Stewart. I used to call him Daddy but he's not my daddy and I've got to call him Stewart but sometimes I forget.'

'This other man?' Donna said.

'He came to see Stewart. They were very noisy. I couldn't get to sleep. Was it him, the man, who did that to Annabel?'

'No,' Donna said.

'I thought they'd wake Charlie and then there'd be trouble. Except Gaynor wouldn't know so it might be all right. Then when it was quiet I went to the toilet and he saw me coming back down. He was in the kitchen. I went in my room but he came in.' She stopped. A tremor shook her thin shoulders.

'What happened then?' Donna said gently.

'He was drunk and I didn't know what he was saying and he told me to stay still. After, he said if I ever told anyone he'd come and kill me.'

'Did you see him again?'

'No.'

'Did he visit Stewart again?' Donna said.

'No. I don't think so. I have to stay in my room when people come.'

'Did you tell Stewart or Gaynor about what had happened?' Donna said.

'No,' she said quietly. She gave a little sigh.

Donna's heart went out to her. She heard a clicking sound, glanced at Jade and saw her gnawing at her nails, rocking on her feet.

Donna turned back to Evie who was gazing at her, trust in those clear brown eyes.

'And when you had Annabel, can you tell me what happened?' Donna said.

'It hurt so much. I was crying and shouting, and Gaynor came in and then Stewart, and Annabel was crying and I was crying. Gaynor and Stewart were mad and they were shouting, She was shouting at Stewart, saying what have you done. And swearing. Then he said, "It's not mine!" And he wanted me to tell him who it was but I didn't dare because then he'd come and kill me. And I didn't know his name, like I said.'

'Evie, yesterday you said that Gaynor and Stewart were talking about getting some money for Annabel. How did you know that?'

'Gaynor was saying what a bloody mess. And she said she hated me and I always ruined everything. There was no way I could have a baby. It was against the law. And they had to find it a home. I didn't want them to do that. And then another day, they were in the office and you can hear from my room if they don't whisper and if the washing-machine isn't on. And she said there were people desperate for a baby, people who'd give it a good home and pay thousands. And Stewart said OK. And then she said it's a shame we can't flog them both.'

'Evie, what that man did to you was very wrong. He shouldn't have done that. And it was not your fault. No one should ever hurt you like that. And the way Gaynor and Stewart treated you was wrong. You haven't done anything wrong, Evie. You've been really brave and you tried to help Annabel and keep her safe, and we are going to punish those people who treated you so badly. And those who hurt Annabel.'

There was a moment's quiet, Evie's face so young. Then she said, 'If I hadn't tried to run away, then Annabel might be still alive.'

'You did everything you could do to try to protect your baby. None of this is your fault. None of it,' Donna said.

'Gaynor always said I was a moron. Was it Gaynor?' Evie said. 'Did she kill Annabel?' Her face was alive with apprehension.

'Yes, we think so,' Donna said.

'Because she hated her too?' Her voice wavered.

'No, we think it was an accident. Annabel was crying and we think Gaynor tried to keep her quiet. And Annabel couldn't breathe properly.'

271

Evie nodded slowly once. A tear ran down her cheek, dropped off her chin. 'I want to see the boys,' she said.

'Yes. I'll see what we can sort out,' Stella told her.

Afterwards Donna said to Stella, 'Have you any idea how the boys regard her? If they've been raised to see her as less than them, as a moron or whatever?'

'I don't know. We'll have to assess their relationships before we decide on any contact.'

Jade interrupted, the first time she'd said anything since they'd arrived at the hospital. 'They'll probably blame Evie for what's happened.'

'It's possible,' Stella said. 'Children are remarkably loyal to their parents and they invariably model behaviour on their example. In this case ostracising the one seen as other, the outcast. Demonising them. There's a lot to sort out. If we can find a way, and we judge it to be in Evie's interests, we'll make it happen. The boys have each other. Evie's lost everyone.'

'I'll see you back there,' Jade said, and was out of the room before Donna could reply.

Stella, picking up on the atmosphere, looked quickly at Donna to give her a chance to react but moved on when Donna didn't take it. 'If Evie has to testify, will you be able to provide special measures?'

'As a vulnerable witness? Yes, I'm sure.' Evie would be able to give evidence by video link and not have to face the Harringtons in the intimidating atmosphere of open court.

'We should be able to get the name of the man who raped her from Stewart Harrington,' Donna said. 'Get him locked up too. I'll be in touch when we've any news. Do you know how long they'll keep Evie here?'

'Another day at least. I'm trying to find a suitable foster place for her, someone with the right experience,' Stella said.

Out in the corridor, they paused to let a child on crutches, escorted by a nurse, pass by. The walls were full of children's drawings, a riot of colour. Donna thought of the picture Aidan had drawn, six of

272

them. Evie with the family. Aidan, at four, too young to understand that Evie was a secret, a dirty secret. Invisible. Silent. Hidden.

Had the boys been told not to talk about Evie? *She's not your sister. Evie is nothing but trouble. We don't talk about her. Nobody wants to hear about Evie. She should be ashamed of herself.* And if one of them did let something slip, how would Gaynor or Stewart explain? A visiting cousin? An imaginary friend? *Crazy imagination, this one.*

Chapter 62

Donna and Jade fed through the new information Evie had provided to the rest of the team at a hastily convened briefing.

Jade was describing the circumstances of the rape. 'So Gaynor was away when Harrington had this man round. It's likely she knew nothing about it.'

Donna was reminded of her own ignorance about Jim. She pictured the woman with the red hair and freckles looking across to him at the inquest. Had Jim been on his way to fuck her when he'd had the accident? Or on his way back? How often did they meet? Donna thought of all those little end-of-day conversations.

'You have many lessons?'

'Just a couple. Had a girl pass her test first time. Then she drives into a junction box on the way home afterwards. Oh, and I stopped off for a quick shag with Pen after lunch. Used that hotel near the Parrswood complex.'

Her stomach ached and acid rose up her throat. She couldn't scrub away the images any more than she could unsee those text messages with their cheery emojis. Hearts and wine glasses. Red devils. *Drive me crazy, babe. Sexy beast. She's someone I'm seeing.*

'Boss?'

Donna started. Jade was staring at her, impatient. Donna's mind was blank, frozen in panic, until Jade said, 'Harrington – shall we ask the prison to get him ready for interview?'

'Yes, of course. Do you want me to hold your hand?' Donna heard herself snap. Hated the vicious edge in her tone.

She saw a flare of surprise in Isla's expression, Calvin stroking the top of his head. Displacement activity, uncomfortable with her. Donna felt the rush of heat in her face but carried on speaking, stumbling a little over the words as she brought the meeting to a conclusion, and told Jade that she'd visit Harrington on her own.

Harrington was on remand in HMP Manchester, or Strangeways as everyone still referred to it. His wife had been sent to Styal women's prison a few miles south.

The man Donna met looked exhausted. At the age of thirty-eight he'd never been in trouble, never locked up before. The shock, the struggle to adjust, would be enormous. Taken from his family, home and work. With no privacy, no comforts, no freedom. The experience would be demeaning, frightening – he probably feared for his own safety. Prisons were horrible. Anyone who thought otherwise needed their head examining.

Donna explained to him that she wanted to interview him under caution, specifically about the statutory rape of Evie Potter. And he was entitled to a legal representative if he wanted one.

He declined, which she was thankful for. If he had asked for a solicitor, there would have been a delay while provision was made.

'You've told me that you didn't know who fathered Evie's baby,' Donna said.

'I don't,' he said flatly.

'Evie has been able to tell us the circumstances although she's not able to name the person responsible.'

He looked up from under his brows.

'The crime took place back in January. A weekend when Gaynor was away. You had a visitor, a large man with a beard?'

She saw the realisation filter through, his expression change, an awful recognition.

'Can you tell me who that was?'

He pinched his lip between thumb and forefinger, avoiding eye contact.

'That man raped your stepdaughter and vowed to come and kill her if she ever spoke about it. She was just thirteen years old at the time. Is that someone you're prepared to protect? A sexual predator and a paedophile?'

He didn't speak. The man Evie used to call Daddy, back when he was married to Alison. What was his relationship with Evie like then? Had he cared about her, like his own? He'd chosen to bring her to Manchester with his son William. After that, how easily had he accepted Gaynor's attitudes, her rules about Evie's place in the household? How quickly had he got used to the sight of a nine-year-old cooking and cleaning? How readily had he agreed to the bed in the utility room? How easy had he found it to hold his tongue and stand back when Gaynor belittled the girl, when she pinched her for daydreaming, when she denied Evie her freedom and stole her childhood?

He just shouted.

'We will find him by other means, if necessary,' Donna said. 'But this is something you can do to help us, to help Evie. You might want to think about that.'

Harrington cleared his throat. 'Michael Rushton,' he said.

'You have an address?' Donna said.

'Ellington Drive, in Withington. Number eight.'

'How do you know Michael Rushton?' Donna said.

'He did some work for us. He's a chippie.' A carpenter. 'We'd have a drink sometimes at the pub.'

'But you drank at the house on this occasion?'

'I was babysitting—' He stopped dead. His face working. He should have been caring for his children but his stepdaughter was being raped.

And he wouldn't be tucking his kids into bed or playing kickabout or doing anything like that with them for the foreseeable future.

'You weren't aware of the incident?' Donna said.

'No.'

'How come?'

'I don't know. I passed out at some point. It was a heavy session. When I woke up the next morning he'd gone.'

'Did you see him again after that?' Donna said.

'Yes.' Harrington set his teeth.

'And did he visit your house again?'

'No.'

'And will you be prepared to testify to this, if required, in court?'

He hesitated, then gave a nod. 'Yes,' he said. He looked empty, hollow. Hopeless, she realised. He had no hope, nothing to look forward to.

Chapter 63

'I'd like to interview him,' Jade said, when Donna gave her the information on Rushton.

'Hang on. Just a minute. Let's get some air,' Donna said.

'Why?' Jade looked panicky.

'I just want a word. Come on, we'll go outside for a bit.'

Around the corner from the station there was a small park, landscaped with grasses and ferns and bamboo.

When they reached it, Donna could see a free bench near the entrance.

She sat and Jade followed her lead, hands in her jacket pockets, chin tucked in. Hiding?

A stocky woman, dressed from head to toe in cream, walked past with a French bulldog on a lead, the dog snorting and wheezing, like a little white asthmatic pig.

Donna remembered Matt begging for a dog. Might that be some sort of consolation if Jim and she split up? Was that inevitable, them parting? Could the relationship be fixed? Did she even want that? Donna chased the thoughts away.

'I'm worried about you, Jade.'

'Don't be.'

'Just listen—'

'I know, I swore in the interview and I went to find the store when you told me to go home but—'

'It's not just that,' she said. 'You've been distracted, on edge. Bailing on me at the hospital. Losing your thread in interview.

Getting agitated. Losing control. I'm just trying to understand what's going on.'

'Nothing.' Jade began to drum her feet on the ground.

'Jade, it's not nothing. Don't tell me it's nothing. I'm just trying to help. You said the other day there was some personal stuff going on. Now if—'

'That's sorted,' Jade said. 'She's gone.'

'Who's gone?' Who was she talking about? A lover? A friend? A relation?

'No one. It's fine. It's cool.'

This was getting nowhere.

A man pushed a buggy along the path, the baby inside grizzling. The man wore earbuds. Could he even hear the crying? Or was that the point?

Donna pictured Evie creeping out of the house, Annabel in her arms, then the baby wailing, the pair of them discovered.

Donna tried again. 'I don't know whether it's this case, or work in general, or stuff at home, but whatever it is you've not been yourself. As your manager I have a responsibility—'

'Boss, I'm sound. OK, I need a good night's sleep. But that's all. Yeah? Sorted.'

Donna thought of Jade's twitchiness, the scratching. The way she kept looking behind her, refusing to sit. 'Are you ill?' she said. 'I know you've not been well before. Are you finding it hard to cope?'

'No!' Jade turned, scowling, a blush darkening her brown cheeks. She stopped drumming her feet.

'Would you even tell me if you were?' Donna said.

'Of course,' Jade said. 'Look, I'll see to Rushton then I'm home. I'll be fine. Yeah, things have been a bit crazy but it's OK now.'

Donna was torn. 'There's no shame in taking some leave, Jade. There was a case I did, two lads, best mates. A stupid fight and one kills the other. We knew them. My eldest, Bryony, she was friends with the guy who did it. That was hard. Separating it out, you know?'

Jade didn't say anything.

'We brought it to a conclusion. Sent it through to the CPS. Job

279

done. I thought I was OK, thought I'd coped but . . . then . . . well, I realised I hadn't. I'd just run with it, buried it. I don't know. Anyway, I crashed. I needed time off. And to talk to someone. It really helped. We have to protect ourselves. This job, it's so easy to burn out.'

Jade's feet resumed their tattoo.

'I can send Calvin, you know,' Donna said. 'It's not a problem.'

'No, boss, please. I should go.'

'Why should you?' Donna said.

'I don't know. For Evie—' She broke off. Sniffed.

Two women joggers ran past, their breath steaming in the air.

'Please? And then I'm home,' Jade said. 'Soon as.'

'All right, then. But listen, I want you to take a day off tomorrow. Just a day to recharge. We'll manage. Will you do that?'

'Yeah, all right.' Jade nodded.

'I'm just looking out for you, Jade. Your work is important and so is your health. You understand?'

'Yes, cool.' Jade stood. 'What about you? You OK? You know, with everything? With your— With him?' Jade raised a shoulder and lowered it. Hid behind her fringe.

'One foot in front of the other,' Donna said. Not wanting the reminder but at least Jade made the effort to ask.

There were times at work when Donna could go for an hour, more, absorbed in the tasks of the investigation, focused determinedly on how all the evidence fitted a narrative, and what they still needed to prove, then it would hit her out of the blue. Like a crowbar to the back of the knees.

'Right, I'll get on,' Jade said.

'OK.'

Donna watched her walk quickly away. A slight figure, all in black. Tension vibrating through her. Donna prayed she'd come to the right decision. She had to trust her, didn't she?

Like you trusted Jim?

Ah, Christ. Her heart turned over again.

Chapter 64

Jade stared at the tape recorder, sitting there looking all innocent. And above on the wall the cameras were readied. Were they filming her already? Her neck was tingling, ears ringing.

Are you ill? You've not been well before. The boss suspected her. Thought she was going mental. Was she watching her, like the others were? Waiting to swoop in and what . . . Jade's thoughts scattered, broken beads.

Then a knock at the door and they brought in Michael Rushton.

Rushton was a lump of a man, with a beard like a preacher from the Wild West.

As soon as he'd heard why he was under arrest he'd clammed up.

In interview he looked at Jade with glassy, hate-filled eyes and, after stating his name, address and date of birth, said, 'No comment,' to every question put to him.

It wouldn't do him any good. His DNA sample would prove he was Annabel's father. The very fact of Evie's age meant Rushton was guilty of statutory rape. And with testimony from both Evie and Stewart Harrington to draw on, it was a done deal.

Jade had been twelve. That foster dad had been thin and weedy-looking but still strong enough. Hand on the back of her neck. *Dirty little slut. You get what you deserve.*

Jade stood abruptly. Her skin crawling. 'Interview suspended.' She stopped the tape.

'You might as well wait here,' she said. 'We'll be laying charges immediately. And recommending that you're remanded in custody.'

He said nothing but she saw the bitter twist of his mouth. With any luck he'd get eight years, as well as a lifetime on the sex offenders' register. But nothing would compensate for what he'd done to Evie.

Chapter 65

They were alone at last. It was after ten and Donna wanted nothing more than to go to bed, to sleep and dream, but knew she had to tackle him and not hide or prevaricate any more.

Without asking she turned off the television.

He gave a small sigh.

'Are you going to keep seeing her?' Donna said.

He looked at her, impassive. Shifted in his chair. 'She makes me happy,' he said at last. 'I'm in love with her.'

And me? Donna's throat tightened. Her heart hurt. She would not cry. At least he's honest, she thought. But it didn't help.

What did he expect? That Donna would accommodate the situation? Play nice for the sake of the children? That she'd swallow the rejection, the humiliation? Let things chug along as they had been? *Seriously?*

'You need to move out, then,' she said, as calmly as she could. 'And soon.'

'What do we tell the kids?'

We? We? It's your fucking mess! You fucking tell them. That you don't love me any more. You don't want me. You've been off shagging Lady fucking Penelope.

'The truth,' she said.

'You can't manage everything here on your own,' Jim said.

'No,' she said. 'So find somewhere close by. I'm assuming you do still want to be a father?'

His face darkened. She bit back all the other barbs. She would not expose herself. She didn't want his pity.

'OK,' he said, after a moment.

She couldn't imagine it. The way all their lives would be shaken and jolted. Especially the younger ones. But the twins, too, with GCSEs ahead, and Bryony studying A levels. It was hateful and sordid, and she was sadder than she'd ever felt.

We'll be OK, she told herself. We'll make it OK.

'I want mediation,' Donna said. 'To sort things out as best we can.' She'd seen other couples locked in vitriolic separations that never seemed resolved. She'd worked murder cases where adultery had triggered carnage.

He nodded.

'I'm going to have a bath,' she said. She never had a bath, these days – there wasn't enough time in the day and they were trying to do their bit to save water – but she didn't want to be in the same space as him. She would fill the bath, drink a large glass of wine and maybe let herself weep in private.

'I could . . . well, tonight . . . if you'd rather. If you want to be on your own,' he said.

'Yes,' she said, the agreement bitter in her throat. Knowing where he was going, who he was choosing. Thinking of them together pierced her heart. She fought to swallow.

As she reached the door, Jim said, 'I am sorry.'

But it was meaningless. Far too little, and far too late.

Chapter 66

Donna found Jade at her desk, papers spread out but her monitor dead. 'Jade, I thought you were taking a day off.'

'Wanted to finish this.' Jade didn't turn around.

'Has the system crashed?' Donna said.

'What?' Jade looked alarmed.

'The computer.'

'Mine's fine,' Isla called. 'Was it updating, Jade? I can check.'

'No. Don't touch it,' Jade shouted. 'Leave it off.'

Isla glanced at Donna. Concerned.

Oh, Christ. Donna's stomach fell.

The room hummed with tension.

'Jade, I'd like to talk to you. Let's go in my office.'

'But this.' Jade pointed to the mess of papers. Half the reports were the wrong way round, the lettering upside down. 'I just need to sort it.' Jade began grabbing at the papers, heaping them in random piles. She was breathing quick and shallow, shaking like a leaf.

'It can wait a bit,' Donna said. She'd dealt with enough people who had mental-health issues in the course of the job to recognise that Jade was ill. Donna had suspected as much yesterday, but she'd let Jade persuade her otherwise. Giving her the benefit of the doubt. Why? Because Donna had *wanted* to believe her, had hoped it could be fixed with a day at home. *Idiot.* All she'd done was leave Jade to deteriorate.

'Come on,' Donna said.

There was a pause, and Donna wondered what she would do if Jade outright refused, but then Jade slid back her chair and rose.

'Do you want to sit down?' Donna offered, as she shut the door.

'I'll stand.' Jade stayed close to the door. She kept looking over her shoulder. Hypervigilant.

'When did you last sleep?' Donna said.

'I'll do the reports now, Evie's witness statement.' Jade was batting her knuckles together.

'Jade. When did you last sleep?' Donna said.

'I can't remember. I've got loads to do so—'

'What about food?' Donna said.

'I'm not hungry.'

'When did you last eat?'

Jade didn't reply. Looking over her shoulder again, distracted.

'Have you got your medication, Jade?' They didn't talk about it, hadn't, not since Jade had persuaded Donna to keep her condition a secret, by threatening blackmail more or less, because who trusts a detective being treated for psychosis?

'What?'

'Your medication?'

'It's at home?' Jade said uncertainly, as though guessing for the right answer.

'Did you have some today?' Donna said.

Jade's face was blank for a moment. Then she recoiled. Eyes on Donna's desk, on the monitor.

'Turn it off,' she said, in a rapid whisper. 'Everything electrical. They can hear us. They sent Shannon to plant the devices.'

'Shannon?'

'She's not my sister. Just because we've the same name on our birth certificates. I was in care before she was even born. They sent her to mess with my head, Shannon.'

Donna felt a chill down her back.

'They can put them under the skin now, too. Like trackers. Bugs. Like maggots. They eat flesh. They eat secrets. Dead inside.' Her eyes were wide, glassy.

Donna struggled to follow. Jade was ranting, speaking so fast, hand rubbing at her wrist, unable to keep still.

286

Donna got out of her chair. She was worried for her, frightened for her.

'Who's they?'

'Sssh!' Jade put a finger to her lips. 'They're listening.'

'No one's listening, Jade. This is just me and you talking,' Donna said.

Jade was trembling, her whole frame shaking. She leaned towards Donna, whispered, her words broken up, chopped and jerky, by the spasms. 'They're listening. They can hear everything. I'm not like her. You've got to be careful. Watch what you say and anything electric. Or solar. They can find me, hear me.'

Donna's stomach clenched in an instinctive response to Jade's mounting terror. She took a breath, resisted the infectious nature of the woman's panic. 'Who are you talking about?'

'The CIA,' Jade said. 'Black ops. They have helicopters. They plant the bugs inside. I'm dead inside. They get inside and multiply, they breed. Not fit to have children.'

Oh, Jesus.

Jade kept glancing round petrified, as though dangers lurked in the corners of the room. 'They're coming for me.'

'Jade, I think you need to go to hospital.'

'I have to work,' Jade said. 'There's all the work. It's important. Evie. And Vasile and DD.'

'Who's DD?'

'I don't know him,' Jade said. 'You need to turn that off.' She pointed to the desk.

'You're anxious and I think you're confused and we need to get a doctor.'

'You think I'm going mad? That's what they *want* you to think. Don't you see?' She gave a brittle laugh. 'Why won't you listen?'

Donna's phone rang. She hurried to answer it, to stop the noise before it panicked Jade even more. *Kenton, Press Office.*

'Hi, Donna, we'd like you to make a statement on the baby Rosa case, thanking the public, that sort of thing. A follow-up to the appeals.'

'Sure,' Donna said. 'I'll ring you back.'

'What we'd really like is to catch the—'

'Sorry. I'm right in the middle of something.' Donna killed the call.

Jade was staring, fearfully. 'Was that them?' She was plucking at the fabric of her top, at her breastbone.

'No,' Donna said.

'They can hear,' Jade mouthed. Terror stark on her face. 'Turn off the phone!'

'I'll turn it off while we talk. OK?' Donna did. Set it down.

'Is it off?' Jade's head whipped round, to the door and back.

'Yes,' Donna said.

'They use the sockets too. They know where I am. They're coming for me. Extraordinary rendition. There wouldn't be a trial. I'm guilty, that's what they'll say. I'm guilty. If you turn everything off. Tell them I'm not here. You've got to. They can hear us. Hear us here. Hear us here. Guantánamo's still open and Muslims don't count. Pakis don't. Black ops. Brown ops. Guilty.'

Her speech was disjointed, looping round and round.

'Jade, you haven't done anything wrong.'

'You don't know.' She whirled about as if there was something behind her.

'You're frightened?' Donna said.

'I don't want to die.' Jade reached out and gripped Donna's hands, squeezing hard as though the pressure might carry her message. Anxiety coming off her in waves. She had never touched Donna before like this.

Donna swallowed. 'I can take you to hospital. You'll be safe there.'

'No,' Jade said. Her expression changed, shuttered, suspicious. She moved back towards the door.

She was going to run. Was she? Oh, Jesus. 'Who's your doctor?' Donna said.

'She tied me up in the cot. Like handcuffs.' Jade laughed. No humour in it. She scratched violently at her wrists.

'Jade, don't.' Donna put a hand out, careful not to touch. 'She

288

shouldn't have done that. That was cruel. But now we need to get you somewhere safe, where you can rest. Come on, Jade. It's me – Donna. You need a break. Get your medication sorted out.'

'I have to work.' Jade came close to Donna, looking at her directly, face only a few inches away. 'I have to work. No psychos allowed.' She hit at her own temples.

'Jade, don't. Listen, I'll help. I promise. We'll call it stress. You take a few weeks and you come back when you're better. You won't be the first. We're all feeling the pressure. We're dealing with trauma, with horrendous events, day in, day out. One job after another. It's a pressure cooker. You know that. You need to take some leave.'

Jade was twitching again, jerking her head around, rubbing her wrist. 'You're going to section me?'

'No, Jade, not if you'll go in voluntarily. You'll get help. You'll get better. Do you understand? It would be harder to come back if you're sectioned. Do you understand? It's going to be OK. It's going to be all right.'

Jade slid down the wall, arms crossed over her head, rocking. 'Come back here?' she said.

'Yes, back here. You're on my team, Jade. What would I do without you?' Donna lowered herself to sit beside her. She felt like crying, her heart aching for Jade.

Jade started to weep. Desolate cries that cut Donna to the quick.

'Look at everything you've done for Evie. For Annabel. For the case. You're a gifted detective, Jade. You've still got a lot to learn. You can improve. But you can't do that if you're not well. So you need to rest and get better, then come back. And your job will be here waiting for you.'

'Really?' Jade was wiping her face hard but still her tears fell. 'You're not lying to me, are you? Are you lying? Did Shannon tell you to lock me up? Did they tell you to say this? Are they coming?'

'I'm telling you the truth. Me, Donna, telling you the truth. Now let's get that doctor, eh? We'll sit here and I'll ring for help, yes? And I'll wait with you, Jade. We'll wait for help together. It's going to be OK. You're going to be OK.'

Chapter 67

Halloween, and there'd been a half-hearted attempt to decorate the team office. Someone had strung plastic bunting, a row of orange jack o' lanterns, over the door. Stuck a black spider's web on one wall.

Donna hoped there wouldn't be too many spiders in evidence when Jim took Matt and Kirsten trick or treating or Matt would end up hysterical and have to go home. Then again, maybe exposure to comic cartoonish versions of the creatures might blunt his fear a bit.

Donna checked the time, saved the document she was working on and stretched in her chair. The team were preparing the file of evidence for the prosecution against the Harringtons. Days of paperwork: pulling together and checking all the reports and statements, interview testimony, electronic and physical evidence. Steady, painstaking work.

'What were you scared of as a kid?' Donna asked Calvin.

'Snakes.' Calvin didn't hesitate.

'Lot of snakes in Ashton, are there?' Donna said.

'More than you'd think. Guy next-door-but-one had a python in a tank. I was awake all night imagining it coming through the drains or up the toilet.'

'My lad's scared of spiders. And cats, monsters, flying insects and thunder.'

Isla came in, cup in hand.

'And you?' Calvin asked Donna.

'It used to be mice, when I was little. And wasps. I couldn't bear wasps.'

'Clowns,' Isla said. 'Absolutely terrified. There was one in the toybox at infant school. Total meltdown.'

'That's a common one,' Calvin said. 'There's a name for it.'

'Coulrophobia,' Isla said. She gave a shudder.

'You grew out of it, though?' Donna said.

'No. Clowns still give me the heebie-jeebies.'

'Wrong answer,' Donna said. 'I'm looking for a little bit of hope here.'

Isla grinned.

Donna gathered her things together. She and Jim had their introductory mediation session at two o'clock. They hadn't told the children that they were planning to separate or why. And they couldn't agree when it would be best to do that.

There is no good time. Perhaps they should have one last Christmas together before they shared the news. Or was that dishonest? Didn't the children have a right to know sooner? Her thoughts snagged and tangled. She honestly didn't know what was best – or least worst. She hoped mediation might give them some guidance.

Outside it was a fine day. Sunshine soft and golden, low in the sky. The air still, trees turning lemon and russet and crimson.

Tomorrow was Colette's funeral. Odelia would be there. She had been shaken and upset to hear about Colette's death and later told Donna she was starting volunteering with A Bed Every Night, the Greater Manchester mayor's campaign to assist rough sleepers.

Colette's death was such a waste, Donna thought. The woman had died haunted by the belief that she had somehow failed to save Annabel. But that had never been possible. If only she could have lived to learn that her actions had helped save Evie.

Donna imagined them meeting, the woman who had cradled Annabel, carrying her in her arms in the dark along the road to the police station. A woman who had seen everything taken from her, work, home, dignity, health. Colette, who'd worked and had friends, who'd planted a tree in her garden, cherries for the birds. Who'd saved for a holiday abroad each year and had given to charity. An ordinary, decent woman, like millions of others. There was a statistic

Donna knew: one in three families were only one pay cheque away from losing their homes.

And Evie had lost almost everything too, when her mother died, but had loved her little brothers and the baby, who'd come as such a surprise.

'Why did you pick "Annabel"?' Donna had asked on one of her visits.

'I'd a doll called Annabel when I was little. It's my favourite name. It sounds so beautiful. And she was beautiful too, my baby.' Tears glittered in her eyes.

If only they had met, Colette and Evie. What Donna would have given for that to happen.

If wishes were horses.

I'm sad, she thought. So very sad. Of course I am. It'd be weird if I wasn't.

She stood a moment by the car, tilting her face up to feel the sun's warmth, hearing the chatter of sparrows in the hedge by the road, stealing a moment's peace. Before she had to go.

Chapter 68

Jade was discharged in late December after nine and a half weeks in hospital.

The first fortnight on the ward was a blur of exhaustion and paranoia. Of walls rippling with snakes and cockroaches, icy hands grasping her neck, blood in the sink and enemies gathered outside the doors and windows. Ready to execute her. A helicopter over open sea.

Locks and chains, pills and needles. Shouting. The skitter and slap of bare feet on plastic floors, the stink of body odour. Afraid of the water, the lightbulbs, the switches, the dark, the rain tapping to come in.

Slowly the drugs had worked, knocking her out, suffocating her, switching her off. Then slowly, slowly letting her sleep, breathe, eat again.

Weekly meetings with the doctor: are you still hearing voices, still having hallucinations, still thinking suicidal thoughts?

Then unescorted leave. For the last ten days she'd been judged well enough to come and go at set times during the day. Able to wander round the rest of the hospital, to the shop, to the café. Shaken, raw, subdued. Bored.

Fit for visitors.

The boss came twice. Talked about her kids, not that Jade was especially interested but Jade had nothing to talk about so it filled the silence.

The second time Jade asked her about Evie. The girl was settled with a foster family and they were working with the local school to support her resuming education. The boss said Evie had picked up quite a lot over the years, watching what William did for homework, so they hoped she'd catch up in time.

'Did Evie see them, the other kids?' Jade said.

'Yes. Well, the two little ones. They've had contact. There's every hope that will continue. There's a bond between them. But William, he chose not to go. He doesn't want to see her at the moment.' The boss pulled a face, shame.

But it made perfect sense to Jade.

When Jade arrived home Mina insisted she come in for tea and cake.

Jade would rather have been left in peace to get on with things, to settle back in, and said, 'I've things to do—'

'Half an hour, Jade,' Mina said. 'No arguments.'

Jade sat down and Mina went into the kitchen, and then there was a knock at the door.

'You get that,' Mina called.

For a sickening moment Jade imagined Shannon there. She couldn't move.

'It'll be Bert,' Mina said.

Bert?

'What's the occasion?' Jade said. Mina and Bert never entertained each other. They were neighbourly but not chummy.

'You are!'

Jade opened the door.

'Welcome home.' Bert grinned. He teetered in the doorway and she waved him in.

'Good news,' Bert said, once he was seated. He lifted his arm, hand shaking, and Jade saw his watch, sliding round his spindly forearm. 'They found it. Gold merchant in the centre of town. But the lad who'd taken it in says he bought it off someone else. Claimed he'd no idea it was stolen.'

'He wasn't called Ryan, was he?'

You're all mental.

294

Not wrong there.

'No. Some French-sounding name. Pascale or something.'

Jade said, 'The money, I can—'

'Don't worry about that. I'll manage.'

But she *would* pay him back. She must be earning Bert's pension several times over: she'd pay him a hundred quid a month. Whether he liked it or not.

Mina came in carrying a stack of side plates with a chocolate cake on top. 'Jade, can you fetch the drinks through?' she said.

Jade did as she was told.

'Bert's is the blue cup,' Mina said. 'Three sugars.' She divvied up the cake. 'How was the food in there?' she said.

'Rank,' Jade said.

'It wasn't bad in Wythenshawe as long as you chose carefully,' Bert said.

'How've you gone on with your shopping?' Jade asked Mina. It was usually Jade who did it, Mina giving her a list once a week.

'Barbara Atwell on the second floor. Her daughter does hers and she's been getting mine as well.'

'Great,' Jade said. It had always been a bind trying to fit in trips to Aldi and M&S around work. When the job got busy Jade could just ignore her own chores, live out of the freezer and on takeouts but there was still Mina's shopping to think about. To be rid of that would be brilliant.

'I'm so glad you're back,' Mina went on. 'She never gets the list, says they don't have any, brings the wrong things. I tell her you're home. I'm all right until the weekend, you get sorted out.'

Across the room Bert winked at Jade, maybe it was a wink, could just be one of his facial spasms but Jade raised her eyebrows at him anyway.

She took another slice of cake.

'So when are you back to work?' Bert said.

'Couple more weeks. I'm going in the day after tomorrow to talk about a phased return,' Jade said.

She would rather have gone straight back full-time. She'd adjusted to the meds now and although she felt sleepy at times the fog in her head had cleared. She could think straight. But the boss said it had to be this way.

'I'll see you in the afternoon,' the boss had said. 'Annabel's funeral is at eleven. I'll be going to that but it's entirely up to you, see how you feel. Either way I'll meet you in the office after lunch and we can talk about your schedule. Say, two o'clock?'

It was mild for the turn of the year. A steady breeze rattled the bare branches of the huge plane and beech trees and sent ripples through the skirts of the conifers that ringed the cemetery. A grey squirrel darted away as Jade walked up the driveway to the chapel.

She was a bit late but no point in hurrying: these things didn't always start on time, did they?

There was music playing, some violin. Jade didn't know the tune. It sounded miserable. The entrance doors were wide open, and when she stepped inside the vestibule a man in a suit held out a programme. Jade took it and went forward.

She opened one of the interior doors a few inches and looked inside. A tiny coffin, not much bigger than a shoe box, a spray of white flowers on it. A handful of people on the front row, backs to her. The social worker Stella, then the boss, hair mostly grey. When had that happened? The boss was bending over talking to Evie. The other side of Evie sat a black woman with a smart hat. The foster mother?

Evie turned, looked at Jade. Jade ducked away, let the door close. Not quickly enough. Evie's eyes, hollow, harrowed, her nose and mouth red and swollen from crying, filled her with a sense of desolation, a feeling of loss so wide and deep and wild it unmoored her and the floor lurched beneath her feet.

She ignored the murmur of concern from the usher and stepped outside. Shivering.

They'd manage without her. The boss was there representing the police, after all. Jade didn't need to be.

It'd be fine.

She'd go into the station. Get ready for the afternoon's meeting.

As she walked back down the drive the wind blew harder, making her eyes water. She sniffed and blinked.

It wouldn't be long till she was back at work. Till they got the call again.

Another body. Another murder. Another life cut savagely short.

It was never very long.

And it was what she lived for.

She zipped up her jacket and raised her eyes to the horizon where the city waited beyond the towering trees.

Acknowledgements

Thanks again to my writers' group – Anjum Malik, Livi Michael, Mary Sharratt and Sophie Claire: it's always such a pleasure. Thank you to all the team at Constable, especially Krystyna Green, Jess Gulliver, Hannah Wann, Brionee Fenlon, Anna Boatman, Lucy Howkins, Bekki Guyat and Rebecca Sheppard. Thanks to Hazel Orme for copy-editing, knocking it into shape and spotting my glaring mistakes. And a big thank-you to all the readers who asked for more Donna and Jade.